Acclaim for the authors of *Regency Christmas Parties*

ANNIE BURROWS

"As soon as I picked this book up I didn't want to put it down... [A] wonderful romance!"

—*Rae Reads* book blog on
A Scandal at Midnight

LARA TEMPLE

"A passionate, gorgeously romantic story about two people at crossroads in their lives, the chemistry between them sizzles, and Ms. Temple's talent for writing sparkling, witty dialogue shines once again. Highly recommended!"

—*All About Romance* on
A Match for the Rebellious Earl

JOANNA JOHNSON

"An excellent book and a real page turner and a lovely historical romance—it is 5 stars from me for this one, very highly recommended!"

—*Donna's Book Blog* on
A Mistletoe Vow to Lord Lovell

Annie Burrows has been writing Regency romances for Harlequin since 2007. Her books have charmed readers worldwide, having been translated into nineteen different languages, and some have gone on to win the coveted Reviewers' Choice award from CataRomance. For more information, or to contact the author, please visit annie-burrows.co.uk, or you can find her on Facebook at facebook.com/AnnieBurrowsUK.

Lara Temple was three years old when she begged her mother to take the dictation of her first adventure story. Since then she has led a double life—by day she is a high-tech investment professional, who has lived and worked on three continents, but when darkness falls she loses herself in history and romance...at least on the page. Luckily her husband and her two beautiful and very energetic children help her weave it all together.

Joanna Johnson lives in a pretty Wiltshire village with her husband and as many books as she can sneak into the house. Being part of the Harlequin Historical family is a dream come true. She has always loved writing, starting at five years old with a series about a cat imaginatively named Cat, and she keeps a notebook in every handbag—just in case. In her spare time, she likes finding new places to have a cream tea, stroking scruffy dogs and trying to remember where she left her glasses.

REGENCY CHRISTMAS PARTIES

—

Annie Burrows
Lara Temple
Joanna Johnson

HARLEQUIN®
HISTORICAL™

ISBN-13: 978-1-335-72353-6

Regency Christmas Parties

Copyright © 2022 by Harlequin Enterprises ULC

Invitation to a Wedding
Copyright © 2022 Annie Burrows

Snowbound with the Earl
Copyright © 2022 Ilana Treston

A Kiss at the Winter Ball
Copyright © 2022 Joanna Johnson

For questions and comments about the quality of this book, please contact us at CustomerService@Harlequin.com.

Harlequin Enterprises ULC
22 Adelaide St. West, 41st Floor
Toronto, Ontario M5H 4E3, Canada
www.Harlequin.com

Printed in U.S.A.

CONTENTS

INVITATION TO
A WEDDING

Annie Burrows

Author Note

Christmas is a time when people without families can feel very lonely. My heroine, Clara, has always dreamed of experiencing a real family Christmas, and when she receives an invitation to a wedding that will take her into the heart of a wealthy family, she is absolutely thrilled.

I hope you enjoy my story of how Clara discovers there is more to Christmas than eating, drinking and exchanging gifts.

And hope that you all enjoy your own celebrations at this festive season, whether you can meet with family members or not.

Chapter One

What an adventure!

Clara Isherwood was in a coach, on her way to a wedding. A wedding to be held on Christmas Day, what was more. And she had an invitation to stay with the bride, a former pupil of Heath Top, the school where Clara now acted as assistant teacher, for three whole days.

She could still hardly believe it. Christmas in a family home.

How often she had yearned to celebrate Christmas in a family home again. She could dimly remember, as a little girl, scenes of jollity and extra-special dinners, and people crowding into overheated rooms and exchanging gifts. Nowadays, she had to stifle the envy she felt, watching the local people bustling about, making preparations for their own family Christmases. And eyeing with something like pain the cheery faces of those leaving church after the morning service, who would be going home to roast dinners, probably followed by plum pudding and custard.

But never mind what had happened any other year, this year she had received an invitation to not merely an ordinary family Christmas celebration, but to a Christmas wedding in a ducal residence! For Bella Fairclough, who'd once been the naughtiest girl ever to attend Heath Top, had, according to the *Oakwick Chronicle* in which Clara had read the news, captured the heart and hand of none other than the Duke of Braid.

Miss Badger, the headmistress, had naturally been furious that Clara had received an invitation, rather than her. Although why on earth she'd thought Bella might have extended the courtesy to the woman who'd done nothing but give her stern lectures about her behaviour, before meting out increasingly harsh punishments, Clara couldn't imagine. Nevertheless, Miss Badger had seemed so offended that at first Clara had feared she was going to refuse to let her attend. But then she'd sighed and admitted that since Clara had been the only person who'd ever managed to get the girl to listen, she could see why she should go to represent the school, rather than someone more official. And had granted Clara permission to attend, providing she would promise to use the opportunity to ask the Duchess-to-be for donations to the school.

And so here she was, stepping into the third coach in which she'd travelled so far, ducking her head to dodge the hares and turkeys dangling from the luggage racks, squeezing into a seat next to a farmer's wife and placing her feet on the wicker basket, which, the farmer's wife informed her, would take no hurt, since it contained jars of pickles and some well-wrapped fruit cakes she was taking to her daughter's.

Clara couldn't help reflecting, as three schoolboys scrambled into the coach with moments to spare before it lurched off on to the next stage, and took up the whole of the facing seat, how different this all was from the last time she'd made a journey in a coach.

That time, she'd been eight years old, scared and trying not to cry. And the three elderly men dressed in black, who'd sat in the coach with her, had done little to help. Solemnly urging her to be grateful for the provision of a home and lecturing her about the generosity of all those patrons who'd made it possible for her to still get a good education, even though her parents had been improvident by leaving her without means, was not the sort of thing a recently orphaned child wanted, or was really able, to hear. She'd wanted someone to hold her and dry her tears, not look at her gravely, and tell her to count her blessings.

Which was perhaps in part why she'd had such a soft spot for Isabella Fairclough. She had known exactly how it felt to be ripped from a comfortable home and sent to a joyless and austere boarding school when she was still less than ten years old. She had even been able to understand why she was so angry. For although Clara had been a genuine orphan, Miss Fairclough's father was not only still alive, but also comfortably off.

'*Heath Top is supposed to be a refuge for daughters or sisters of indigent or deceased clerics,*' the little girl had wailed. While Clara had lent her a handkerchief and a shoulder upon which to cry.

But nobody travelling on any of the coaches Clara had been on so far, this time, had been in the slightest bit solemn. The drivers and guards might have been stern, or impatient. Some of the passengers might have been querulous, or sickened by the swaying of the vehicle. The landlord of the inn where she'd stayed overnight had looked right through her, while the waiters he'd employed had been downright rude. But solemn, no.

She couldn't help smiling at the way the schoolboys opposite kept on wriggling and bouncing, because they were incapable of containing their excitement at escaping their school and going home for Christmas. As a schoolmistress she supposed she ought to be trying to make them settle down. But how could she, when she felt just as excited as they evidently were, at her own escape from school? She only wished she, too, could bounce and wriggle, or that she had someone to chatter nineteen to the dozen with about what she hoped to do when she got home.

But then she was single female, with a reputation to

maintain. And she wasn't going home, either, was she? She didn't have one. Not a real home, where there was a family waiting. The nearest thing she had to home was the school and it was the very last place she wanted to spend yet one more dreary, dissatisfying Christmas. She might not know much about what life inside a ducal palace was like, but she was sure she wouldn't have to spend most of Christmas Day, once she'd returned from church, sitting before a meagre fire, with a shawl round her shoulders, attending to a pile of darning, or reading a book of sermons to a group of bored schoolgirls.

Knowing Miss Fairclough, if she had any books about her they were bound to be frivolous. Probably with pictures in them. Were there books with lots of pictures in them? Well, there were magazines with the latest fashions printed in them, she knew that much. And Miss Fairclough was just the type of girl who was likely to buy them.

But the Duke himself was bound to have a library, even if he didn't read much himself. Some of his forebears would have done, wouldn't they? She'd be able to sit and read in his library without feeling guilty about some pile of bed-sheets that wanted turning sides to middle. And his house would no doubt be set in the middle of a massive and well-tended park.

She hadn't had time to find out anything about the Duke of Braid's winter residence before setting out, but no Duke worthy of the name could possibly not have a park with deer roaming free and mazes, and lakes and views, could he? Which would be so vast that nobody would notice one small, insignificant schoolmistress wandering about exploring.

But even if she never set foot in any of that magnificent, imagined parkland, she was absolutely certain that at every mealtime there would be a table groaning with all the kinds of food she'd always dreamed of eating at Christmas and never had the chance. Turkeys and beef and raised pies, whatever they were. And puddings stuffed with fruit and possibly even jellies and creams. And oranges galore.

Clara's mouth watered at the prospect. Sometimes, at Christmas, the girls who stayed at Heath Top received an orange from the board of trustees. When she'd been a boarder, she'd been a recipient of one of those charity oranges herself. But since she'd graduated to the position of assistant teacher and started receiving a nominal wage, she'd lost her right to such Christmas treats.

When Clara finally got out of the last coach on the final stage of her journey, she wasn't a bit surprised when the guard ignored her, while bustling around taking down the luggage of all the people who looked as if they could give him a good tip. It was entirely Miss Badger's fault. Miss Badger might have obtained all the necessary tickets for the journey, but she hadn't given Clara any money to waste on things like tipping guards, or drivers, or waiters. 'I have to answer to the board of trustees for any unexpected expenditure,' she'd explained. And, remembering those black-clad, solemn men, Clara could see exactly why Miss Badger was always so careful with money.

She amused herself, while she was waiting, by watching all the people milling about the inn yard. Those with jobs, like ostlers, unharnessing the tired horses and leading fresh ones to the coach. Passengers descending. Passengers alighting. And through the windows of the inn she could see waiters bustling about with trays held aloft, containing jugs and mugs, trailing steam in their wake.

She actually smiled wryly when she saw the schoolboys getting better service than her. She could hardly blame the guard for leaving her case till last, although it was a little galling that when he finally did get round to unloading it, he rudely tossed it to the ground on the far side of the

coach from where she was standing, before hurrying on
to his next task. It meant that Clara was going to have to
make her way right out into the busiest section of the yard
to retrieve her little carpet bag. And she'd better not leave
it lying there for long, lest one of the laden porters, or scurrying passengers, tripped over it.

She darted round the back of the coach, so that she
wouldn't get in the way of the business of changing horses
that was going on at the front end, and was just bending
down to pick up her bag when a hard, masculine arm suddenly clasped her by the waist and swung her off her feet.
She was so surprised that she'd barely opened her mouth
to utter a protest, when a massive horse, with feathered fet-
locks, went trotting across the very spot where she'd been
standing. And she perceived that if she'd managed to get
hold of her bag, the horse would have knocked her down.
And possibly trodden on her.

Her stomach lurched and her heart beat a rapid tattoo
against her ribs, which was silly, really, now that the danger was past.

'Have you no more sense than to run out in front of a
horse that size when it has blinkers on?' The voice came
from just behind her ear, the mouth so close that the breath
fanned warmly down the gap between her collar and her
neck. 'Didn't you see it coming? Or did you think that whatever is in that bag is worth risking your life for?'

Clara screwed her head round as far as it would go, although, thanks to the brim of her bonnet, she could see no
more of the man with the angry voice and the arm like a
mahogany banister than the darkly stubbled plane of his
jaw.

*Don't be stupid...of course I didn't see the horse com-
ing*, she wanted to say. Although, thanks to the pressure
of the arm still constricting her stomach, and the pattering
of her heart, all that came out was a small mewling sound.

'You are trembling,' the man observed, as though surprised that such a thing could happen after a brush with death in the form of a draught horse and the shock of being lifted off her feet by a dark and determined-sounding stranger. 'You had better sit down.'

The arm round her waist slid so that instead of him being behind her, and completely out of her sight, the man appeared at her side. He still held her firmly, but now he was ushering her into movement. In the direction of the inn.

'My bag,' she managed to squeak as his grip altered.

'Leave it where it is,' he said irritably. 'It has caused you enough trouble.'

'Oh, but…'

'I will go and fetch it once I have sat you down in a safe place.'

'Oh. Well, thank you,' she said as he thrust her down on to a bench right beneath the window she'd just been peering through. And before she got the chance to have a proper look at him, he was striding away, nimbly dodging between the other people scurrying hither and thither, his heavy dark blue coat brushing the cobbles. He then swooped down, snatched up her bag and turned to make his way back to her in one deft movement, putting her forcibly in mind of some great dark bird of prey.

Now that he was facing her fully, Clara got the impression of a tight, lean face that matched the irritability of his voice to perfection.

'Here,' he said, dropping her battered and now muddy carpet bag at her feet. Then he stood still for a moment, looking at her, with his head tilted to one side.

From beneath the dark blue bicorne hat he wore on his head peered a pair of snapping dark eyes, accentuated by black brows and framed by black lashes. Yet, for all the harshness and darkness of his face, there was something very attractive about him. Which puzzled her. Why on earth should she be attracted to a man who'd manhandled her, told her she was foolish, dumped her on a bench and who was scowling at her as though she was an inconvenience he could well have done without?

'Have you taken any hurt?' he asked, his scowl deepening when she remained silent. Which reminded her that she ought to have thanked him for rescuing both herself and her bag, rather than just staring up at him.

'Do you need me to summon anyone? It is just that...' he half turned and glanced round the busy inn yard '...I have come to meet someone and I don't want to miss her in all this crowd.'

Her heart gave a funny lurch. He had a sweetheart. Well, of course he did. A man who looked like that, wearing clothing she could tell, now that she was nearer to him, was of good quality, of course must have a sweetheart. And of course he resented having to waste precious moments he could have been spending with *her*, rescuing a clumsy, foolish schoolteacher from the result of her own short-sightedness.

'I am fine,' she said, lifting her chin. Because she was fine. The pang of hurt was nothing more than a reaction to her brush with danger. It wasn't real. And she didn't care that he was too busy to linger. He'd done enough. He'd rescued her. It had been an adventure which was now over, and no harm done.

He glanced down at her again. 'Well, if you are sure? It's just that she was supposed to be on the coach you got off and...' He trailed off, looking at her sharply. 'I say, you don't go by the name of Miss Isherwood, do you?'

Only on weekdays, she wanted to reply, flippantly. Because she never got the chance to be flippant and there was something about this day, the improbability of going to spend Christmas in a ducal residence, and then getting swept off her feet by a man, that was giving everything an air of unreality.

But common sense prevailed. If he was here to meet Miss Isherwood, then the chances were that he was going to provide her transport to the ducal palace. Miss Badger had told her, after grumbling about having to work out the complicated itinerary and before pressing a sheaf of tickets into her hand, that this inn yard was the closest that the stage would take her to her final destination and that she was going to write and ask somebody to come and meet her.

And the somebody must be him.

'I am Miss Isherwood, yes,' she said.

He scowled at her. 'You are not…'

She had a suspicion that he'd been going to say *not what he'd expected*. But he gathered himself up, altered the expression on his face from one of disbelief to polite enquiry and said, 'That is, are you the bride's guest of honour?'

Clara felt a moment's perplexity. 'Guest of honour? I don't know about that. But I did receive an invitation to Miss Fairclough's wedding to the Duke of Braid. Would you like to inspect it?'

Without waiting for his response, she pulled open the strings of her reticule and delved inside for the thick cream card, edged with what looked like gold. She was jolly glad now that she'd decided to bring it with her. It had been just as she'd been tucking it between the pages of her prayer book, in order to keep it in pristine condition, that she'd had a sudden dreadful premonition that without it, people might not believe that such a humble creature as she had any right to enter such a grand place as the ducal palace sounded. But it had her name on it. And a personal note, scribbled on the reverse, from the bride herself. With that in her hand, nobody could deny her admittance.

The man glanced at the invitation she showed him. Removed his hat. Gave her a curt bow.

She tried not to sigh with relief, although she felt as if she had just surmounted what might have been an uncomfortable hurdle.

'I am pleased to make your acquaintance, Miss Isherwood. I am Lieutenant Warren.'

Lieutenant? Well, if he was in the army, or navy, that would explain his curt manners. He was probably more used to ordering people about than making polite conversation.

Clara got to her feet and dipped a respectful curtsy. 'And I am jolly glad to make yours, too, Lieutenant. If not for you, that horse might have trampled me.'

Something that was not exactly a smile, but was definitely a lessening of the severity of the line of his lips, softened his expression somewhat.

'If you would care to come this way,' he said, gesturing with his arm, 'I have a vehicle waiting out in the street. Because I have come, as you've probably already guessed, to convey you to Saxony Palace.'

'Thank you,' she said, her spirits lifting.

When he took her bag and strode off, the crowds parting before him and giving her a clear passage in his wake, it was all she could do not to skip along behind him. For not only had she escaped from the school for the duration of the Christmas festivities, not only had she had an interesting journey, not only had she been rescued from dire peril by a handsome, dark stranger, but she was now going to spend however long it would take to reach Saxony Palace in his company.

What an adventure! What a lot of tales she'd have to tell the girls when she went back to Heath Top!

Chapter Two

Hugo took a good long look at the slender, rather poorly co-ordinated young woman who claimed to be Miss Isherwood as he led her across to where he'd parked his new curricle. Could this really be the person that the Duke of Braid's bride-to-be had been describing in such glowing terms? The only person she said she could possibly consider as her maid of honour?

From what he'd learned so far about the silly chit who was about to become the Duchess of Braid, he would have expected her closest confidante to have been cut from the same cloth. So he had been expecting a dazzling creature to step out of the one-thirty coach, someone stylishly, if not gaudily dressed. Someone who would have simpered and batted her eyelashes, and sighed up into his face—and that only after he'd prised her from the gaggle of besotted swains she would have attracted on her journey thus far.

Instead, she'd been so effacing he'd hardly noticed her step out of the coach at all. Not until she'd wandered out into the middle of the yard, to collect the only piece of luggage he'd since learned was all she'd brought with her, and damn near been knocked down by a draught horse that was being trotted through the yard.

Which only meant she was silly in a different way to the bride-to-be.

Although…could that very gaucheness make his task

somewhat easier? he wondered as he helped her up into the passenger seat.

Before setting out, he'd wondered if the fashionable woman he'd expected to be collecting would complain about him coming to fetch her in the curricle. He'd been prepared to argue that he could ask the carrier to bring any luggage that he couldn't strap on to the back.

But there was no need. He could simply stow that one, shabby little bag at her feet.

As he did so, he couldn't help noticing that the coat, which he'd at first only thought was severe to the point of drabness, was also a touch threadbare.

'I hope,' he said, his conscience smiting him, 'that you do not object to travelling in my curricle? The air is mild today,' he said, as much to comfort himself as to stave off any reproaches from her. 'And I thought you might appreciate some fresh air after being cooped up inside public stage coaches all day.'

She turned to him with a smile of such sweetness that he completely revised his first impression of her. Clumsy and poorly dressed she might be, but underneath it all, and in spite of the bonnet that looked as if it had been designed for the purpose of repulsing the entire male sex, she had as much potential to turn the heads of an unsuspecting chap as her protégée.

And where else, after all, could little Miss Fairclough have learned her many tricks, but at the hands of a cunning preceptress?

'Oh, that was kind of you,' said Miss Isherwood. 'And I must confess I will enjoy the novelty of travelling in a rig like this,' she added, looking about her from her perch with bright, inquisitive eyes. 'Until today I have never had the chance, you see. It is all such an adventure!'

'The trouble with adventures,' he pointed out, having had far too many in recent years, 'is that they can very soon become uncomfortable.' And if it was true that she'd never ridden in a curricle before, she would have no idea how very cold it could get once they reached top speed. 'Here,' he added gruffly, taking a rug from the boot and draping it over her lap, 'this should help protect you from the worst of the chill.'

'Oh, thank you,' she breathed, as though the act of seeing to her comfort was a feat of great significance.

Preceptress, he reminded himself as he went round to the driver's side. *Beware*, he added as he climbed up beside her.

Nevertheless, since he needed to persuade her to help him achieve his aim, he allowed none of his suspicions to show on his face. He'd had plenty of practice at maintaining a teak-jawed inscrutability. A man couldn't hold command without learning how to prevent his subordinates from guessing what he was feeling or thinking. They had to have complete confidence in the orders he gave. Even when he himself suspected they were foolhardy to the point of criminality.

She jerked as he set the horses in motion with a flick of the whip and grabbed at the side. He glanced at her warily in case she was going to set up a screech. If she really hadn't ridden in a curricle before, he supposed she might find the height above the ground, and the swaying sensation of being suspended over only two wheels, a touch alarming. And he didn't want her scaring the horses.

But he need not have worried. Far from looking alarmed, she was smiling again, this time with a touch of glee.

'I am glad to see that you are enjoying your first experience of riding in a curricle,' he said, once he'd negotiated his way through the narrow, bustling streets.

'Oh, yes, it's marvellous,' she said. 'One can see so much from up here. And it feels as if we are going so *fast*.'

'Once we get on to a clear stretch of road, I can show you

just how fast my horses can go, if you like,' he offered. And then wondered why on earth he was offering to do any such thing. If he'd heard any other man speak like that, to a girl he'd only just met, he'd accuse the fellow of showing off.

'Oh. I don't know,' she said uncertainly. 'I might…that is…you won't take any risks, will you?'

'You will be perfectly safe with me,' he assured her. Before thinking that made him sound even more of a coxcomb. Even though it was the truth. He would never risk the life of a passenger, no matter what he thought of them, for the sake of showing off his prowess as a driver, or the peerless perfection of his newly acquired pair of chestnuts. 'And if you feel frightened, just tell me and I will slow down at once,' he added.

'Thank you,' she breathed. 'I don't want to sound cowardly. Indeed, I don't know if I am a coward or not.'

'Nobody does until they've been tested. Well, here goes,' he said when they reached the long straight section of road that led from Market Gate to the lane which led, via a series of winding undulations, to Saxony Palace. 'Hang on to your bonnet.'

She took his comment literally and he gave the horses the signal to speed up. Which they did, smoothly and without fuss.

Miss Isherwood said nothing, but whenever he glanced her way to check on how she was faring, it was to see her smiling.

'That,' she said when he slowed to take the turn through the gateposts, 'was…exhilarating!'

'I am glad you enjoyed it,' he said. And then cleared his throat. 'Miss Isherwood, I have to confess to having an ulterior motive in coming to fetch you in this rig. Apart from hoping you might appreciate the fresh air, that is.' And wanting to try out the gift his uncle had so unexpectedly given him as an early Christmas present. He'd never had such fine horses before. Never had a chance to as much as drive a matched pair like this. He'd come up with several plausible reasons for having them harnessed up, when he'd agreed to come on this errand, but he had to admit that mostly he just hadn't been able to resist the temptation.

'Oh?' She turned to look at him, those bright, intelligent eyes making him feel as if she was examining some species she'd never come across before.

Or perhaps that was just his guilty conscience coming into play.

'Yes,' he said firmly. 'I was hoping we could have a talk. A serious talk. I know that we might have had more privacy for doing so in a closed carriage, but I could not in all conscience have travelled in one all the way to Saxony Palace with you without a chaperon.' Which was a perfectly good excuse. It was. 'Which would have defeated the object.' It *would*. 'And for some reason, although we are just as much alone, and sitting far closer than we would have done in a coach, nobody seems to think it improper to sit with an unmarried female in a curricle.'

'Is that true?'

He glanced at her, wondering if he'd detected a note of sarcasm in her response. But she merely looked faintly bewildered.

He cleared his throat again.

'The fact of the matter is,' he said, deciding it was well past time he got to the point, 'that we, that is, the Duke's family, are all rather concerned about this marriage.'

Him in particular. He might not think very highly of Miss Fairclough's intelligence, but he couldn't stand back and let the silly chit make such a dreadful mistake with her life. Not if he could do something to prevent her. He would never forgive himself. Just as he'd never been able to forgive himself for failing to save his neighbour's daughter, Julie, from marrying a man she'd sworn would make her life a misery. Every time he'd heard tales of Lord Waring's cruelty to his much younger bride, in the ensuing years, he'd wished he'd just eloped with her and married her over the anvil, as she'd begged him to do.

His passenger's look of faint bewilderment deepened into one of utter confusion.

'What,' she asked, 'do you mean?'

'Well, it is just that His Grace is at least three times Miss Fairclough's age,' he blurted out. 'And just about four times her girth. His three daughters are all pretty much old enough to be her mother. And they are all hoping that you might be able to persuade her...' Because it had to be the lady who cried off. No man of honour could break a betrothal, no matter how unsuitable, especially not mere days before the ceremony. 'That is, to warn her...that is, that you might be able to ask her to make sure that she is absolutely sure that she can stomach, that is...that this union is what she really, truly wants. And if not, that she may apply to me for help in removing from the Palace and making sure that she is safe from any recriminations her own family might heap upon her head.'

For that was the main difference now. He might not be a wealthy man, but he was no longer a boy with no income at all. He could just about support a girl who had nowhere else to go and nobody to depend on. Somehow.

Surely, once the woman sitting at his side had seen the Duke of Braid with her own eyes, she would remember his offer to help and would have the sense to talk Miss Fairclough out of going through with what was bound to be a disastrous match.

If not...well, it didn't bear thinking about.

Chapter Three

For the first time since setting out Clara became aware of the cold. Like a disembodied finger, it trailed a path down her spine.

Miss Fairclough's intended was three times her age?

And four times her girth?

And all the Duke's family wished to prevent Miss Fairclough from marrying him? No wonder she'd invited Clara to come. The poor girl must feel in desperate need of someone, *any*one, to support her.

Before Lieutenant Warren might have expected her to form some kind of response to the information he'd just imparted, they rounded a bend and she caught her first sight of the Palace. There was no other way to describe it. And luckily, it was so breathtaking that nobody could have blamed her from being dumbstruck by its magnificence. In fact, if she hadn't been so worried that Lieutenant Warren would think she resembled a landed trout she would not have been able to prevent her mouth from opening on a gasp of amazement.

It was huge. With rows and rows of windows, set like panels of pure gold in a façade of mellow stone which was also glowing warmly in the reflected rays of the setting sun.

A lady came bustling out to greet her as the curricle swept round a gravel turning circle in front of a set of steps flanked by pillars and shielded by a portico.

'I am Mrs Cromwell,' the lady informed Clara, 'His

Grace's housekeeper. I shall conduct you to your room myself,' she added, in a tone that told Clara she was doing her
an immense favour.

'I'd better…' Clara said apologetically to Lieutenant
Warren as she clambered hurriedly down from her perch
seat. And, indeed, before she had time to do more than grab
her bag and fling her thanks to Lieutenant Warren, Mrs
Cromwell was ushering Clara into the house.

She'd thought the outside was impressive, but the inside
was even more breathtaking. Clara had never been inside
the house of anyone of note, but even she could see that the
many paintings and ornaments, and even the wood used to
construct the banisters of the staircases she was ascending,
were all of the very finest.

'This is your room, Miss Isherwood,' said Mrs Cromwell, opening the door to a room that was as big as the
dormitory in which she'd slept when she'd been a junior
pupil at Heath Top. But that was the only resemblance to
anywhere she'd ever been before. She had never trodden
on a carpet of such lush softness, or seen walls adorned
with what looked like real silk. Nor had she ever seen a
bedroom possess such a massive fireplace and with a fire
blazing away in it cheerfully, to boot!

But then she noted a mound of what looked like gowns,
gloves, feathers and crumpled heaps of velvet on the massive, oak-posted, silken-canopied bed.

'There must be some mistake…' she said.

'No, this is the room Miss Fairclough insisted you must
have,' said Mrs Cromwell, bustling over to the window and
twitching the curtains, as though to draw Clara's attention
to the view. 'From here you can see the formal gardens,
which she said she was sure you would enjoy.'

'Oh, but then…' Clara pointed to the muddle of articles
on the bed '…to whom do those belong?'

Mrs Cromwell was drawing breath to reply, when there

came a pattering of feet and then a familiar squeal from the doorway.

'You are here!' Miss Fairclough bounced into the room and enveloped Clara in a crushing embrace. 'I am so sorry I did not come to the door to meet you, but I *swear*,' she said, pressing her hand to her bosom, 'I came the moment I heard you'd arrived. Did you have a good trip? Do you like the room? Do you want some tea? And a wash? Cromwell, do be a darling and fetch some tea and a can of water. Or several cans. You can have a bath if you like, Miss Isherwood, before dinner...'

Clara took both Miss Fairclough's hands between her own and gave them a squeeze as she searched her face for signs of distress. After what Lieutenant Warren had told her and her suspicions about why the invitation had arrived, almost at the last minute, she'd half expected to find her former pupil looking distraught.

But she didn't.

'Yes, I would love some tea and a wash,' said Clara. 'And the room is lovely. Only, won't whoever is already staying here mind me sharing it with them?' It had dawned on her that this must be the explanation for the jumble of dresses and so forth piled on the bed.

'You aren't sharing the room with anyone, dearest Miss Isherwood. Those things are...' She turned to the housekeeper, raising one imperious little eyebrow. 'Are you still here? My maid of honour requires tea and enough water for a bath.'

She then giggled as the affronted housekeeper stalked from the room. 'She doesn't approve of me,' she told Clara. 'Well, none of them do, but what do I care?' She tossed her head with the kind of defiance she'd so frequently offered Miss Badger.

'Yes, I did hear,' Clara said hesitantly, 'that the family

are concerned that the Duke is, perhaps, rather older than one would wish…'

'Pooh! I don't care how old he is. Buttons is an absolute darling. And,' she said, tilting her head to one side and adopting a shrewd expression, 'you can only have heard that from his nephew, since he is the one who went to fetch you from the stage. And *he* is suffering from a massive case of sour grapes, because if I give Buttons an heir, it will cut him out.'

Cut him out? 'Are you telling me that Lieutenant Warren is the nephew of the Duke of Braid?' Because she had to assume that Buttons was the pet name Miss Fairclough had given her husband-to-be.

Miss Fairclough nodded. 'His heir, too, since he hasn't so far had anything but daughters.'

His heir? Had it been from envy, or even malice, that Lieutenant Warren had expressed those misgivings about her pupil's impending marriage to the Duke of Braid?

All of a sudden she remembered the curt way he'd spoken to her before he'd known who she was. The harshness of his face when he'd chastised her for almost walking out into the path of that draught horse.

And the abrupt change to his manner when he'd found out who she was and that she might have some influence over the woman who was about to marry his uncle and possibly provide him with a male child.

Oh… She had never felt such a crushing sense of disappointment since…well, she couldn't ever remember feeling so disillusioned. He'd seemed so perfect. The epitome of all the manly virtues, from the moment he'd wrapped his strong arms round her and swept her out of harm's way.

When she'd thought about how she was going to relate her adventure to the girls back at Heath Top, she'd had every intention of making him the hero of the piece. After telling them a handful of anecdotes about the funny people she'd met and what it had been like to spend a night, alone, in a bustling coaching inn, she'd been going to describe her first impressions of the handsome young man who'd come to meet her. How he'd rescued her, then borne her off to the Palace in a fashionable vehicle pulled by glossy horses that blew out smoke like dragons as they thundered along the wintry track.

She might not have shared with the girls how…cherished he'd made her feel, with the attentive way he'd tucked the rug round her knees to protect her from the cold and then the way he'd asked her opinion before setting his horses into that thrilling gallop.

Nobody had ever been so considerate. Nobody had ever asked her what she'd thought about what they planned to do, not even if it involved her welfare, let alone alter their course in order to please her. And she definitely wouldn't have told them how her heart had fluttered when he'd swept her into his arms. She'd planned to make it a wholesome adventure, suitable for the impressionable girls who'd enjoy hearing such a story, rather than having yet another sermon read to them.

But he wasn't a hero at all.

He'd been manipulating her.

Which just went to show how vulnerable a woman could be to the glib tricks of a passably attractive man, when she'd had so little experience of what men were really like.

'Which is why,' Miss Fairclough said, 'well, partly why,' she amended, with a slight flush, 'I insisted on having you brought here to be my maid of honour.'

Ah. So she wasn't as untouched by all the opposition to the marriage as she was trying to make out.

'I need someone here who is totally on my side,' Miss Fairclough continued. 'And I knew you would perfectly understand why I jumped at the chance of marrying my dear Buttons. Even if he *is* older than my own father,' she added with another defiant toss of her head, a gesture with which Clara was all too familiar. 'He is offering me a home, and a position, that nobody can ever take away. Even if we should fall out, or if he should die, I shall still be the Dowager Duchess, with an income and a home of my own that *nobody* can turn me out of,' she concluded fiercely.

She looked so very much, in that instant, like the hurt and furious little girl who'd arrived at Heath Top, declaring she ought not to be there since she wasn't an orphan. Who'd wept angry tears night after night at her father's betrayal in sending her away the moment his second wife had presented him with a son.

Clara patted Miss Fairclough's hand. 'Yes, I *do* understand the desire to have some security in this uncertain world. And, as long as he is kind to you…'

'Oh, Buttons is the most generous creature imaginable! He insisted on treating me to an entire new set of bride clothes, from the very best modistes. Says he doesn't want to see me in any of the rubbishing things I wore during my Season. Which is why I'm giving them all to you,' she said with a look of triumph, completely missing the implicit insult that she'd just given Clara, along with the mountain of clothes.

'Well,' Miss Fairclough continued, 'I knew you wouldn't have anything to wear suitable for a house party where his stiff rumped daughters would be in attendance.' She cocked one eye at Clara's shabby little bag. 'And I see I was right.' Her face resumed her fierce expression again. 'I am not going to give those vile women any opportunity to make you feel bad. You are going to have a different gown to wear for every meal and all the accessories to go with them.'

'Oh, I know that you and I are of a slightly different build,' she said, understating the case completely. Miss Fairclough was shorter than Clara, with far more abundant curves. 'But I've taken care of all that. Once you've had your bath, I am sending a woman to measure you up and pick something she can make ready for you to wear to dinner tonight. Because I am *not* going to expose you to the nasty tongues of those so-called ladies for want of having a fashionable gown.'

Clara didn't know what to say. Because she *did* only have her Sunday best in her overnight bag and she had been intending to wear it every evening, as well as for the wedding itself.

Besides, what woman could resist the lure of a set of new gowns? One for every night of her stay and another for the ceremony, she would warrant.

Even if Miss Fairclough now did consider them rubbish, to Clara, the multi-coloured, sumptuous mound of fabric on the bed looked to her like a sort of treasure from Aladdin's cave. If Aladdin had been a dealer in women's clothing, she smiled to herself.

'Miss Fairclough,' she said. 'That is very kind of you…'

'Oh, but you must call me Bella, you know.'

'Then you must call me Clara,' Clara felt obliged to respond.

With a beam of triumph, Miss Fairclough swept from the room, leaving Clara feeling a bit as though she'd just had an encounter with a small blonde whirlwind.

Which made her smile.

Because, even though she was about to become a duchess, it didn't look as if Miss Fairclough had changed one bit.

Chapter Four

After Hugo had dropped Miss Isherwood off at the front entrance, he drove the curricle round to the stables and had his groom, Steeple, saddle up his mare, Remembrance. He simply wasn't ready to enter the Palace and do the pretty with all his uncles and aunts, and cousins particularly now with all the satellites they were trailing in their wake.

Ever since he'd come one step closer to the coronet, with the death of his older brother Malcolm, he'd suddenly become interesting to a certain type of woman. The type who wanted to wear ermine themselves. The type who would feign friendship with any relation of his in an attempt to get near him. Or at least, that was how it had appeared last night and again this morning. He could barely sit and eat his breakfast without one or another of his aunts introducing him to a *lovely young lady*, the daughter of a *close bosom companion* of theirs.

He had spent an informative hour or two exploring the outermost limits of the estates, only returning to the Palace when it grew dark enough that he risked injury to Remembrance, should she step into a rabbit hole, or some such hazard.

Having stabled her and taken a lingering look at the magnificent chestnuts he'd driven earlier, he entered the Palace through a door that led to the servants' quarters and, from there, took the back stairs to get to his room.

He hadn't reached the second flight before he came across a sight that made his blood boil. Lord Baguley, who was married to the Duke's eldest daughter, had cornered a housemaid on the half-landing. He could just see the edges of her pinafore round his great bulk and guessed she was pressing herself close into the wall, in an attempt to dodge the older man's slobbering lips.

Or at least, he'd thought it was a housemaid. But when Lord Baguley half turned at the sound of his approach, he caught a glimpse of the girl's face. And saw that it was Miss Isherwood.

'What the devil do you think you're doing, Baguley?' Hugo strode right up to the man and, with no thought for the family connection, he pulled him away from the clearly terrified Miss Isherwood.

'Just a bit of fun with a pretty little maid,' snapped Lord Baguley. 'Not that it's any of your business, Warren.'

'It isn't fun when you are clearly scaring the poor girl out of her wits,' he retorted. 'Besides which, she isn't a housemaid. She's one of the guests.' Not that it should have made any difference. Though Hugo knew only too well that men like Lord Baguley saw the servants in houses that they visited as fair game. He wouldn't even be surprised to learn that he preyed on his own staff.

Lord Baguley raised one eyebrow. 'That so? What's she doing on the back stairs then? Lost your way, did you?' he said, turning back to Miss Isherwood who, the moment Hugo had distracted her oppressor, had begun creeping crabwise along the wall, to get out of his reach. 'Then allow me to show you the way to wherever it is you were hoping to go,' he said, with an oily grin as he held out his arm, his elbow crooked.

'I can escort Miss Isherwood wherever it is she wants to go,' said Hugo, stepping between Lord Baguley's arm and Miss Isherwood's shrinking form.

'Do you think so?' Lord Baguley trailed a mocking eye over Hugo's less than presentable attire.

At which point, Miss Isherwood settled the matter by stepping up to Hugo and clutching the sleeve of his mud-splattered coat, even though he hadn't as yet thought to hold his own arm out to her.

'I see,' said Lord Baguley, a rather nasty smile twisting his fat lips. 'Then all I can say is that I look forward to furthering our acquaintance over the next few days.' He swept Miss Isherwood an ironic bow and made off down the stairs. In the direction, Hugo couldn't help noticing with unease, of the servants' quarters. Where he was clearly going to make a nuisance of himself if his attitude just now had been any indication.

'A word of advice, Miss Isherwood,' he said, forcing his attention away from the potential trouble Lord Baguley represented as he rolled wheezily down the stairs. 'If you don't wish to be molested, stick to the public areas in future.'

'That's—that's an outrageous thing to say! As if any woman would wish to be molested!'

Her remark stung him a bit, since he'd already been thinking that housemaids had as much right to be treated with respect as a guest and ought to be as safe on the back stairs as a lady would be on the grander ones.

So naturally he retaliated with some irritation.

'But you have no business loitering on the back stairs. Just where were you sneaking off to?'

'I was not sneaking,' she protested, removing her hand from his sleeve and drawing herself up to her full height. Which brought her level with the bottom of his chin. 'I was merely hoping to explore the house a bit while I was waiting for the seamstress to finish the alterations to the dress I am to wear to dinner. I believe there is a very fine library on the ground floor, which I thought I might just have time to take a swift look into. And since Miss Fairclough told me that what I am wearing will only cause certain people to mock me…' She swept an indignant hand over the drab and extremely unflattering gown she wore. He supposed he ought to have known that whatever she had on under that threadbare coat of hers was likely to be equally as unfashionable, but he hadn't expected her to be wearing something that resembled a voluminous apron.

Still, at least being angry with him had brought some colour back to her cheeks, he observed. He hadn't liked the white, drawn look Lord Baguley had caused.

'Perhaps you would be better to stay in your room until then,' he suggested. 'You certainly don't appear safe to be let out on your own. You have no more sense than a…'

'I beg your pardon?' Now her eyes were sparkling, too. He'd never understood what chaps meant about women looking attractive when they were angry, until this moment. But Miss Isherwood, roused, was a rather interesting figure.

'I will have you know that I am a very capable, intelligent woman, and that I routinely take charge of girls in need of not only an education, but also counselling and compassion. That is not a job that just any female can do, I will have you know!'

'That may be so,' he replied. 'And I concede that within the walls of your school, you probably fare very well. However,' he pointed out, 'this is the second time today I have had to rescue you from the results of your own folly. You walked right out in front of that horse without looking, then went waltzing down the back stairs dressed like a servant straight into the path of a notorious lecher.'

'How dare you imply that I need a…some sort of…man to look after me! I was trying to clear the path of an obstacle so that nobody might trip over my bag when that guard tossed it into the middle of the yard,' she protested. 'And as for using the back stairs, well, how was I to know it wasn't safe? You must know that I've never visited an establishment like this before. And anyway,' she said, her eyes narrowing, '*you* are using the back stairs.'

'Well, yes, because I'm covered in filth from riding. Besides…'

'Besides what?'

'Well,' he admitted, 'just as male predators lurk on the back stairs, the female ones have a habit of lurking on the public ones.'

A frown pleated her brow. 'What is that supposed to mean? Oh. That you think you are a catch and any woman would go to any lengths to attract your attention.'

'It's true,' he protested. 'A certain sort of female will do her utmost to get an invitation to an event such as this, just so she can have the excuse to claim the right to accost me.'

She stiffened. 'Are you accusing me of accosting you? Of wheedling an invitation to this wedding because I am trying to catch *you*?' She made the kind of noise a horse might make if its oats went down the wrong way. Though in her case, it clearly denoted fury.

'If I *was* on the catch for a man,' she flung at him, 'which I am not because I am perfectly able to look after myself, both financially and…and in every other way, then you would be the very last man I would target.'

'It didn't look like it to me,' he said, half wondering why he was prolonging this altercation, rather than just bowing ironically and stalking away, which was what he would have done, he was certain, had this been any other woman.

She looked baffled.

'I only meant,' he said provokingly, 'that you were not averse to taking *my* arm, though you were positively cringing away from Lord Baguley.'

'You are,' she gasped, 'without doubt, the most obnoxious, arrogant and *pedantic* man I have ever met!'

And with that she turned and flounced away back up

the stairs. Back in the direction of where he happened to know her room lay. Back to safety.

Objective achieved, then. She'd learned her lesson. And wouldn't venture out on her own again in a hurry.

What a pity it was that he'd had to make her so cross with him in the process.

Chapter Five

Some time later, Clara was standing observing her reflection in the full-length mirror, a luxury to which she'd never had access before.

She couldn't say that what she saw in that mirror brought her unmitigated pleasure. The seamstress had insisted that the gown she now wore was exactly the kind of thing to wear when dining with a duke and all his noble relatives. But Clara couldn't help thinking that it revealed rather too much of her. It clung to her in such a way that she appeared to have a far fuller bosom than she'd ever suspected. And the neckline emphasised that impression by plunging much lower than she felt was decent. So low that she was surprised that she wasn't covered all over in goose pimples. But the apparently flimsy undergarments she was also wearing, courtesy of Bella, did a much better job of insulating her lower limbs than she would have thought possible.

She was just starting to wonder if she would ever pluck up enough courage to leave her room, with the tops of her breast on show like this, when, after a brief knock, the door burst open and Bella herself dashed into the room.

'You are ready! Good,' she exclaimed. 'Oh, and don't you look elegant! I just knew that shade of amber would suit you, with you having dark hair and eyes. And I also knew that you wouldn't have anything to go with it, so I've brought you some baubles to hang round your neck, just in case you didn't have anything of your own.

'Here,' she said, opening the drawstring of a little velvet bag, which Clara hadn't even noticed, until that moment, that she was carrying, and pulling out a string of amber beads. 'Only trumpery, really, I'm afraid. But it will go perfectly with this outfit. My uncle, Mr Lyons, the husband of my mother's sister Clarissa, you know, the one who launched me into society, when she *finally* remembered my existence,' she put in tartly, 'bought it for me for the purpose.'

'Then I couldn't possibly…'

'Now don't go spoiling my evening by refusing me! It's only a loan, after all, so you won't have to be the only lady there who isn't dripping in jewels,' retorted Bella with a pout, as she draped the beads round Clara's neck and did up the clasp. 'There,' she said triumphantly, looking at their reflections, side by side, in the mirror. 'The finishing touch!'

'I cannot deny that…that somehow I don't look so… undressed as I did before…'

Bella giggled. 'I know just what you mean. The first time I wore a fashionable neckline, I felt very, very exposed. It's all the bare skin. Once you have a string of beads to break up the expanse, it does look very much more acceptable, doesn't it?'

Clara wasn't sure. But it was so hard to refuse a gesture of such generosity. She'd sound churlish if she complained about either the gown, which was the finest thing she'd ever worn, or the loan of the amber beads, which did, as Bella had predicted, set off the gown to perfection.

'I… I…'

Before she had time to form a coherent sentence, Bella gave her a quick hug. 'You don't need to say anything, dear Miss Isherwood. Clara. I know you aren't used to having anyone give you anything. I spent all those years at that miserable school as well, didn't I? And it is such a joy to me to be in a position to be able to spoil you a little, after all the friendship you showed to me while I was there. If it hadn't been for you, I don't know how I would have survived. So it's only right that I share a little, just a very little, of the good fortune that has come my way, isn't it?'

'Well, if you put it like that, I suppose…'

'Exactly! Now, come on. Let's go down. The timing will be just right. Not so early that the tabbies will have much of a chance to sharpen their claws on us, but long enough before the meal that dear Buttons won't grow anxious. There is nothing,' she said, drawing Clara across to the door, 'that vexes him more than having to hold back a meal because someone is late. He is so worried that a particular sauce might spoil, or curdle, or…or…well, things like that,' she said in a confiding manner as she headed in the direction of the main staircase.

The one which Clara had felt, earlier on, that she didn't have the right to use, what with its sumptuous carpets, and its intricately carved banister, and all the works of art poised precariously in little niches between portraits of such skill that they looked just like real people, frozen in the act of looking down their noses at schoolteachers who had the effrontery to pose as guests in their home.

Bella led Clara unerringly to a vast room, which was more like a wide corridor, stuffed with chairs upon which none of the gorgeously garbed people gathered there deigned to sit. Instead, they were all standing in little clusters, murmuring to each other, while looking askance at her. Or, perhaps at Bella, since it was no secret that most of them disapproved of her.

As ever, when one of her pupils was under threat, Clara felt a surge of angry protectiveness surge up. She lifted her chin and gave back look for look, while holding on to Bella's arm a little more tightly. Even so, she was not holding it tightly enough to prevent her from breaking away, with a little cry of, 'Buttons!'

Bella went scampering across the room to the only person who was sitting down. A man who was clearly the Duke of Braid, since Miss Fairclough was peppering his face with kisses and surely she would do no such thing to any other than her betrothed. Besides, he matched the description Lieutenant Warren had given her, to the letter. And Lieutenant Warren himself was standing behind his chair, watching her approach with a wooden countenance.

Even though it was impossible to tell what he might be thinking, she was really glad that she was wearing the gown Bella had loaned her. For the golden, silky material swirled round her legs as she walked, shimmering as brightly as that of any of the other ladies past whom she had to make her way.

If she'd worn her Sunday best, as she'd intended, she would never have been able to withstand the scornful looks the other ladies were giving her. She would have felt even more of an impostor in this glittering crowd in the garb of a penniless schoolmistress—the kind of gown that had made that lecher mistake her for the sort of person upon whom he could prey without suffering any consequences.

At which point, she noted the lecher in question, lounging against the wall between an arrangement of greenery on a pedestal and a painting of nymphs cavorting in a forest, looking for all the world like a satyr lurking in the shrubbery in hopes of catching some other poor maiden unawares. Making her aware, once more, of the low cut of her neckline. And she was going to have to walk right past the spot where he was lurking, in order to reach the Duke's chair.

Her cheeks began to heat. But then Lieutenant Warren came marching up to her.

'Miss Isherwood,' he said, moving into a position that blocked her from Lord Baguley's view before making his bow. For which action she ought to have been more grateful. Only it had the unfortunate effect of reminding her that he'd witnessed the horrible scene on the staircase. And had felt obliged to rescue her. Both then and now.

'Allow me,' said the Lieutenant, 'to present you to my uncle, His Grace, the Duke of Braid.'

Clara tried not to mind that he'd had to step in to cover for Bella's thoughtlessness. And tried not to blush when she caught a very haughty-looking woman shoot her a look which somehow conveyed the information that Clara had made a poor job of teaching Bella anything about etiquette, if she couldn't even perform an introduction in the proper manner.

She lifted her chin as she laid her hand on the arm Lieutenant Warren had so gallantly offered her and took her first good look at Bella's intended. And, after only one glance, she could scarcely believe that her pupil could truly be thinking of marrying a man so much older than her. Even for the security his position would bring her.

Hoping that her own expression was as inscrutable as that of Lieutenant Warren, Clara made her curtsy to the grand old man.

'Forgive me for not rising to greet you,' wheezed the Duke. 'The old legs not what they were.'

'N-not at all,' Clara murmured, since she was aware she had to say something. She couldn't just stand there and gape at the mountain of satin-covered flesh, as though he was an exhibit in a museum. Although she couldn't help seeing exactly why Bella might have decided to call him Buttons. Every single one that adorned the front of his vast waistcoat was under such strain that it looked as though it might pop off and fly into someone's eye at any moment.

'My nephew can introduce you to the relevant people,' said the Duke, waving one hand vaguely, before returning his attention to Bella.

Lieutenant Warren towed her, immediately, to a middle-aged couple who were standing not far off, arm in arm, as though providing each other with moral as well as physical support.

'Mr Lyons, and his wife, the maternal aunt of Miss Fairclough,' said the Lieutenant in an expressionless tone.

The couple looked at her, then at her gown, and then, their expressions darkening, at the beads round her neck. Clara suddenly realised that they must have paid for everything she was wearing and were not at all pleased to see her in the clothes they'd bought for their niece. But before they could say anything unpleasant, or she could begin to stammer excuses for Bella, Lieutenant Warren was steering her over to another family group. The man had a red sweaty face. The tall, slender woman at his side was deathly white. And the two plump youths who made up the family party looked as though they thought a great deal of themselves.

'I do not know if you have already had the pleasure of meeting Miss Fairclough's father,' said Lieutenant Warren, 'or his wife?'

'No,' said Clara, dropping the obligatory curtsy as he gave them her name. Nor could she say it was a pleasure now, not knowing how badly they'd all treated poor Bella.

Then a set of double doors at one end of the room opened. As though it was a signal for them to leap into action, two footmen stepped smartly up to the Duke's chair, took one elbow each and heaved him to his feet.

'Nevvy!' The Duke's bellow made just about everyone jump, apart from Lieutenant Warren himself, who merely turned to his uncle and raised one eyebrow. 'You will escort Miss Isherwood in to dine,' said the Duke. 'As our guest of honour, she will, naturally, sit on my left at table. And I want you on her other side, since you already know her. And since you are, out of all the family, the only one I can trust to behave like a gentleman.'

Lieutenant Warren bowed. Then held out his arm to her.

As yet another footman was handing the Duke an ebony cane, adorned with scarlet and silver ribbons, Clara couldn't help hearing several people muttering in muted outrage at the Duke's proclamation. Or noticing that Bella's father and stepmother looked as though someone had just driven a coach at speed through a puddle next to which they had been standing.

The Duke, paying no heed to anyone else, smiled benevolently at Bella as he set his pudgy hand on top of the cane. She positively beamed at him as she set her hand on top of his and they began to make their ponderous way to the open doors.

'We have had our orders,' said Lieutenant Warren in a quiet, but firm voice, as she hesitated. 'And whatever we may think of them, it is best to simply obey.'

Whatever they might think of them? What did he mean by that? That he didn't want to sit next to her?

Well, she didn't want to sit next to him, either! If it wasn't for the fact she knew nobody else here but Bella, she would have...

No. She would not have stalked off with her nose in the air and sat next to somebody else. She wasn't made of such stern stuff.

Acknowledging this flaw in her own character made her feel resentful as she laid her hand upon Lieutenant Warren's sleeve, so that they could follow the Duke and his bubbly bride-to-be into the dining room. She'd never thought of herself as being a fanciful sort of person before, but she could feel the icy-cold stares of the people following along behind them, stabbing into her back like knives.

In turn, she poured some of her own resentment into the backs of the couple walking ahead of her. For she had come all this way to support Bella, who had just cheerfully abandoned her to the prospect of social discomfort and was behaving as though the Duke was the only person in the room.

She took a deep breath. It was foolish to feel let down. She knew what a…mercurial temperament Bella had.

And at least the Duke had taken steps to protect her, by ordering his nephew to escort her to table.

Even if, she suspected, he ought not to be trusting him all that much, since he'd told her he didn't want the marriage to take place.

Although the Duke had been right about him being a gentleman. He'd proved it by rescuing her from another of the Duke's relatives, who was most definitely not. Even if he had also been rude enough, while coming to her rescue, to imply she was not fit to be let out on her own.

Although he'd redeemed himself by leaping into action just now, when Bella had left her stranded alone in the middle of a room full of strangers.

She pursed her lips.

He might not approve of Bella's marriage to his uncle. He might not like Clara. But at least he had a strong moral compass. If she had met him under different circumstances, she could imagine them seeing eye to eye about a great many things.

What a pity they'd got off to such a bad start!

Chapter Six

Hugo could hardly believe the transformation in Miss Isherwood's appearance. Gone was the shapeless, threadbare gown that had given Lord Baguley the impression she was one of the maids. Instead she wore a golden confection that made her look positively regal.

Particularly with that raised chin and cool attitude to everyone in the room apart from Miss Fairclough. And the positively condescending way she had laid her hand upon his sleeve as she accepted his escort to the dining room.

The queenly attitude lasted only until they reached the dining table. As he handed her to the seat next to his uncle's, he caught a rather nervous look in her eyes as they flicked round the room. Once he'd taken his own seat, next to her, he followed the direction of her gaze, wondering what on earth she'd seen to provoke that slightly nervous look.

Could it be the sight of Lord Baguley, taking his place next to his wife who, as the eldest of the Duke's daughters, was acting as his hostess? Surely not. He'd gained the impression that, if he hadn't rushed to her side the moment she'd seen the man propping up the wall of the reception room just now, she'd have stalked past him with her nose in the air. Yet she was touching each item of cutlery, in turn, then flicking anxious glances at all the crystal glasses ranged round her place setting as though she had no idea what she was supposed to do with any of them.

Ah. Perhaps she didn't.

He looked with fresh eyes at the table the length of a ship's deck and draped with yards of snowy-white linen, upon which stood silver epergnes containing displays of fruit, along with the many works of art created in his uncle's kitchen from sponge cake, icing and marzipan. Then at the titled, bejewelled guests who were elbowing one another aside in their determination to get the best seats. And lastly, at the veritable troop of bewigged footmen in their scarlet livery who were bearing down on the table, carrying covered dishes and tureens.

She might look as though she belonged here, in that silken gown, but he'd seen her arrive with just the one small case that she treated as if it contained all her worldly possessions, when in fact it could not possibly hold more than a change of nightwear and a few odds and ends such as hairbrush, comb and toothbrush. Which meant that Miss Fairclough must have lent her the gown. It wouldn't have occurred to anyone else to do so. And, in spite of giving a show of defiance, underneath that borrowed gown Miss Isherwood was still very aware that she was merely an impoverished, unconnected, unsophisticated schoolmistress who'd been thrust into a world about which she knew nothing.

It made him recall just how he'd felt when he'd grown old enough to sit at table with the adults, on an occasion very much like this one, in this very room. How overwhelmed by the grandeur, formality and opulence of it all he'd been, since it was in such contrast to the far more simple surroundings in which he'd grown up.

Once again, the moment he suspected she was feeling vulnerable, he had an overwhelming urge to try to put her more at ease.

He cleared his throat. 'The first time I ever dined with my uncle, in this very room,' he said to her, 'I was so scared of using the wrong fork, or committing some breach of etiquette, that I could scarcely eat a thing.'

She whipped round to look at him, those brown eyes that he knew could flash fiery scorn, or anger, now clouded with trepidation. He wanted to pat her hand. But that was out of the question. All he could do was try to think of some words of comfort.

'You need not worry that you will do anything of which the Duke might disapprove. Once he starts eating, pirates could fire a broadside into the room and he wouldn't take a bit of notice.'

What had pirates got to do with anything? She frowned as she wondered why on earth he'd brought up such an odd topic of conversation and noted a look of concern in Lieutenant Warren's eyes.

He'd been trying to distract her!

Or amuse her, or something of the sort.

How...how thoughtful.

She attempted a smile. 'I had been wondering what on earth I could find to say to a duke,' she admitted. Although that had only been one of her concerns. 'So it is a relief to learn that I won't have to say anything after all.'

He gave her a brief nod, then sat back with the air of a man who was pleased at having just performed his duty.

She tried not to mind that he saw her as a duty. After all, sitting between the Duke's vast and uncommunicative bulk and the Lieutenant, who was ready to leap into action to defend a woman on the slightest provocation, was the safest place at the table to be. The ladies present might shoot dagger glances at her, but they could hardly lean round either of her dining companions to say anything hurtful. And that man who'd accosted her on the stairs—well, he might be leering at her over the soup tureen, but she need not take any notice.

So she would concentrate on just enjoying the experience of sampling the kind of meal she'd fantasised about, for as long as she could remember.

She began by allowing one of the attentive footmen to pour her a glass of rich ruby-red wine and then encouraging others to put a selection of delicious-looking food on her plate. Then, when she'd eaten that helping, had seconds of all the things she'd enjoyed. Seconds!

However, no matter how tempting it might be to go for thirds, she simply had to leave enough room for an orange. She'd seen a whole pile of them, sitting in a dish a little way down the table, with all sorts of greenery twined into the mound, making the oranges look even more vibrant against the dark glossy leaves.

She was just laying down her knife and fork and plucking up the courage to ask the Lieutenant to pass her one—a whole one—when one lot of footmen whisked away all the dishes from the table and another lot of them set out another array of meat, jellies, cakes and pies.

She gazed wistfully after the pile of oranges as one footman bore them away and another set a jug of custard down before her plate.

'You do not need to keep on eating,' murmured a voice in her ear. 'That custard is not a challenge,' Lieutenant Warren added, sounding amused.

'I know,' she snapped at him. And then sighed wistfully. 'But oh, how I wish I could. I have never seen so many delicious-looking things. And I have dreamed of custard. But…' she placed one hand on her stomach '…I enjoyed the first course too much. Because I didn't realise there would be another.'

His smile faded. 'Custard?' He gave her a strange look. 'Don't you usually get enough to eat?'

Clara was torn between telling him not to ask such personal questions, because it was impertinent, and a bewildering yearning to confide in him that, no, she never felt as if she got enough to eat. That this table, spread with so much bounty, was the stuff of fantasy.

'My only regret,' she admitted, by way of a compromise, 'is that I didn't snatch one of those oranges from the display before the footmen whisked it away. I could *always* make room for an orange.'

'His Grace prides himself on the bounty of the food he provides for his guests,' said Lieutenant Warren. 'You have only to make your wishes known. Here,' he said to a footman whose sole job seemed to be to go round topping up everyone's wine glasses. As he came to answer the Lieutenant's summons, Clara put her hand over the top of her glass. Wine might look rich and enticing, but she didn't like the taste and couldn't say that she ever wanted to sample any more.

'Could you,' said Lieutenant Warren to the footman, 'go and fetch this lady an orange?'

'Of course, sir,' he said, before darting off.

Clara blinked in surprise. She'd assumed the Lieutenant had summoned the wine waiter to pour him more wine, not so that he could go and fetch her an orange. Besides…

'I really don't think I could possibly manage an orange,' she admitted.

'Take it to your room, then,' said Lieutenant Warren with a shrug. 'Have it later on. Or when you wake up tomorrow.'

An orange for breakfast? What a marvellous idea!

'Thank you,' breathed Clara, through a throat suddenly thickened with an almost overwhelming surge of gratitude.

'Don't thank me,' said Lieutenant Warren, looking a touch uncomfortable. 'I told you His Grace prides himself on being a generous host. Particularly when it comes to food. Whatever time of day you might fancy something to eat, you will find a selection of things laid out in one of the rooms.

'The breakfast room, of course, at breakfast. And then during the day, the side tables in the south drawing room are constantly kept refreshed in case anyone might feel the slightest bit peckish between breakfast and the nuncheon that is set out here at about two of the clock. And after that light meal, tea and cakes are always available in the conservatory until just before we dine here at six. Should you wish to, you could spend all day drifting from one room to another, grazing.'

All day? She could spend all day, wandering from one room to another, eating?

She was so stunned by the heavenly prospect that she absentmindedly poured some custard into her bowl.

'Oh, but…' she said, setting down the jug with deliberation, 'I shouldn't.' Not custard now and not eating all day, either. 'There were so many other things I wanted to do while I was here.'

Lieutenant Warren was giving her a quizzical look. As though he couldn't believe what she'd just said. And nor could she. Why was she confiding in him? *Him*, of all people?

'Such as?'

'I had hoped to be able to browse in the library, if…' She blushed, recalling that horrible encounter with that lecherous man on the stairs, when she'd tried to slip down quickly to take a peep at it before dinner. 'Or if the weather is fine,' she continued, hastily stumbling away from the memory of those grasping hands, those bewildering, yet somehow shaming words, 'I would like to go exploring outside. For I am never likely to get another chance to wander round grounds that are bound to be as fine as they are here.'

'You could do both,' he said, startling her. 'Explore the grounds first, then come back for a hot drink and a slab of cake, which you will enjoy all the more for having worked up a healthy appetite on a brisk walk.'

'I don't know about brisk,' she said. 'I was just thinking it would be lovely to wander about, looking at gardens,
without having any duties to rush back to attend to.'

He nodded. 'I keep forgetting. You know what it is to
work for a living.'

'What do you mean by that?' Was he trying to remind
her that she didn't belong with all these grand, titled people? There was no need. She *knew* it.

But he was turning the upper part of his body to her and
looking at her intently.

'Well, it is just that it is something that few of those sitting round this table understand. In fact, it is probably only
you and I who have ever known the rigours of working
under the command of a superior, or what it is to be routinely hungry. Most of these people have no idea how the
rest of humankind have to struggle, as a matter of course,
for the necessities of life. Whenever I come here and witness
all this…excess…' He snapped his mouth shut, as though
biting back on the rest of whatever he might have been
thinking.

'But… I thought you were the heir to all this?'

His face hardened. 'Well, yes. But inside, I still feel like
a mere half-pay officer waiting for my next post. His Grace
is trying to persuade me to abandon my career by offering me an allowance to stay ashore indefinitely. Kicking
my heels…' He screwed up his mouth as though he'd just
tasted something unpleasant.

It gave her a funny feeling to see that he felt as if he
ought to be earning his living. And that he didn't feel as
if he belonged here, either. As though they were both cut
from the same cloth. Although that was nonsense. Even if
he did find all this opulence not to his taste, he'd spent what
he thought of as his working life at sea, doing all sorts of
heroic, manly things. While she spent her life in a dusty

schoolroom, or trying to comfort girls going through the worst years of their impoverished lives.

The Duke chose this moment to set down his knife and fork and lean back in his chair. And, as though waiting for the moment, the lady who was sitting at the foot of the table got to her feet. Which was the signal for the ladies to withdraw. For a moment, Clara was a bit surprised that it hadn't been Miss Fairclough who had done so, but then she worked out that until she had actually married the Duke, she could scarcely act as his hostess.

As she was getting to her feet, Lieutenant Warren tapped her arm.

'I say, tomorrow, if you are serious about exploring the grounds, I could show you around. Only if you like… I mean, I know some good walks, with splendid views, and…' He petered out, looking a touch baffled, as if he couldn't believe he had just made that offer.

'You don't need to. Truly, I shall be happy wandering about on my own.'

'With predators like Lord Baguley lurking behind the bushes? Are you sure that is what you want?'

'No. Of course I don't.' She eyed the rest of the ladies, who were laying down their napkins, getting to their feet and making their way to the door through which the hostess had already gone. 'I just didn't want to put you to any bother. Oh, dear, whatever shall I do?' She eyed Lord Baguley, who was leaning back in his chair, watching the procession of ladies with what she felt was an unhealthy interest.

'Agree to meet me, after breakfast, wearing stout walking shoes and a warm coat, and let me take care of you.'

Take *care* of her? He might as well have thrown a glass of water in her face.

'I don't need any man to *take care* of me,' she snapped.

His face closed up. 'Have it your own way,' he drawled.

Just as Miss Fairclough came round the back of the Duke's chair, caught her arm and smiled at her.

'Come on, Clara! Time to stop flirting with the most eligible man in the room and come with me to face the gorgons.'

'I wasn't flirting,' Clara protested. Probably to no avail. Everyone left in the room would have heard Bella's tactless remark. And would probably believe that was exactly what she had been doing. Even though nothing could have been further from the truth.

Chapter Seven

Clara had been looking forward to this part of the day, very much. She was sure Bella would have arranged all sorts of fun and games in which she could participate, after dinner, without having to worry about being in charge of impressionable girls, for once.

And at first she did enjoy herself with the younger set, who followed Bella to one end of the massive drawing room while the older guests drifted in the direction of the card tables at the other. She didn't mind when everyone laughed when she lost the first game of bullet pudding and ended up with a face covered in flour. And was pleasantly surprised when the next activity Bella suggested was a sort of guessing game. Until, that was, she became aware that the purpose of the game was not so much to exercise the mind with clever riddles, but more about making lewd jokes under the guise of using words that had more than one meaning.

But worse was to come. One of the young men produced a large silk handkerchief and declared it was time for a game of Hoodman Blind. Clara thought it strange for grown men to wish to play such a childish game, until they turned it into a sort of…free-for-all, with the young men grabbing whichever female form they could get their hands on and, brandishing sprigs of mistletoe, claiming kisses as forfeits if they guessed the name wrong.

Finally, Clara escaped from the increasingly boisterous and indecorous games by pleading exhaustion from the long day of travel.

The first thing she saw, when she reached the safety of her room, was an orange, sitting on a porcelain saucer on her bedside table.

Her conscience smote her. Lieutenant Warren had kindly asked that footman to fetch her one, but he hadn't returned with it by the time the ladies withdrew from the table. And the footman hadn't approached her at any time since. So Lieutenant Warren must have given orders to have it brought here. Even though she'd flounced off so rudely at the end of the meal.

Even though she'd spent the rest of the evening ignoring him. Or trying to do so, anyway. She hadn't been able to help noticing the disapproving frowns he kept flinging her way. Or wishing she hadn't been caught up in behaviour about which she felt so uncomfortable.

He'd made her feel so…foolish.

And to cap it all, now he'd made sure she'd received the orange she'd told him she wanted.

After that, it was impossible to get to sleep, in spite of what a long and arduous day she'd had. Because she couldn't stop thinking about how she was going to have to approach him in the morning, to thank him for the orange.

And to accept the offer of his escort that she'd so rudely told him she had no need of.

Oh, how she wished she'd just said *yes*, in the first place. Then she wouldn't have to appear to back down. What was it about the man that made her so ridiculously sensitive? Or act as though she had any right to pride? She was a *nobody*. And ought to just gratefully accept any crumbs anyone cared to toss her way.

Yet it still felt like one of the hardest things she'd ever done when she made a bee line for where he was sitting at breakfast, tucking into a plate of sausage and eggs.

'Good morning,' she said.

He looked at her with suspicion, his forkful of eggs suspended halfway to his mouth. She couldn't blame him for that look, not one bit. Not after she'd made a point of ignoring him all last evening.

'I believe I must thank you for making sure I received that orange.'

He gave her a brief nod, before raising the fork the rest of the way to his mouth, taking the eggs from it and chewing methodically.

Clara's heart sank. He wasn't going to make this easy for her, was he? 'And,' she continued, drawing upon every reserve of courage she could find, 'you said that if I would like you to show me round the grounds, I should let you know, this morning, at breakfast, and well…' She spread her hands and shrugged her shoulders, hoping that she looked as though she saw nothing wrong with approaching a man and asking for a favour, after spending an entire evening being extremely rude to him. But she could feel her cheeks heating.

He swallowed. Tilted his head to the sideboard, on which stood dozens of silver domes, on chafing dishes. 'You had better get some breakfast, then. And go and find some warm clothing to wear. For, although the sun is shining,' he said, tilting his head to the windows, through which, indeed, the sun was shining, 'it won't be giving out much heat—besides, the glass is falling, and the wind rising. I shouldn't be surprised if we don't get some showers later. I beg pardon,' he added, looking a touch chagrined. 'Habit of mine to keep an eye on the weather.'

'I suppose you need to, when at sea,' she said, completely understanding his fascination with weather.

'Yes. Might have to trim the sails at a moment's notice,' he said, feeling relieved that she was not going to accuse him of being peculiar for knowing exactly what the barometric pressure was and what was likely to happen, weather-wise, during the course of the day, when he was about as far inland as it was possible to get in England. That was what any of his aunts would have pointed out, tartly, should he have said anything so gauche to any of them.

But then she wasn't habitually spiteful, like they all were, he mused, as she turned away and went to the sideboard. Oh, he'd annoyed her, just about every time their paths had crossed, but that was his own fault, he reflected as she lifted the lid of one dish after another, an expression of awe, mingled with indecision, crossing her face. He kept on blundering in with the kind of phrases that were bound to set up any female's back. It came of being more used to the rough-and-ready ways of sailors. Of being in command. Of getting into the habit of barking orders and expecting them to be obeyed, instantly.

Life on land, with civilians, ran on an entirely different set of rules, as his uncle, the Duke, kept on reminding him. If he was going to step into his shoes, one day, he was going to have to learn to speak more diplomatically. Especially to females, who seemed particularly hard to get along with.

By the time Miss Isherwood returned to the table he could see that she'd dealt with the vexing problem of what to choose for breakfast by taking a little portion from every single dish, for her plate was piled high with a selection of food guaranteed to give anyone indigestion.

'I shall meet you at the door to this room, in half an hour,' he said. Then, since he'd just decided he ought to try being a bit more diplomatic, added, 'Will half an hour be long enough?'

She looked at him, then at her plate, then at him again, her lips compressing into a mutinous line. Then, with a visible struggle, merely said, 'Thank you', before tucking into the mountain of eggs, sausage, rice, steak, ham, fried potatoes, tomatoes, mushrooms and cheese on her plate.

It felt like a minor victory to see that his own attempt at diplomacy had resulted in her shutting the gun ports rather than firing back at him. Even though he'd clearly annoyed her, somehow. He eyed her breakfast plate again. And the speed at which she was working her way through it. Then considered how long it might take her to change from the gown she had on to something more suitable for an expedition out of doors.

'Better make it an hour,' he decided. And was rewarded when she smiled with relief and began to wield her cutlery with less frenzy.

It didn't take him anywhere near an hour to fetch a coat, pull on some boots and return to the door of the breakfast room, of course. Which meant that by the time she turned up, he'd practically worn a furrow into the floor with all the pacing up and down he'd been doing.

She was wearing what looked like a new coat, with a matching fur-trimmed bonnet, which she touched self-consciously when she noticed him looking at it.

'Bella gave me this coat and hat,' she said, looking flustered. 'She has been so generous. Though she keeps insisting she would never have worn any of the things she has given me, again, I can't help feeling a bit—' She broke off, with a frown. 'She just says it is Christmas and I ought to accept gifts. Only, I have nothing to give her in return. It is—' she gave a brief smile '—rather lowering.'

'I know exactly what you mean,' he said with feeling. 'My uncle keeps on giving me gifts, like those horses I was driving yesterday, as well as pressing me to accept an allowance, just because I am his heir. But I…well, I've been used to earning my pay. It's bad enough that with Napoleon beaten at sea, there's a surfeit of young lieutenants at present, so that I cannot foresee getting promotion any time soon. And at least you have done something to deserve Miss Fairclough's largesse, what with my family being pretty much united in opposition to her marrying my uncle and making no secret of their opinions.'

She lifted her chin. 'Yes. There is that,' she said, giving him a look he couldn't interpret. 'Thank you for reminding me.'

They walked to the door of the rear terrace, where he'd decided the tour might as well begin, in silence. A silence that swirled with undercurrents. Undercurrents he became increasingly determined to fathom. 'What,' he blurted when his curiosity finally reached boiling point, 'made you change your mind? About exploring the grounds with me?'

'It wasn't so much a change of mind,' she said, sticking her nose in the air as she passed through the door while he held it open for her, 'as a making up of my mind. I didn't precisely turn your offer down last night, did I?'

He cast his mind back, trying to remember the exact sequence of words they'd flung at each other. He seemed to recall her saying something about not needing a man to take care of her and then Miss Fairclough accusing her of flirting with him.

He frowned. Perhaps it was no wonder she'd been reluctant to accept his offer to show her round the place. He'd told her of his aversion to predatory females during their encounter on the back stairs. Which made it all the more puzzling for her to have backed down.

'There is no need to scowl at me like that,' she said.

'Like what?' He hadn't even been aware he was scowling.

'As though you suspect me of some nefarious motive for getting you alone. If you must know, the truth is, that…' She bit down on her lower lip.

'You cannot leave me in suspense after hinting at nefarious motives,' he objected, after she'd remained silent for several paces.

'On the contrary. I mean,' she said, looking vexed, 'that my motives are not a bit nefarious. It is just that, well, as I said last night, I might never get another chance to just wander round the grounds of a place like this, as a guest of the owner, with a perfect right to go where I please without being accused of trespassing. And although I truly did not wish to monopolise your time, when I am sure you have far more important things to do, there simply isn't anyone else who would come with me!'

'Ah. I see it now. I am your last resort!'

'Yes,' she admitted, without the slightest sign of realising that she'd just insulted him by doing so. 'You see, after last night, I knew I couldn't just wander about on my own. And not only because of Lord Baguley. *None* of the males seem to think there is anything wrong with sneaking up on a girl, brandishing a sprig of mistletoe and claiming a kiss. And as for the games they were playing! Why, they were, well most of them were, merely an excuse for the men to... to take liberties with the females.'

He'd noticed, from the card table where he'd spent the evening playing whist, her growing more and more uncomfortable as the evening progressed and the level of sobriety dipped, and the behaviour of the youngsters grew more boisterous. He'd almost stepped in to intervene, once or twice, before recalling her indignant assertion that she didn't need any man to rescue her. And had been glad that he hadn't, when she'd extricated herself neatly, all by herself.

'I did think Bella might—I mean, Miss Fairclough might show me about, but then her brothers, her half-brothers that is, said they intended to go out gathering greenery today, since it is Christmas Eve, and she said that she would not set foot anywhere outside where she might run the risk of meeting up with them and being obliged to be polite.'

'She doesn't get on with her half-brothers?'

Miss Isherwood looked torn. Then she glanced up at him. 'I suppose there is no harm in telling you, since you are going to be related to her after tomorrow and you are bound to find out eventually. They have been the cause of most of her unhappiness. Oh, not deliberately. I am sure they are perfectly charming boys. That is, they seem to behave no worse than any of the other young men here.'

They'd been ambling along a gravel path which led past the east wing of the house, but now they reached the broad, shallow steps which would take them up to the formal gardens. She glanced round at the neatly clipped box hedges, laid out in geometric patterns, and let out a sigh of pleasure.

He allowed her to meander along at her own pace, though he kept subtly nudging her in the direction of the herbaceous border, which he hoped she would enjoy as much.

'You were telling me,' he reminded her, after an interlude during which he'd studied the changing expressions on her face, as she studied the various plants and the settings in which they grew, 'why Miss Fairclough does not get on with her brothers.'

'Oh, well,' she said, pausing before a gigantic specimen of cardoon, her nose wrinkling in confusion, 'it is just that the moment he had a son, her father sent her away to school. The school where I teach. Which is, more properly, a place for orphans, although it has such a sterling reputation for the quality of the education we provide that, from time to time, we do get boarders from…oh, but I am getting away from the point. Which is that they hurt her, no matter what they may say, or do, merely by virtue of being alive.'

He frowned. 'I had noticed that she doesn't spend much time with her father and mother.'

'Stepmother,' Miss Isherwood pointed out, setting off along the path once more.

'Stepmother, yes. I had wondered at the cause. I believed

it might be because they were putting some pressure on her to marry my uncle…' Just as Julie's parents had obliged her to marry Lord Waring.

'No. In fact, at a guess, I would say their delight in the match is the one thing that might tempt her to cry off.'

'Really?'

'And don't look at me all hopeful like that. I didn't say she was really thinking of crying off. She won't. Don't you understand? Once she is the Duchess, she will have security for the first time in her life. A security that was ripped away from her, as a child, when her father married a woman who didn't want the daughter of his first wife under her feet. And a chance to be in control of her fate. Not at the mercy of a strict regime of a charity school, or the whims of relatives who launched her into society more from duty to her late mother, than from any genuine affection for her.'

'I admire your defence of her. Your loyalty and your obvious affection for the girl. But shouldn't that affection make you wish to save her from taking a step, that, though it may have financial advantages, can never make her happy? You must have seen, even last night, that while her husband-to-be sat playing cards, she was happier frolicking about with his grandchildren!'

Clara bit her lip. She couldn't deny that she had been shocked to see the vast difference in ages between the bride and groom. And by the way Bella, and the other young ladies, would allow, nay encourage the young men to grab them and plant sloppy kisses on their cheeks, or even their mouths. Though at least *their* enthusiasm to get in the way of a pair of questing, blind male hands had made it easier for *her* to stay well out of reach. She didn't want any male to grab her and kiss her.

Although she hadn't minded when Lieutenant Warren had grabbed her, had she?

Oh, but that was different. He'd been rescuing her from that horse!

She glanced at him, warily. And had to admit that had *he* been playing Hoodman Blind last night, she might not have been so determined to stay out of the way. Because she didn't think she'd mind if he wanted to kiss her.

In fact, she'd rather like it if he wanted to kiss her. She only had to cast her mind back to the way she'd tingled, all over, after he'd swept her up in his arms, in the inn yard. And how those feelings had returned last night when she'd been drifting off to sleep, remembering the highlight of her day, while planning how to approach him with her apologies.

Heavens, what a thing to be thinking! She was supposed to be defending Bella's decision to marry her Buttons.

The fat, ageing man who saw nothing wrong with his bride-to-be romping about the drawing room with a selection of several much younger, fitter men.

Ah! There was her answer to Lieutenant Warren's objection.

'The Duke himself didn't appear to mind Bella's behaviour. Whenever I watched him, watching her, he was smiling at her. Fondly!'

'So you think he will be a complacent husband if she decides to play him false, is that it? You think that is a recipe for a successful marriage? For the husband to turn a blind eye to his wife's infidelities?'

'That is not what I was implying! I told you, she craves security and the Duke seems kind…'

'Good God, woman, will you listen to yourself!' Lieutenant Warren paced away from her, then turned round, looking not angry, as she'd expected, but agitated. 'I am doing what I can to rescue that silly chit from making a dreadful mistake! Why won't you help her? Why can you not see that all the money in the world cannot make a girl happy if she is shackled to a man who is not, and can never be, an equal match for her?'

'Well,' she said tentatively, 'although it is not the kind of match that would make *me* happy…' But he was clearly too angry to listen to her properly.

'But you are benefitting from the union already, aren't you?' he said, pacing closer, raking her with scornful eyes. 'Look at you, dressed in the kind of finery I don't suppose you could ever afford to buy for yourself, not in a million years!'

'I didn't *ask* Bella to give me these things,' she protested. 'She didn't want me to feel uncomfortable, when all the other ladies are so wealthy…'

'But what else are you hoping she might do for you, eh? Once she is married and has an allowance of her own? That if you stay in her favour you might be able to benefit from her wealth? That she will rescue you from that school? That she will take you on as some sort of companion, perhaps?'

Clara felt her cheeks flushing guiltily. Oh, not because she hoped to gain anything for herself. But because, since she'd promised Miss Badger that she would do so, she had already asked Bella if she might ever consider making some sort of donation to the school.

'You are! For all your vaunted friendship for that girl, you are planning to use her to further your own ends!'

'That is not how it is at all! You of all people should be able to understand that…'

'Me of all people? What do you mean by that?'

'Only that you've just told me the Duke keeps showering you with gifts. To try to make you dance to his tune.'

He flinched. Turned away. And as he did so it struck Clara that Bella was very much like the Duke, in the way she was using gifts and treats to gain Clara's support.

Which meant… What?

'I think,' she said, feeling the beginnings of a headache forming, 'that I'd like to go back to the house now.'

'Miss Isherwood,' he said, turning to her as she began to walk away.

'Alone,' she flung at him over her shoulder. She had too much to think about. He would only be a distraction.

As would all the frivolity going on back at the house. Glimpsing a shimmering body of water in the distance, Clara set off for what she hoped might turn out to be an ornamental lake. The waves lapping on the shore would help to calm her, wouldn't they?

She hadn't gone very far before she became aware of footsteps, doggedly following her. She glanced over her shoulder, nervously.

Lieutenant Warren.

She sighed. Either he was being ridiculously chivalrous, by respecting her privacy, yet remaining close enough to make sure nobody molested her.

Or he was being annoyingly protective, because he thought she was such a silly helpless woman she wouldn't be able to find her way back to the house on her own.

And whichever it was, she didn't know what to make of it.

Chapter Eight

When Clara awoke on Christmas Morning she couldn't say she was looking forward to it—not the way she'd hoped. For instead of it being a day of celebrating Christmas itself, she could now only think of it as the day that Isabella Fairclough was going to marry her elderly, overweight Duke.

And either Lieutenant Warren, or some other member of the Duke's family, might try to put a stop to the wedding.

If they did, what could she do? As if there was anything *she* could do! She was merely a schoolteacher. And Lieutenant Warren was a...well, an officer in the King's Navy. And the Duke's daughters were all married to lords.

Bella's own aunt, Clarissa, would be the one to take her home and shelter her, should any of those powerful opponents somehow prevent the marriage from taking place.

She had rarely felt so useless.

Her gaze lingered on the gown which had miraculously appeared overnight, courtesy of Bella's seamstress, as she wondered just what anyone could do to prevent a wedding from taking place. Not if there was no lawful impediment. And there couldn't be one, could there, if things had progressed this far?

Clara had barely finished washing and donning the sumptuous gown, which was of primrose satin, with the most delicate overdress of lace, when Bella herself bounced into the room.

'Are you almost ready? Have you had any breakfast? Oh, but I am far too excited to eat anything,' said Bella, flinging herself on to the bed where she landed in a most unladylike sprawl. 'You look amazing in that gown. I knew you would. Well, you have looked splendid in every single gown I have given you.'

'Have I?' Clara glanced at her reflection in the full-length mirror, wondering if it was wicked of her to yield to a feeling that was so dangerously close to vanity.

'Everyone says so. Just before they remark what a pity it is that you didn't manage to teach me to convey the natural elegance that just oozes from you,' she said, wrinkling her nose. 'But that isn't why I've come in. I have come to take you to my room. I want you with me while I prepare, so that I can make sure you know *exactly* what to do.'

'But I haven't had my breakfast.'

'Not a problem. I will ring for whatever you want. But you must not leave my side today. Not for one minute. Not until I am safely wed to my Buttons.'

'Oh.' So Bella was prey to the same suspicions that had been troubling Clara. 'Of course not. If that is what you really want.'

'It is.' Bella sat up, clenching her hands into fists. 'You mustn't let anyone into my room, unless I have sent for them. I don't want to have to listen to any more lectures about my unsuitability, or appeals to put in a word, once I am married, for those lumps of brothers of mine, or, or anything like that. And I want you to walk with me to the chapel. Nobody else,' she added fiercely.

'Once we get there, you will have to let my father lead me up the aisle.' She pouted. 'Buttons say he *has* to be the one to give me away even though the truth is that he did that years ago. But,' she added earnestly, 'you must sit on the front pew, next to my stepmother.'

'The front pew? Are you sure? But…' She didn't manage to finish what she'd meant to say about not being family, because Bella bounced off the bed, grabbed her hand and dragged her up to her own room. Where Clara spent the rest of the morning watching the bride prepare for her bridegroom and shooing away anyone who had the temerity to attempt to speak to the bride before the ceremony. Apart, that was, from a stately man who claimed to be a valet, bearing a gift from the bridegroom.

Both Bella and Clara gasped when they opened the large, flat, wooden box to see nestling within it a necklace, bracelet and earrings of glittering diamonds. Bella snatched up the necklace, held it to her throat and ran to the mirror.

'Do up the clasp for me, will you?'

It would probably be the only time in her life Clara had the chance to handle genuine diamonds, she reflected as she helped the bride drape the jewellery about the appropriate parts of her body.

As a teacher and mentor of young girls, Clara should probably have uttered some moral platitude about the pitfalls of vanity as Bella preened in front of her mirror, turning from side to side to make the diamonds flash fire from every cut facet. But it would be a bit hypocritical when, not an hour since, she'd been doing pretty much the same thing.

She'd never thought she could be so shallow, but now that she'd had the chance to dress in fine clothes, and, yes, even wear jewellery, even if it was only what Bella described as trumpery stuff, she had to admit that she was just as susceptible to the lure of fine things as any other woman. Although she would never *seek* them, deliberately, she had enjoyed knowing that she looked elegant, rather than drab and dowdy. Which she would do, tomorrow, when she would have to leave here and return to the dreary life of a schoolteacher.

She would just have to make the most of today's festivities, she vowed, rather than allowing herself to become despondent because this was her last day of living in such luxury. Of wearing fine clothes and eating sumptuous food, and sparring with a certain dark-haired man with a face of teak.

The chapel, where Bella was going to marry her Duke, was situated in the oldest part of the Palace, just off the great hall, so they didn't have to go outside to reach it, let alone get into a coach. Instead, when the time came, they walked, arm in arm, along carpeted corridors and down staircases with intricately carved banisters, their respective bouquets held in their free hands.

It was only when they reached the door of the chapel and she saw her father waiting for her there that Bella's smile faded. Her little chin went up. She barely glanced at him, making it obvious that she would rather have done without his escort altogether, and that it was only because she wanted to please the Duke that she was yielding to this tradition at all.

Clara followed the pair along the ancient flag way to the very front of the chapel, where the Duke was waiting, with Lieutenant Warren at his side. It had never occurred to Clara that the Duke would ask Lieutenant Warren to stand up with him. But then who else, but his heir? The Duke did not have any sons of his own, Bella had told her.

The Duke was smiling.

Lieutenant Warren was not.

When the bridal party reached the altar, Clara went to the front pew, as directed, and sat next to Bella's stepmother. The woman inched along to give her room, but glared at Clara as she did so.

As the ceremony got under way, things that had been puzzling Clara from the moment she'd received the surprising invitation to this wedding began to make sense.

She'd never been able to believe that Bella had invited

her from motives of friendship. If Bella had thought of Clara as a friend, she would have written to her regularly, sharing her impressions of life with her Aunt Clarissa and details of her debut ball, as well as how on earth she'd managed to wrest a marriage proposal from a duke. But she hadn't.

It had always felt as if Bella had come up with the notion of summoning her at the very last minute.

And now she thought she knew why. Bella couldn't have come up with a neater way of offending every single person who was hoping to gain something from her good fortune, than showing them she'd rather elevate a lowly teacher from the school she'd hated than acknowledge that she owed any of them a single thing. Not her stepmother, who'd ousted her from her childhood home, or her father who'd had her sent to an orphanage… Why, she'd even shown her Aunt Clarissa how she felt about their reluctance to do more than launch her into society by giving Clara every item of clothing they'd ever bought her.

Clara shifted on her seat as she recalled all the arguments she'd had with Lieutenant Warren over Bella's determination to go through with this marriage. How she'd insisted the poor girl wanted security, above all else.

Why, oh, why had she put out of her mind what a very naughty girl Bella could be? Why had she forgotten all the misdemeanours she'd committed and instead recalled all the times she'd been affectionate? And grateful to Clara for her help?

As she watched Bella repeat her marriage vows, looking as though butter wouldn't melt in her mouth, Clara was filled with foreboding. Because she could see Bella not only using her position to settle old scores, the way she'd done with the stepmother, by making her give place to her on the front pew just now, but also in taking a lot of pleasure in thumbing her nose at anyone who tried to cross her in future. And, far from being beaten down, or upset, Clara could foresee Bella revelling in the skirmishes.

No wonder Lieutenant Warren had such a grim expression on his face. She wouldn't say he'd been completely right, in all respects, but she could concede that he might have had good reason for having his doubts about this marriage.

But it was too late now. The Duke's personal chaplain was proclaiming them man and wife.

Bella let out a most unladylike shriek, jumped up and down on the spot, and raised both hands in the air in a sort of triumphal dance. She then flung her raised arms round the Duke's neck and kissed him full on the lips, making him chuckle fondly. She then turned from him, grabbed Clara's hands and, in a gesture that took her so much by surprise she was unable to resist the momentum, pulled her to her feet and whirled her round in a way that would have been more fitting in the middle of a country dance than the chapel of a duke's palace.

The Duke's family, unsurprisingly, looked down their noses at this display.

'Disgraceful,' sneered Lady Baguley, the Duke's eldest daughter, who had been acting as his hostess.

'How can he,' hissed his next daughter, 'have given her the family diamonds to wear?'

'She will *never* be fit for the role our dear mama filled with such grace and decorum,' said the third, rather more loudly.

Although the Duke gave no sign that he had overheard, he surely must have done. Bella certainly had, because, having given Clara one extra twirl, she turned to the Duke's daughters, making sure she had her back to the Duke himself, and stuck out her tongue at them, provoking a collective, shocked gasp.

She then turned to her new husband and, with a huge

grin, linked her arm with his so that they could leave the chapel and make their way to the dining hall for the wedding breakfast.

Lieutenant Warren stepped forward, his arm outstretched, making Clara realise she was going to have to accept his escort, along with his disapproval. Because he clearly saw her as an accomplice to what his whole family seemed to regard as something very like a crime.

And, for the first time, it occurred to Clara that perhaps she could not blame them.

Chapter Nine

Hugo felt as if he'd swallowed a rock.

How had he managed to get it so wrong? Wrong about the bride, wrong about his uncle's motives for marrying her and, to his way of thinking worst of all, wrong about the girl who was clutching at his sleeve now as they followed the bridal couple from the chapel.

He'd just worked his tongue round his mouth to try to dislodge the imaginary rock lodged in his throat, so that he could explain himself, when Miss Isherwood cleared her own throat.

'Lieutenant Warren,' she said timidly, 'I have an apology to make.'

'*You* do? No, no, it is I who must apologise to you.'

She frowned up at him. 'What? But you were right, all along. About the unsuitability of this match,' she said, nodding at the couple who were sauntering along in front of them. 'I had forgotten just what a very naughty girl Bella could be. How she would take it into her head to…to defy anyone in authority for the mere sake of it, sometimes. What pleasure she took in getting away with mischief.'

'You…you think she has married my uncle for some sort of mischievous reason? But you claimed you believed she did it to gain security.'

Miss Isherwood hung her head. 'I wanted to believe the best of her. It has always been a weakness of mine, according to Miss Badger, that is, the head teacher. She says I am too soft-hearted and allow compassion to overrule my better judgement. That I should never have unpicked Bella's embroidery and done it over, when she'd made a mess of it. That I should not have opened the window to let her back in when she'd run off to go to the fair, but made her sleep on the back step all night. That I should have known better than to allow her access to improving books when I might have known she'd only asked for them so she could tear out pages to use as curl papers.

'Although, in my defence, I was the only one who could get through to her, on occasion, the only one she would listen to. And I did make her behave better. Often. I did!'

'I am sure you did,' he said soothingly.

'Don't patronise me when I am trying to apologise,' she hissed. Probably because they'd reached the Chinese gallery and two footmen were standing in the doorway, handing out glasses of hot negus.

'Is that,' he asked, steering her to a cabinet full of ugly chinoiserie, which everyone else was avoiding, 'what you are trying to do?'

'Yes. And to admit that,' she said, lifting her chin, 'you may have had reason to oppose the wedding. And I am sorry that I have come to this realisation too late for it to do any good.'

He shook his head. 'You did more than you know.'

She looked up at him sharply.

'You challenged my assumptions, which led me to share my concerns with the Duke himself.'

'You did?'

'Yes. Last night.'

'Clearly, you didn't persuade him to change his mind.'

He took a sip of his drink before replying, 'No. But then a man of honour cannot withdraw from a betrothal. However, he did confide in me, a little, about his motives for marrying your former pupil. His first marriage had been far from happy.' Lord Braid had actually described his first wife as a cold fish. As Hugo's eyes strayed to where that very woman's daughters were standing, shooting their father and his new bride poisonous looks, he could well believe it.

'And that he felt that at his time of life he had every right to snatch at what happiness he could, *while* he still could. Then I…ah…' He paused, wondering why he felt the need to make a clean breast of it. Pushed the doubt aside and just plunged headlong into his confession. 'I am afraid that then I used something you told me to try to, well, at least put him on his guard. I told him she was only marrying him for his money.'

'I never said that!'

'You used the term security, but it amounts to the same thing.'

'It absolutely does not.'

'Well, anyway,' he put in swiftly, 'it made no difference. He just said he was glad an old buffer like him had *anything* to offer a lovely young creature like her. And then he began to sing her praises. He believes she is genuinely fond of him and that therefore he doesn't need to worry about…' Well, the Duke had used the word cuckolding, but he wasn't sure if an innocent like Miss Isherwood would know what that meant. 'Well, he has seen how loyal she is to those who show her kindness, because so few people have done so, during her short life.'

Hugo also skipped the part of the conversation where the Duke had used the way his bride had invited her *withered-up spinster schoolteacher* to be her maid of honour, rather than someone of fashion or influence, as an example of that loyalty, for obvious reasons.

'Then he chuckled and said he knew she was a minx, but that he was looking forward—and I'm quoting him as accurately as I can recall—to watching her "setting his starched-up daughters in a bustle, before going on to ruffle the feathers of all the stuffy society matrons who would thoroughly disapprove of her antics". It seems that, of late, he has been growing increasingly jaded and felt he had nothing to look forward to, during what he termed his twilight years, but boredom and fatigue. But no longer, because he would never know what she might take it into her head to do next.'

Miss Isherwood gaped at him. 'You mean he regards her in the light of an…an amusing sort of…*pet*? They both,' she continued, before he could form a suitably tactful response to that, 'if you don't mind me saying so, appear to have taken leave of their senses.'

'No,' he mused, 'actually, I think they will both be getting what they want from this match. And I can imagine them both being content with one another. At least for some time.'

She glanced up at him sharply. 'But you were so set against this marriage. Whatever has made you change your mind?'

He drew in a deep breath. 'It was the way she flung herself at him. With such exuberance, once she'd become his wife, legally. It was…well, so different from what I'd been dreading. You see, I got her all muddled up, in my thinking, with another girl I knew, whose parents forced her to marry a much older man because he was rich and titled. Julie begged me to help her escape her fate, but I could do nothing. I was a young man with no influence, and no hope of marrying her myself since we were both underage. My failure to do anything for that poor creature has weighed on my conscience ever since.

'And when I heard of my own uncle's intention to marry a girl barely out of the schoolroom, I… I suppose I acted without looking at all the facts. And today I have seen that although neither of them is marrying for reasons that I would consider essential, they are both going into it with their eyes open, of their own free will.'

'Oh, I see. Oh, but that makes perfect sense,' she said,

draining her glass. 'You were, in fact, trying to rescue *her*, not trying to protect your uncle, which was what I assumed at first.' She set her empty glass on a tray proffered at the precise moment she'd finished, by one of his uncle's extremely efficient footmen. 'It is all of a piece,' she added, with a shake of her head.

'All of a piece? What does that mean?'

'Only that you seem to go round trying to rescue females all the time. Whether we need it or not.'

'May I remind you that if I hadn't stepped in when I did, you would first have been trampled by a horse and then kissed, or perhaps worse, by Lord Baguley.'

'If I had been trampled by the horse, I would not have been in danger from Lord Baguley. Since I presume I would have been lying down somewhere having my broken bones set.'

'And you accuse *me* of being pedantic! Look, I have just tried to apologise to you, d—' He stopped himself before uttering a curse word.

Now it was her turn to sigh. 'You are right. I seem to have dropped into the habit of arguing with you for the sake of it, don't I? Which is foolish, since we are, at last, coming to some sort of understanding.'

'Are we?' He felt suspicious of her sudden about-turn. Her valiant effort to be conciliatory.

'Well, yes. I mean, you said that it wasn't your idea of what marriage should be about and I can totally agree with that! I mean, I would never gain any pleasure from thumbing my nose at people, just to see them bridle, nor could I glean any satisfaction from spending my time working out how I could settle scores with all the people who have wronged me.'

As she gazed round the room at the various factions in his family who clustered in groups, disdainfully eyeing those with whom they'd fallen out, he found himself wondering which people had wronged her. And wanting to run them to earth so he could settle their hash.

Only she didn't want him to 'rescue' her, let alone avenge her, did she?

'And I,' he said, as the butler dramatically flung open the doors to the dining room, 'would take absolutely no pleasure in having a bride who saw me only as a provider of life's luxuries. Who would expect me to turn a blind eye to her escapades. Or even laugh at them.'

'No, you would only marry a woman if you truly cared for her,' she sighed.

'And if I could be certain she cared for me,' he replied bitterly, as he caught sight of one of his aunt's protégées darting him a languid look over her shoulder as she began to follow her group in the direction of the open doors. 'Rather than just fixing on the possibility of a coronet.'

'Any sensible woman would see that there is more to you than the potential to offer her a position in society,' she declared, with some heat. 'I mean, although I do not, myself, have any ambition in that quarter, since I have a secure place in my own right, being valued by the head teacher for my skill and intelligence…'

'Even though she thinks you are too soft-hearted with the naughty girls?'

'A secure place,' she continued, adding a degree of frost to her words, but carrying on as though he hadn't spoken, 'because the world will never run out of orphans in need of a decent education.'

More and more people were putting down their emptied glasses and drifting from the room. He supposed, as groomsman, he ought to be leading the procession, rather than lingering in a corner. But he wanted to hear what Miss Isherwood had to say first. And she wasn't likely to confide in him where anyone else could overhear.

'So what,' he asked, lowering his voice as he moved

closer and stepped in front of her to obstruct her, should she decide to walk off just when things were getting interesting, 'do you think I have to offer a woman, then, even though you, yourself, do not wish to avail yourself of my person?'

'I... I... Oh, you are so infuriating that I forget!' Her eyes darted right, then left, before she raised them to his face. 'Even if I did think, for a moment, there was something, right now I cannot imagine why I ever thought there could be.'

'You do not find me physically attractive, perchance? You do not sometimes wonder, when all those kissing games are going on, what it might be like to kiss *me*?'

Her face turned bright red. 'How dare you accuse me of any such thing? Why, I...' Her eyes darted away. She wrung her hands. And then she looked up at him in puzzlement. 'How did you know?'

His heart skipped a beat. What was she saying? That in spite of all the animosity she'd shown him she found him attractive? As attractive as he found her?

'Because I have been thinking exactly the same thing,' he said thickly. 'And I'm damned if I know why. You are the most infuriating, argumentative, ungrateful woman I have ever come across.'

She stopped wringing her hands. She looked up at him. Looked to the doors through which everyone else was already making their way.

'And you,' she said, as a very determined look came to her face, 'are the most overbearing, insufferable male I have ever met.'

Then she stood on tiptoe, rested her hands flat against his chest as if for balance, before planting her lips fleetingly, yet firmly against his own.

And then, while he was still reeling from the shock of it, she darted away from him.

Leaving him so stunned he was completely unable to move.

Chapter Ten

Could Clara blame her behaviour on the negus? For she'd drunk it on an empty stomach since, in spite of Bella saying they could have breakfast sent to her room, neither of them had actually ordered any. And she wasn't used to strong drink, at any time of day.

No. It would be feeble to blame anything but her own overwhelming need to seize the moment. Nor, she decided mutinously, was she going to allow guilt to creep up on her and ruin a moment that she would much rather treasure like a precious Christmas gift. After all, when would she ever get the opportunity to kiss a handsome man, again? When was she ever likely to *meet* another man like Lieutenant Warren, come to that? Handsome men weren't exactly thick on the ground at Heath Top School. Miss Badger did her utmost to keep them away. Which was why girls like Bella had to climb out of windows to meet them.

Clara wasn't, and never had been, that type of girl. And so she made sure they were never alone again, for the rest of the day. It wasn't that hard, since the Duke had organised no end of festivities to celebrate his wedding. There was the lengthy feast, to start with. After which a troupe of carol singers came from the village to sing to them.

Then there was a professional ensemble, imported direct from Drury Lane, who performed a comic piece, followed by some operatic arias. And then everyone went to change for dinner. Then there was dinner. And then there were more boisterous games for the younger set, while the older guests gambled enormous amounts of money on whist or piquet.

Lieutenant Warren hovered about, eyeing her darkly. But she had no intention of giving him any chance to accuse her of being like all the other women he said kept on trying to trap him into matrimony. Or to say he'd been right to suspect she was the sort of woman who could have somehow trained Bella to develop the wiles she'd deployed to entrap her wealthy Duke. Which was laughable! How could she, a spinster, with no experience of men whatsoever, have been able to teach a girl like Bella anything to do with anything worldly? If anything, it was the other way round.

It was exposure to the atmosphere of this place that had changed her. Somehow, she must have absorbed the lax morality and become corrupted. Had excused her behaviour by saying what all the gentlemen had said as they'd brandished their sprigs of mistletoe. *It's only a kiss.*

It was just as well she was returning to her school in the morning. There, she would no longer be tempted to feast until she felt as if her stomach would explode. Or have to play games that entailed dodging the questing hands of lecherous men. Or puzzle over riddles that had answers which made all the worldly wise, titled people shriek with laughter, but which had left her sensing that if she had understood the joke she would have been rather shocked.

And no more encounters with a man who set her pulses racing, her temper soaring and her heart yearning for something which could never be.

She rose early the next morning to begin her long and complicated journey back to Oakwick. She tried not to mind that nobody was there to wave her off. She couldn't possibly expect Bella to get up that early on the first morning of her married life. But she had shown her care by ordering her maid to pack all the new clothes she'd given Clara in a set of luggage she'd provided. And, when Clara got into the carriage, provided by the Duke, which was to take her to the first stage, she saw, on the seat, a string bag full of oranges. With a note attached.

Clara snatched at it, her heart pounding as she looked first at the signature. Could it be a parting gift from *him*? A peace offering?

No. She sighed, recognising Bella's scrawl on the label. *For the girls of Heath Top*, was all it said. *With fond memories from a former pupil.*

Clara turned to look out of the window as the coach lurched into motion. The frontage of the Palace wavered and grew misty, the longer she kept her eyes fixed on it. But she craned her neck as the carriage wound down the drive, until the last possible moment, fixing every detail of the Palace in her mind. And telling herself it was foolish to wish just one person had come out to wave her farewell.

Then she dabbed at her eyes and blew her nose resolutely.

It was over, her little Christmas adventure.

That was all it had been. All she'd ever expected when she'd first held that little gilt-edged square of card, with her name inscribed on it.

She sniffed, then blew her nose again. This would not do. She'd promised the girls she'd left behind at Heath Top that she would regale them with tales of what it was like to spend Christmas with a duke. She should be recalling details of Bella's dress and jewels, and what she'd eaten for her Christmas dinner, to amuse them while she handed out the oranges she was still cradling on her lap.

So she'd better start working all the things she'd experienced into a series of amusing anecdotes. And not sit moping over the way she'd allowed her feelings for a man to

overwhelm her. Most of all, she must never, *never* confide
in anyone that she'd flung herself at him and kissed him.

Although the harder she resolved never to speak of him,
to anyone, let alone a group of impressionable schoolgirls,
the more he invaded her thoughts. Every time she came
up with an amusing way to relate the story of Bella's wedding, Lieutenant Warren kept on creeping into the narra-
tive. Whenever she thought of the Duke's awful family, she
wanted to add that one of them wasn't so bad.

When she considered how to describe the games that the
Duke's family played in the evenings, her mind conjured
up the image of him, sitting at the card table with his aunts,
a frown of concentration pleating his brow, the light from
the candelabra making his hair gleam like a raven's wing.

It felt as if it took three times as long to return to Oakwick as it had to reach Saxony Palace. For one thing, every
other passenger who got on or off any of the stages seemed
as miserable as she felt. As if they, too, were reluctant to
return to their workaday lives. The weather conspired to
make the whole experience more wretched, the windows
steaming up inside from everyone's damp clothing, ob-
scuring any views that might have been visible through
the sleeting rain. Many had to keep blowing their reddened
noses every five minutes and most grumbled with increasing irritation as the roads turned into ruts over which the
wheels slithered and jolted.

It was as if, with Christmas behind them, nobody had
anything to look forward to. Just taking that journey would
have depressed Clara's spirits, even if they hadn't been so
low when she'd set out.

But at last she reached Oakwick. She left most of her
luggage with the innkeeper of the Red Lion, to collect at a
later date, and set off up the hill to Heath Top School, her

oldest case, containing her overnight things, in one hand and the string bag of oranges in the other.

It was growing dusk and, once she left the well-lit inn yard, it was like plunging for a moment into a dark chasm between the buildings. But then she saw light glowing from the upper windows of the school, like a beacon guiding her home.

Home. How strange. Before she'd set out, she'd never thought of it in that way. In fact, she'd envied the towns-folk their snug little houses and the relatives, blood relatives, they lived with. But now she'd seen what it was like to sit down to a Christmas feast with a family, she no longer envied any of them. The animosity simmering between the Duke and his relatives, and Bella and her family, had been extremely uncomfortable to witness. She'd imagined a rosy, storybook sort of family Christmas, before experiencing the reality. But now she'd learned that with families came family feuds.

And as for her dreams of eating delicious food and smiling and laughing through a series of celebrations—hah! Either the licentious behaviour of the male guests had made her downright queasy, or the vast quantity of rich food she'd eaten had given her indigestion.

If it hadn't been for a certain dark-haired, oak-timbered man, she would, she discovered with surprise, be jolly glad to be returning to her quiet, sober, prudish little life.

Only she *had* met him. And been held in his arms. And had kissed him, when it had become apparent that he was never going to dream of kissing her. Not even under the pretext of it being Christmas and the mistletoe granting him the licence to do so.

Unlike the other male guests, he'd avoided mistletoe. And quiet corners. And even the games, when he might, legitimately, have taken her hand, or had her sit on his lap while paying a forfeit for breaking some silly rule.

She sighed, her breath billowing out like steam escaping from a kettle set on the hob as she trudged up the hill.

She admired him for having principles. Of course she did. It was just a pity that he didn't care enough about her to have wished to break them. The way she'd abandoned all hers, so that she might know what it would feel like to kiss him.

The truth was she was of no importance to anyone, not really. Bella had only invited her to her wedding to snub her stepmother and aunt. Lieutenant Warren had only spent time with her because he'd hoped she had enough influence over Bella to be able to talk her out of the match. And as for her boasts about her position at school... Hah! Of course they didn't employ her because they *cared* about her. She was good at her job, that was all.

It didn't seem fair. All her life she'd tried to do her best. To be good. While Bella never heard a rule without wanting to break it, stuck her tongue out at anyone in authority and ended up marrying a duke and gaining untold wealth. Not that she envied Bella her particular Duke, it was just...

She raised her eyes once more to gaze despondently at the lights of Heath Top, the only home she could ever expect to have, and saw, standing just in front of the gates, a male figure. A familiar male figure.

No. She must be imagining it. She missed him so much, already, that she was seeing things that weren't there. The man was so muffled up against the cold that he could have been anyone. It was probably a...a crossing sweeper. Or a traveller, wanting to ask the way to...to...somewhere or other.

But then he spoke. And there was no doubting his identity any more.

'Miss Isherwood,' he said, stepping out from under the coping stone of the school walls, which had provided a bit of shelter. 'Clara, I thought you'd never get here.'

Chapter Eleven

He'd had one hell of a day.

No, to be honest, his troubles had started when she'd kissed him. That kiss had completely bowled him over. And confused him. Did it mean she felt something for him? It must, after what she'd said about him having more to offer a woman than a mere title. Only then she appeared to regret her moment of boldness, taking great pains to prevent any chance of them being alone, to talk further and explore... possibilities.

And then he'd spent a sleepless night wondering if she might even have found the touch of his lips upon hers disappointing. Distasteful, even. And counselled himself to just let her go and put it down to experience.

But he couldn't. He needed to *know* why she'd kissed him, what she'd thought about it and why she'd subsequently avoided him. Then he discovered she'd left. And he'd experienced a cold, clutching sensation in his gut. She'd gone. And he might never see her again.

Gone, without one word of farewell. As if he meant nothing.

Even if that were true, he couldn't help wondering how she was faring on her journey. It couldn't be comfortable for a single woman of limited means to travel alone. In such inclement weather, too. It seemed that the moment his uncle had married his flighty little bride, the sun had stopped shining, the clouds had massed and the temperature had plummeted.

He imagined her shivering in shabby overcrowded coaches. Having to endure the rudeness of guards and drivers, waiters and landlords at every change. And knew that he'd get no rest until he'd made sure she reached her destination safely.

'Miss Isherwood,' he exclaimed, the moment he saw her trudging up the hill with her sparse luggage. The fact that she was safe was not what was making his heart leap with joy, though. It was just seeing her. 'Clara!' He stepped forward, instinctively wanting to pull her into his arms and cover her dear face with the kisses he should have given her on Christmas Day. 'Clara, I thought you'd never get here.' It felt like an eternity since he'd seen her. Spoken to her.

'How on earth,' she said, drawing to a halt at arm's length, 'did you manage to beat me here?'

'Drove my own team of horses, took a direct route and didn't have to stop to wait for any connection, or pick up passengers.'

'But…but why?' She tilted her head to one side and frowned, as if she was trying to work it out for herself. 'I managed to get to Bella's wedding without any assistance from you, so it stands to reason I could find my way home without coming to grief.'

'Yes, I know. You don't need anyone to take care of you.' And he'd be a total idiot to tell her that he'd imagined her stumbling from one disaster to another. It would only lead to another argument. So, to save her from having to remind him again, he declared, 'You are strong, and independent, and have no need to lean on anyone.

'But…' he drew closer to her '…I don't think I can be easy without you in my life. The moment you left and I began wondering how you were, I knew that I would always be wondering what you were doing and if you were comfortable, and safe and happy. Because I want all those things for you. And, dammit, I want to be the person who ensures you know all of that.'

'This is…rather surprising…' she said, looking up at him with an expression he'd never seen before on her face. A mix of bewilderment and, dare he believe it, hope?

'Yes. Well, to be truthful, it took me by surprise, too. The way I feel about you. In fact, it wasn't until you weren't there and I suddenly feared I might never see you again…' He shuddered at the recollection of how that awful prospect had made him feel. 'I felt so…alone. Even though there were lots of other people there, I didn't want to talk to any of *them*. None of them understand me the way you do.

'And—' he gulped '—I know it is probably far too soon to make a declaration, but if I don't tell you how much you have come to mean to me, even though we have only known each other for such a brief time, then I would always regret it. Because some other man is bound to snap you up. And if you fell for him, I would be miserable. And if he made you unhappy, I would feel as if it was my fault. And if he made you happy, well, that would be even worse. I would suffer agonies of jealous torment, knowing that I could have been the one to make you happy if I'd only stepped up when I had the chance.'

'But, when I kissed you, you just stood there, like a statue. I thought you…you must hate me for being so brazen…'

'No!' He seized her by the upper arms. 'I could never hate you. I was just…stunned, that was all. Momentarily. By the force of what you made me feel with that shy little touch of your lips. Which was in such contrast to the boldness of the step you had taken. And, I have to tell you, if you hadn't broken free and run away, I would have taken you in my arms and kissed you back. With all the passion that was roaring through my veins.'

'Oh.' She sucked in a deep breath. 'Oh,' she said again.

It made him grin to see her at a loss for words. Because if there was one thing that told him he'd rocked her off her foundation, it was this uncharacteristic inability to launch a counter-argument.

'Now, Clara,' he said, more seriously. 'I told you how my uncle has been, frankly, bribing me to abandon my naval career with teams of horses and an allowance, and the like. And how I've been resisting, because I haven't wanted to stay ashore, kicking my heels. I'm a bit like you in that respect, I think. I don't want some rich man paying my way.'

'No. It…it wouldn't feel right.'

'Exactly! And I also know that the things that matter to most women don't weigh with you. So I'm not going to try to bribe *you* with an offer of riches, or security, or even the possibility of a title. Which I might not inherit anyway, if Bella produces a son. In which case, I might have to go back to sea, since it's the only trade I know. Not that it would weigh with you, I'm sure. You are the sort of woman who would cope brilliantly on your own. You would be equally as brilliant as the wife of an impoverished naval officer, as you would of a duke.'

'So what,' she asked, looking thoroughly bewildered, 'are you saying, precisely?'

'I'm saying—very clumsily—that even if you don't want it, even if you turn me away, I need to tell you that my heart has been yours from the moment you wandered out from behind that coach without any thought for anything but that shabby little piece of luggage.'

A sob left her throat. Her eyes welled up with tears. 'You came all this way to tell me that I matter to you?'

'More than anything. I… I wouldn't even mind staying ashore for ever, if you stayed with me. In fact, I don't think I would be in any hurry to go back to sea if it meant leaving you behind. I'd miss you too much.'

'You'd miss me?' Her eyes widened.

'Yes. But that's not all. I know you wouldn't marry any-one for any of the reasons Bella married my uncle, but… have you ever thought about marrying someone—' his heart began to pound raggedly as he laid all his cards on the table '—for love?'

She gave a juddering sigh. 'Yes, oh, yes. You understand me,' she cried, dropping both bags to the ground at her feet so she could put her arms about his neck. 'I don't want riches, or titles. I wouldn't know what to do with them. I just want someone who sees me as a partner, not a dependent who needs looking after. I want to be respected and, yes, cher-ished, for my character, not constantly told how to behave.'

He could scarcely credit his luck. He had to make sure he'd understood her response correctly. 'You *will* marry me?'

In answer, she raised herself on tiptoe and pressed her lips against his. This time he didn't hesitate, but kissed her back for all he was worth. With his whole body and soul, and heart.

Something cold brushed his cheek.

'Oh,' she gasped. 'It is snowing.'

'Is it?' He felt another featherlight caress on his cheek and saw a snowflake settle on the crown of her shabby bonnet.

'Now,' she sighed, 'I finally know what Christmas should feel like. Here, in your arms. It isn't about feasting, or gifts, or even having the luxury of a warm fire in my bedroom. It is this feeling of belonging. Of joy. Of hope for the future.'

'And I,' he replied, feeling a smile brim up from the depths of his heart, 'have just decided that my uncle mar-rying your naughty pupil was the best thing he has ever done for me. For it brought you into my life.'

And then, completely without the aid of any mistletoe at all, Lieutenant Warren bent down and kissed her again.

* * * * *

SNOWBOUND
WITH THE EARL

Lara Temple

Chapter One

December 23rd, 1818
—*courtyard of the Boar's Tusk Inn, Somerset*

Bella stepped out of the carriage and a gust of wind slapped her face with a flurry of snowflakes. She cursed and tightened her hold on her travelling cloak. Why couldn't people plan an elopement in July rather than on the longest, coldest day of the year?

And why, oh, why couldn't they have chosen a nice, cosy posting house with cheerfully lit windows and food-fragrant smoke tumbling up from its chimneys? The structure before her was nothing more than a dark, squat lump that glared at her through two grimy windows. If there was smoke at all, she could not see it amid the fast-falling snow. Perhaps this roadside haven looked charming in daylight, but in the dark, it looked…ominous.

Bella glanced back at the awaiting carriage with the first real tingling of apprehension since she'd stepped into it in Bath. It had all seemed so clear when she intercepted Rupert Banister's clandestine letter to Violet. Bella knew her cousin wasn't in love with Rupert, merely enchanted with the idea of marrying a wealthy young man from one of the first families in England. The fact that he was underage was only a minor inconvenience. After all, that was what eloping to Gretna Green was for, wasn't it?

All Bella's arguments—that Rupert's family would consider his marriage to the daughter of a Bath solicitor a sad mésalliance, that Rupert was a nice boy and did not deserve to be used as Violet's social climbing ladder, and most importantly that Violet herself deserved better than a boy not yet of age and still tangled in his mama's leading strings— all fell on deaf ears.

Bella had been very tempted to wash her hands of her spoilt cousin and let her ruin her and Rupert's lives, but she couldn't. For ten years she'd lived in her widowed aunt's home and on her meagre charity. She'd never come to care for her or for Violet, but that made no difference to her duty. Her aunt, beset by a host of imagined ailments, overindulged Violet and let her run wild, and it remained to Bella to try to stop her cousin from ruining herself, or others. One day that might yet happen, but Bella was determined that this was not the day... Or night, for that matter...

A figure appeared in the doorway, casting a shadow that reached almost to her chilled feet. It seemed far taller than Rupert. An illusion, she told herself, tucking her coat about her as the wicked wind crept under her skirts and laughed at her urban idea of winter clothes. She resisted the urge to curse again and strode forward. It was best to be done with this quickly so she could return to Bath.

'You're an idiot, Rupert Banister,' she announced.

The man's head canted a little and the faint light caught the side of this face, forming its contours out of darkness. This was not the pleasant, puppyish face of Rupert Banister, her cousin Violet's hopeful beau. This was a hard face with dark, deep-set eyes that could send men scurrying and women plotting.

The first thought that had entered Bella's mind when she'd met Lord Deverill a month ago had been that Rupert's cousin would look far more at home on the deck of a pirate ship than in the Grand Pump Room in Bath.

Flurries of snow danced about Lord Deverill as he

moved towards her, his expression shifting from disdain to shock and on to glacial fury.

'What the devil? Where is your damned cousin?'

'Where is *your* damned cousin?' she shot back.

'Waiting to meet *your* damned cousin in—' He broke off with something that definitely resembled a snarl. 'Never mind that, what the devil are *you* doing here?'

'Foiling an elopement. What are *you* doing here?' With some effort, she managed to make her '*you*' even more contemptuous than his.

His mouth opened, closed, and he drew a long breath between clenched teeth.

'The same. Of all the bloody bad luck.'

Bella was accustomed to Lord Deverill's ill temper and worse manners. His moniker Lord Devil might simply have been a humorous shortening of his title, but to her mind, he'd earned it fair and square. He was arrogant, condescending and as cold as midwinter. She'd disliked him on sight and nothing he had said and done over the past month had changed her mind one iota. Quite the opposite.

Bella had known from the start that, despite Rupert's five thousand pounds a year, he was no match for someone as spoilt and ambitious as Violet. So when Lord Deverill had appeared in Bath, clearly bent on shoving a spoke in Violet's wheel, she'd had even indulged in the foolish hope they might join forces to prevent the two young people from making a dreadful mistake.

That hope had been dealt a sharp blow during their first meeting when Lord Deverill made it clear he thought Bella a grasping spinster bent on securing a rich catch for her flighty, vulgar and gold-digging cousin. Whatever hope remained after that died a swift death when she discovered that Lord Deverill had hired an actor to charm Violet away from Rupert.

Perhaps it was the result of being a vicar's daughter, but

Bella took her responsibilities seriously. She was damned if she would allow a vain, arrogant rake like Lord Deverill to tarnish Violet's reputation simply because he considered her a social inferior. It had given her great pleasure to tumble his hired actor into a near scandal that sent the poor fellow scurrying out of Bath and she'd made no effort to hide her satisfaction at spiking her new-minted enemy's guns. From that moment on they had been at war.

At times over the following weeks, Bella had even been tempted to allow Violet to entrap the underage boy merely to prove to Lord Deverill that he was not as clever as he thought himself. But when Violet's maid had come to show Bella Rupert's note detailing where Violet was to join his carriage for their flight to Gretna Green, she knew she must put an end to the ruinous affair. So that evening she'd put on her winter cape and had gone to meet Rupert's carriage and hopefully break his heart.

When she'd set out she'd not expected the carriage ride to last several hours and certainly not to find herself facing Lord Devil himself in the middle of nowhere.

'So, where *is* your cousin?' he snapped, his deep voice impatient.

'Still in her bed, I presume. *Your* cousin is not very well versed in subterfuge. I intercepted his note to Violet regarding the arrangements he'd made and replaced it with a note informing her he was very sorry, but their plans to elope must wait until after Christmastide because his mama would be very displeased if he did not attend the family celebrations.'

'And she believed that poppycock?'

'That poor Rupert is terrified of his mama?'

'Point taken,' he said grudgingly, a flicker of something other than anger appearing in his eyes. 'But what the hell are you doing here in her stead?'

She rubbed her frozen hands and stalked past him into

the inn, barely resisting the urge to give him a good shove on to the snow. Lord Deverill thought he was God's gift, an opinion fed by far too many toadies and sycophants of both sexes, but she knew the truth.

The interior of the inn was as even less inspiring than the exterior. It smelt of stale ale and urine, making her grateful for the draught that shoved its way around the warped wooden windows. She positioned herself before a meekly hissing fire and turned to face her nemesis.

'What an idiotic idea to elope in midwinter. What was Rupert thinking?'

'He was thinking that he is about to be sent on a long trip abroad with his mama.'

'Did you arrange that? Don't bother answering, of course you did. That was very foolish of you.'

His jaw tightened, but she ignored that warning and proceeded. 'You ought to have realised it would force his hand. Believe me, Violet didn't wish to elope. She was happily imagining a grand wedding at St Michael's once he came of age where everyone who is anyone would be able to envy and admire her.'

'Then why did she agree?'

'I am not privy to Violet's thoughts, but I presume it is because she is no fool, unlike your cousin. She knows his affections are unlikely to survive a long separation. In other words, this is all your fault, Lord Deverill. And next time you plan to kidnap one of poor Rupert's elopees, kindly provide a foot warmer.'

His chin lowered, rather like a bull preparing to charge. She ought to be worried at taunting him when she was in a way at his mercy, but after observing him with Rupert these past weeks she felt that though he was annoyingly arrogant, he did not pose any real threat to her. He would consider winning her over by violence beneath him.

'I'll keep that in mind, Miss Ingram. And what were you planning to do once you met Rupert? Compromise him?'

Her eyes widened. 'Goodness, what a frightfully limited mind you have, Lord Deverill. Aside from the fact that I am seven years his senior, I would likely run for the hills if I had to spend a week with him, let alone a lifetime. Your nephew is a romantic mooncalf and as far as I can tell he hasn't read a book in his life. Why on earth would I want to compromise him?'

'For a tidy fortune and a possible title if his uncle dies without issue. Isn't that why your cousin pursued him? Five thousand pounds and a leap up the social ladder is quite an incentive to put up with a mooncalf.'

'Well, I wouldn't do it for anything less than twenty thousand. And he only stands to inherit a baronetcy. Paltry,' she added with a snap of her fingers.

For the first time since he'd stepped out of the inn a glimmer of humour pierced his anger. Her shoulders relaxed ever so slightly. He was an unpredictable man, but she rather thought her reading of him had been correct. He was neither violent nor stupid. No doubt as soon as he realised the threat was past, he would send her on her way and that would be that.

'So what *were* you planning to do once you reached Rupert?' It was still a demand, but his voice lacked its previous bite.

'Break his heart by telling him my cousin isn't in the least in love with him. And though I am loath to resort to such underhanded measures, if my words aren't enough to convince him, I might show him a letter my cousin wrote to a friend depicting Rupert in a manner that he would not find at all complimentary and in which she states she has no intention of remaining faithful to him after they wed. If that does not put an end to his nonsense, I don't know what will. Where *is* Rupert, by the way?'

'On his way to the new rendezvous as dictated by the note he received from your cousin.'

'Written by you, I presume?'

'Yes.'

'Dear me. And where did *your* Violet send him?'

'Another small inn where he will cool his heels until the ostlers I hired drive him home tomorrow at the crack of dawn.'

'Poor Rupert. I think my plan was far better. Yours only delays the inevitable and Rupert shall be very cross with you.'

'Excuse me for not being as devious as you, Miss Ingram. My prime concern was to prevent their meeting and convince your cousin it is in her best interest to pursue other options.'

'Ah. You were planning to bribe her. How much?' she asked curiously and his mouth tensed again.

'That point is now moot. Especially if you plan to reveal her perfidy to Rupert. If you give the letter to me, I shall ensure it is delivered.'

She shook her head. 'I think not. Violet may be an ambitious coquette and often misguided, but she *is* my cousin. I have already crossed a line when I took that letter from her desk. I'm damned if I'm handing you her personal correspondence for you to use as ammunition in your campaign to ruin her.'

'The only campaign I'm waging is to save my cousin from making the mistake of his life.'

'Fine words, but I'm afraid I don't trust you an inch, Lord Deverill. You can either allow me to meet Rupert and then decide for myself whether or not I must resort to making use of Violet's letter, or find some other way to put a stop to this nonsense.'

He glared at her, rubbing the side of his face in an ominous fashion. He must indeed have been scrambling to divert the elopement because he looked rather rough around the edges. His jaw was covered in a long day's stubble, his boots and trousers flecked with mud and his cravat a shadow of its former self.

He looked tired and angry and for a moment she felt a twinge of sympathy and even admiration that he was willing to go to such lengths to protect his cousin. Perhaps it was best to extend an olive branch.

'I suggest that once you retrieve your cousin, you send him to me and I—'

'Oh, no,' he interrupted. 'I'm afraid I don't trust you any more than I do your not so sainted Violet. I won't allow you to run back to your cousin and tell her where Rupert is. You, Miss Ingram, aren't going anywhere.'

Chapter Two

For the first time since Miss Bella Ingram stepped out of the carriage, Nicholas saw alarm in her eyes. The tension inside him relaxed a little. There was something rather satisfying at having his enemy at his mercy.

Miss Ingram had become a serious thorn in his side practically from the moment he'd arrived in Bath to rescue his dolt of a cousin from Violet Bartleby's claws. He'd underestimated her at first. He rarely had to take dowdy spinsters into account in his dealings, personal or business. But Miss Ingram, with her plain frocks more suited to a governess than to the companion of a flighty young woman and her hair always pulled back in an unfashionable bun, had somehow managed to foil him at every turn.

Even now she looked as cool as if she was merely waiting for the commencement of one of those interminable recitals Bath delighted in. Yet he knew that calm, blank look was deceptive. Miss Ingram was not at all what she appeared to be.

For someone so outwardly cool, she was composed of vivid colours. Her eyes were more gold than brown and gleamed like a great cat considering a cornered mouse. Even her skin shone warm cream in the candlelight. For the past month that infuriating combination of hot and cold had dogged his steps and blocked his every attempt to detach his cousin from hers.

And yet here she was, apparently also bent on foiling the elopement.

'If you are truly against your cousin wedding mine, why the devil did you try to stop me from easing them apart?'

Her eyes widened. 'You have quite a nerve, Lord Deverill. You did not try to "ease them apart". You did everything you could to discredit Violet, even hiring an unscrupulous actor to act the wealthy suitor and seduce a girl young enough to be his daughter.'

'I didn't hire him to seduce her,' he growled. 'I merely wished to prove to Rupert your cousin valued lucre above love. If you hadn't interfered, we could have put a halt to this nonsense a month ago.'

'If I hadn't interfered, Violet's heart might have been broken…' she ignored his snort of disbelief '…or her reputation ruined. You may regard us as so socially inferior as to render our fates and feelings inconsequential…'

'Now wait one damned moment, Miss Ingram,' he interrupted. How the devil did she always manage to put him in the wrong? 'My objections to your cousin had nothing to do with her family's standing and everything to do with her character. If you have an ounce of decency, you would admit she would eat Rupert alive and pick her teeth with his bones. He's spent his whole life being treated like a lackey by his mother and I won't allow him to condemn himself to a lifetime of more of the same.'

At least he'd managed to silence her. Finally. They glared at each other.

He turned away, considering his options. He hated admitting defeat to the woman who'd become his nemesis these past weeks. He wouldn't allow her to swan off back to Bath and laugh at his failure with her cousin while he was left to deal with Rupert. To hell with that.

Decision made, he turned back to her. 'You shall be my mother's guest for tonight and tomorrow you will show Rupert that letter, after which my carriage will convey you back to Bath. With any luck our paths need never cross again.'

She smoothed her gloves on her thigh and sighed. 'Rupert has such *nice* manners.'

This apparent *non sequitur* baffled Nicholas only for a moment. 'You find my manners wanting, Miss Ingram?'

'I haven't found them at all, Lord Deverill.'

Nicholas once again found himself battling the urge to laugh. That was the damnable thing about her. Even at the height of their verbal duels she somehow managed to appeal to his sense of humour.

'My dear Miss Ingram. I would be delighted if you would honour us with your presence at Hadley Hall. It would be dreadfully remiss of me to leave you here in this country inn all alone at the mercy of the guests and the elements.'

'I wouldn't be at the mercy of either—I would be safely in a private room until I can secure passage on the nearest coach or mail.'

He raised his hand, ticking off his fingers. 'The Boar's Tusk has only two rooms, both of which are presently occupied. As for the nearest coaching house, it is five miles from here in Upper Bradbury, which is also the nearest town with accommodation. I think that might prove a rather difficult, if not dangerous, walk in such weather.'

Her gaze flew to the window where the bottom of the each of grimy windowpane was covered with a white smile of snow.

When she said nothing he continued, 'Much better to surrender to the inevitable and accept my mother's hospitality. Think of it—in under half an hour you could be in a nice room, with a crackling fire and whatever has been prepared for dinner brought up to you on a tray, and tomorrow you may return to Bath at first light. Only someone thoroughly bloody-minded would object to that offer.'

'So you expect me to accept what you yourself would object to?'

'Very amusing, Miss Ingram. What will it be? A freezing trudge through the snow, or the comforts of Hadley Hall?'

'I find it hard to believe your mother wouldn't object to the arrival of an unwelcome guest the day before Christmas.'

She was fighting a rearguard action, he could tell. He ought not to gloat, but he couldn't resist one last barb. 'Christmastide is about charity and hospitality, is it not? What could be more hospitable than taking in one's enemy in their hour of need?'

To his surprise she smiled, amusement crinkling the corners of her eyes. He'd noted before how her smile transformed her. It had been the first indication that she and her cousin were very different. It also made him doubly wary of her. Violet Bartleby was obvious—cunning but obvious. But Bella Ingram was a whole different kettle of fish.

The first time he'd met her he'd made the mistake of trying to charm her into revealing something about her cousin that could be used against her. Before he'd realised what had happened he'd found himself stripped of his fake charm and laughed at to boot. He'd learned from his mistake and changed his tactics, but he'd always felt at a disadvantage after that.

He ought to be grateful she appeared to be against the match between Rupert and her cousin, but all he felt was... wary. The kind of wariness that plagued one when walking into a dark forest filled with brigands and thieves while carrying a sack of jewels and only a rusty teaspoon for protection.

Timeo danaos et dona ferentes. Virgil had the right of it. Enemies bearing gifts were not to be trusted. But as another saying went: enemies were best kept close. So until he was certain Rupert was truly safe, he would keep Miss Ingram very close.

'Well, Miss Ingram?'

For a long moment she concentrated on smoothing her

glove over her thigh. He shifted from one leg to another, as if they were on a boat rather than in Benton's tiny inn. Finally, she looked up, her golden eyes narrowed and intent.

'I have some conditions.'

Bella watched Lord Deverill's mouth curve in a slow, satisfied smile. She looked away from the harsh beauty of his face. It always brought resentment bubbling up inside her like a grumbling volcano. He thought he'd won, the complacent cad. It was clear he didn't believe she wanted something better than his foolish cousin for Violet.

Well, she couldn't prevent him from believing the worst about her. But she could negotiate.

'Three conditions, in fact, Lord Deverill.'

He gave a slight bow. 'I am anxious to hear them, Miss Ingram.'

'I am certain you are. First, I want you to have your silly nephew removed immediately from Violet's surroundings. Under no condition is he to return to Bath before his departure to the Continent.'

His brows rose. 'That sounds rather drastic. Shall I secure him in Hadley's dungeons?'

Her curiosity pricked. 'Are there dungeons there?'

'Miles of them. The Hadleys were once a nasty lot. But you needn't worry you shall grace them. Not if you behave.'

'If you wish for my co-operation, snide threats are not the best approach.'

'My apologies. But your condition is hardly necessary as I have already made arrangements for Rupert and his mother to go on a trip to warmer climes for her health after the holidays.'

'Well, I suggest you keep a closer eye on him until he is safely on board a ship, so he does not outwit you again.'

A flush heated his sharp-cut cheekbones. 'I apologise for disappointing you, Miss Ingram,' he said sardonically.

'Apology accepted. My second condition is that once Rupert is removed, you leave Violet alone. No retribution of any kind.'

'You must think me very petty.'

'I think you can be ruthless when crossed. I want your word on this.'

'If you think me ruthless I wonder that you would accept something as nebulous as my word.'

'I also think you have an abundance of pride and vanity. If you give your word, you shall keep it because you think yourself better than others.'

His brows were already lowered, but now the sharp black wings almost met. 'You hold nothing back, do you?'

'Why should I? As you said, we are unlikely to meet again after tomorrow. At least I very much hope not. And as for my third condition...'

Something very like a snarl escaped him, but he clamped his mouth shut and she continued.

'I want your word that after I reprimand the maid who you have been bribing for the past three weeks, you will not interfere in my aunt's household again.'

The flush deepened and he drew a long breath. She watched his temper teeter on a knife's edge for a moment, but then sense conquered temperament. He shook his head and his mouth softened again into a reluctant smile.

'It is a pity women cannot be called to the bar, you'd have been in silk by now.' She felt her cheeks heat. He had not meant it as a compliment, yet it felt good to have earned at least *some* respect.

'You are too kind. Do you accept my proposal?' She stumbled a little on her poor choice of words and hurried on. 'I want your word on all three conditions.'

It felt like a very long time until he finally nodded.

'I accept.'

Chapter Three

Nicholas woke on the morning of Christmas Eve with a gnawing sensation he'd made a terrible mistake.

As he dressed in the small circle of heat offered by the still young fire, he tried to chase away that sensation. After all, he had every reason to be pleased with himself. Aside from it being one of his favourite days of the year, he'd almost single-handedly foiled an elopement, rescued his idiotic cousin from a mésalliance, and captured his enemy.

Well, forced his enemy to be his mother's guest for a night.

Nicholas took out a length of linen and began tying his cravat absently as he considered the morning's agenda.

Soon the carriage bringing Rupert would arrive and, allowing half an hour for the interview between his cousin and Miss Ingram, he would then bundle her into the carriage and send her post-haste back to Bath.

And he would be rid of her and her family for ever.

He cursed as he pulled the cravat's tail end too sharply, transforming the waterfall knot he'd aimed for into something more akin to a crushed cauliflower. He sighed. His valet, Perkins, would gloat for days. He always resented that Nicholas insisted on dressing himself in the mornings.

His second effort was rather less offensive and as he pulled on his coat and hurried downstairs, he tried to imagine what had been going through Miss Bella Ingram's tricky mind ever since he'd brought her to the Hall.

The sooner she was on her way back to her indolent aunt and avaricious cousin, the better for everyone. Rupert might not enjoy his lesson, but it was important he realise that were people who were willing to feign affection in the hope of gaining a title and a fortune.

Nicholas had been almost the same age as Rupert when he'd learned that lesson and he'd probably been an even greater fool. He'd trailed after Mary Farnsworth for a whole besotted year until he'd drummed up the courage to offer for her, not even realising she was playing him like a harp.

He could still remember every moment of the day he'd ridden to her home, as nervous as a groom on his wedding day, even stopping in the woods outside her house to rehearse his proposal. That had been a fateful decision, for as he paced up and down the wall outside her gardens, he'd overheard her, taunting one of her other suitors that she no longer needed him now she was finally about to land the wealthy heir to one of the oldest titles in England.

Nicholas had done what he could to spare Rupert that horrible shock, that icy disappointment spreading through him like frost on glass. But that avenue was no longer possible.

At least it would be a salutary lesson; Nicholas himself had certainly never again fallen into such a trap. In time he realised that love was merely bottled-up lust which could be addressed in any number of ways, many of which he'd explored quite happily during his years travelling the world.

When he married, as he eventually must, it would be without such foolish expectations. He would find someone sensible who would be a good mother to their children and have as few illusions as he about romantic nonsense.

But first he had to deal with breaking poor Rupert's heart. He might have objected yesterday to Miss Ingram's insistence on doing the dirty deed herself, but as the moment of truth drew near, he was rather relieved she had. He hated the thought of hurting Rupert, even for a good cause. He might dislike his aunt, but Rupert was like a younger brother and Nicholas felt as responsible for him as he did for his own sisters.

But responsibility always came at a price and as he opened the front door and stepped out into the freezing cold to watch a shamefaced Rupert descend from the carriage, Nicholas realised the price of his recent decisions had just risen substantially. Carriage, driver, and horses were blanketed with snow and the road was barely distinguishable from the lawn or the sky. Whatever his personal wishes, it was evident that removing Miss Ingram from Hadley Hall without delay was no longer a possibility.

As the butler, Porter, closed the front door on the storm, Nicholas turned to his cousin. One look at Rupert's mussed hair, downcast eyes, and quivering chin made Nicholas even more grateful it would not be him delivering the death blow.

'We'll save our discussion until you shave and change. Then I want you in my study, yes?'

Rupert nodded morosely and trudged upstairs, and Nicholas went to write a summons to be delivered to Miss Ingram. He spoke with his mother, housekeeper, youngest sister and, finally, inescapably, his aunt.

As suspected, Aunt Agatha did not take kindly to his news that Miss Ingram was now a guest at Hadley Hall.

'It is quite out of the question! I refuse to have that hussy's cousin under the same roof as I,' she announced, outrage raising the tones of her already strident voice.

'You are more than welcome to leave, then, Aunt Agatha,' Nicholas snapped, frustration eating away at his control. 'You ought to be grateful she is willing to help convince Rupert that her cousin isn't in love with him. I told Mama that since the Markhams are unable to join us due to the weather, leaving our numbers at thirteen, I managed to invite one of Papa's distant cousins to even the odds. You will say nothing to contradict that story. While Miss Ingram, and you, are guests under my roof, I expect you make an effort to behave with some of the good breeding I imagine you must have buried under all those layers of spite.'

He sneaked out on that parting shot, closing the door on her sputtering response.

He was still in a temper when he entered his study, but his anger was momentarily knocked off course by the sight that met his eyes. Rupert was seated on the sofa with Miss Ingram, her arm around him and his face buried in her auburn hair.

There was a strange grinding sound in his ears, like carriage wheels straining against the brake, followed by the rushing of wind. It had happened to him once before, when he'd been thrown from his horse as a boy. He could still remember the unpleasant sensation of the world rushing past and yet being absolutely still.

Then he heard a sob. Not Miss Ingram... *Rupert?*

Miss Ingram turned her head, her eyes meeting his with a look of complete and almost comical dismay.

'I thought she loved me,' Rupert wailed, his words muffled against her hair.

She patted his back awkwardly. 'There, there. I'm so very sorry, Rupert. She truly was fond of you, but...well, she's still very young, you know.'

Rupert sniffed and pulled away, hunting through his pockets for a handkerchief. 'Do you think she might yet...?'

Nicholas finally dislodged himself from the strange fixity that had caught him. 'For heaven's sake, Rupert. In her own words she planned to marry you to get her paws on your inheritance. There won't be any Christmas miracle that will suddenly transform her into the sweet-tempered angel you fabricated in your own mind.'

'Go away, do,' Miss Ingram said curtly. 'We were doing very well without you.'

'I dare say you were by the sight of the two of you in each other's arms.'

Rupert looked alarmed. 'I wasn't… I didn't…'

'Oh, pay no attention to him,' said Miss Ingram. 'He's just jealous.'

'Jealous?' both Rupert and Nicholas exclaimed, their voices an octave apart.

Miss Ingram brushed a hand across a crease in her dark grey skirts. 'Of course he is, Rupert. Your cousin has the emotional range of a flea. Men like that resent those who have deeper emotions than they.'

Outrage cleared away the remaining tentacles of the strange fog in his mind.

'Simply because I have no illusions about romantic non-sense doesn't preclude me from having emotions. Not that they are any of your concern, Miss Ingram,' he added as her left brow rose.

He recognised that tell—she was preparing the next stage of her attack and he was damned if he would sit back and let her use him as a dartboard again. 'And you are a fine one to tout deeper emotions. I've never seen you exhibit any emotion at all, not even anger, unless you can call acting superior and smug an emotion.'

Well, apparently he'd been wrong. She most definitely could exhibit anger. Not that her expression changed; if anything her face became even more blank. But her eyes blazed and her hands clenched into two very neat fists.

Rupert cleared his throat, eyeing both of them in the same manner people living in the vicinity of a dormant volcano might react to a sudden burst of smoke rising from its maw. Nicholas gathered his slipping reins and addressed his cousin.

'Rupert. Your mother is looking for you. If you don't wish her to find you, I suggest you go and hide behind my sisters' skirts in the breakfast room. And to be very clear, you have not yet met Miss Ingram and you will not mention her to anyone until I say otherwise, understood?'

Rupert nodded and didn't wait for another warning. Nicholas half expected Miss Ingram to storm out, but she clearly had gathered her reins as well, though she did not look at him as she slipped Violet's letter back into her reticule.

'Poor Rupert,' she murmured.

'Don't get any ideas about comforting him while his heart is broken,' he snapped before he could think better of it. She rose, her mouth curving in that condescending amusement that never failed to make his temperature and temper climb.

'Are you still harping on that, Lord Deverill? You must truly think me very conniving indeed.' She gave a little laugh as she moved towards the door. 'What a pity I shall not have the opportunity to explore this drama you have concocted for me as I dare say you have come to tell me that my carriage awaits. Should I be at all concerned I shall not make it safely back to Bath, but be deposited somewhere in a snowy ditch?'

Right now he almost wished that *was* his plan. That this infuriating woman could somehow be made to vanish, down to the very memory of her. The thought that he must put up with her presence until the snow cleared…

'Well?' Behind the demanding tone he caught a faint hint of worry and he dragged himself out of his uncharitable thoughts and back into the present. Once again he had the peculiar sensation of looking at a painting only to realise there was something altogether different behind it.

'I'm afraid I have some bad news, Miss Ingram. Remember your comment about dungeons?'

She blinked and a faint flush spread over her cheeks.

That involuntary sign of discomfiture further calmed his confusion. She was merely a young woman, after all. Hardly more than a girl, yet, despite her clever mind. He was making a mountain out of a molehill.

'I'm sorry to inform you that the carriage returning Rupert barely made it through the drifts. I'm afraid you shall have to remain until the snow abates.'

She stared at him, stalked over to the window and dragged aside the heavy curtain. He came to stand beside her, inspecting the grey-on-grey world. The trees beyond were little more than lurking hints of darkness through the haze of falling snow. It was still morning and yet it looked like dusk settling on a frozen wasteland.

'You can't blame that on me,' he said mildly. 'Or can you?'

'I would very much like to, Lord Deverill,' she replied, her voice a smouldering grumble. 'But that would boost your vanity even further. But I cannot remain *here*, that is absurd!'

'Why? The house is full to the brim with noisy Christmas guests. You'll hardly even be noticed.'

'How charming of you to put it in such flattering terms. But aren't you worried I shall employ my time to seduce your sainted cousin?'

As she glared up at him he noticed her eyes had icy-green flecks embedded in the gold. Another contrast of coolness and fire. She was also pouting, her lower lip a pale coral curve that mirrored the gentle swell of her bosom above the simple blue gown she wore. She was not a beauty like her cousin, but she definitely had the wherewithal to carry out that threat.

Still, now that he'd voiced his suspicion, he really could not imagine this strange woman settling for someone like Rupert, not even for the benefit of a title and inheritance. She was too... He shook his head. He had no idea what she was, except as annoying as hell.

'How?' he asked.

'How?' she parroted.

'Yes. I'm curious how you would plan to do that. Seduce someone.'

He had the satisfaction of watching the colour streak across her cheeks.

'This is a foolish conversation, Lord Deverill.'

'Is it? I'm known as something of an expert in the field. Perhaps I can give you some…instruction.'

'If you are trying to make clear I have not the faintest ability to attract anyone, I'm well aware of that, Lord Deverill.'

He caught her arm before he could think better of it. 'Don't put words in my mouth.'

She stood with her gaze now fixed stubbornly on the door, but she did not try to pull away.

They'd been at war since the moment they'd set eyes on each other, but he wasn't in the least pleased with himself for having finally succeeded in unsettling her, not in this manner. He was also a little surprised at her misinterpretation of his words, though perhaps he shouldn't have been. She'd never appeared jealous of her beautiful and flirtatious younger cousin. Nor of the fact that Mrs Bartleby indulged her daughter with fashionable gowns, while Miss Ingram wore clothes more suitable for a governess. Yet surely there must be some envy there. Though it wasn't envy he thought he'd detected in her voice. It was something far more elemental…

He tried to find some clue on her face that he had imagined that hurt…that unexpected vulnerability…but she slipped out of his hold and he made no move to stop her as she left the room.

Chapter Four

D̲amn, damn, *damn*.

Her father would have told her it served her right for thinking she could run rings around everyone. Especially around someone as naturally weasely as Lord Deverill.

Well, often she could. It was neither her fault nor his achievement that a snowstorm of biblical proportions had struck Somerset at the worst possible moment.

There was a faint knock on the door and she steeled herself to face the maid. What they made of her and her lack of luggage below stairs she had no idea, but she doubted it was flattering. It had been bad enough when she'd arrived last night, but now she had no choice but to remain…

But it wasn't the maid. Instead, a dark-haired young woman stood hesitantly in the doorway. It was strange to see Lord Deverill's eyes in such a feminine face.

'Hello, I'm Philly, Philomena Hadley. I'm the youngest of the Hadley sisters. There are five of us, you know. Nicholas sent me. He said your trunk was lost in the snow. What a nuisance!' She sized Bella up and smiled, a singularly sweet smile that immediately eradicated any resemblance to her brother. 'I'm a little taller than you, but I'd say you and Cressy are the same size. Well, not now she's married and increasing, but before… That's awfully good luck.'

'It is?' Bella said, simply to say something. What on earth had Lord Deverill told Lady Philly?

'Oh, yes. She had poor George purchase her a whole

new wardrobe and so she left all last Season's clothes here. She's dreadfully expensive, but perhaps now she's to be a mother she might become more sensible. Nicholas says it's about as likely as Napoleon taking up knitting, but Mama is hopeful.'

Bella felt an instinctive tug of liking to the younger woman, but embarrassment prevailed. 'I cannot wear your sister's clothes, Lady Philly. It wouldn't be right.'

'Nonsense. I'll have Sue, that's my maid, bring some to your room and see if they need a few stitches. What lovely hair you have. I always admired auburn hair.'

Bella touched her hair self-consciously. She'd always liked her hair, but fashion was against her.

'Thank you, but…'

'Then it's settled. Once we're dressed we shall go down to Christmas dinner together. Some of the guests haven't arrived and likely won't now, not with this weather. But we shall have plenty to keep us busy, never fear. We always spend Christmas Eve preparing the decorations before dinner. And after dinner we gather for carols and dancing. It shall be quite delightful. You shall see.'

With that parting shot Lady Philly slipped out, leaving Bella even more bemused and inclined to think she might have been safer trudging through several feet of snow to the nearest town.

That conviction faded slightly once the maid arrived. She was a round little whirlwind with freckles and unruly curls that peeked out from under her cap, and she made Bella feel both comfortable and overwhelmed all at once.

'Lady Philly is right, this will look right lovely with your hair, if you pardon me saying so, Miss Ingram,' she said, eyeing Bella from her head to toe as she laid a pale yellow dress on the bed. It shimmered and shone on the blue coverlet like a soft sunset.

Bella opened her mouth to state she could not possibly

wear something so expensive, but nothing at all came out. The maid didn't seem bothered by her silence. She merely set to work, chattering away.

As she spoke she moved Bella around like a loose-limbed doll, undressing and dressing, brushing and tucking, until with a sigh of pleasure she stood back and turned Bella to the mirror. Bella stared in shock at the stranger before her.

She looked…pretty. She touched the fabric of her skirts gently. It was so soft. So different from the plain dark fabrics she customarily wore. She'd never allowed herself to resent that her aunt insisted they could not afford to provide her with new gowns, while Violet was dressed in the best fashions Bath modistes could offer.

She'd never had any illusions about her fate. Poor, plain and penniless women did not find husbands and happiness. She'd laid that childish dream to rest when she'd arrived at her aunt's household as a sixteen-year-old after her parents' death and was told in no uncertain terms that her role henceforth was to ensure Violet married advantageously. Numbed by grief, she hadn't cared much one way or the other and she had soon come to appreciate living in Bath— it had libraries and concerts and gardens to compensate for the tedium of the Bartleby household and those boring society events to which her aunt insisted she accompany Violet. In all those years she had never yet come across anyone or anything who had unsettled her comfortable numbness.

Until the day she'd had to declare war on Lord Deverill.

Lord Deverill had infuriated her, but now, staring at the stranger in the mirror, she didn't feel angry. She felt… frightened. Excited. Hopeful?

She pressed her hand to her abdomen. Queasy.

She ought not to do this. She ought to take off this dress and put her hair back into its bun and hide under her covers until the snow melted and she could return to the stultifying safety of the Bartlebys.

Before she could consider acting on her panicked thoughts, the door opened and Lady Philly entered with an exclamation of delight.

'Sue! You're a marvel. You look simply lovely, Miss Ingram.'

The maid puffed with pride. 'That she does, Lady Philly. You were right about the colour. Now I'm off to help Bess with the others.'

Lady Philly linked her arm with Bella's. 'Don't you worry about a thing, Miss Ingram. I shall see you meet simply everyone.'

With those ominous words she half guided, half propelled Bella out of the room and down into the lion's den.

Chapter Five

Nicholas watched Philly guide his enemy into the drawing room. If not for the colour of her hair and her unusual eyes, it might have taken him longer to recognise her. The pale yellow gown with its fine embroidery and low-cut bodice clung to her curves, accentuating a bosom that would have done a Greek statue proud and which had been obscured by her governess dresses. Her hair was dressed high with pale cream ribbons and long silken tresses captured the candlelight as they framed her face.

It wasn't merely her looks that were transformed, so was her demeanour. Her eyes were wide and blank as his mother approached her with a welcoming smile and extended hands, and she followed her as meekly as a lamb. His mother had accepted without question his story about coming across the stranded, luggage-less distant cousin, merely commending him on finding someone to make up their reduced numbers, and was now introducing Bella Ingram to everyone as if she was the guest they had all been waiting for. Only Aunt Agatha greeted her with cold politeness and quickly turned away as if a poor relation was beneath her.

When they finally reached him, the bemusement in Miss Ingram's eyes faded and a warlike flush warmed her pale cheeks. Battle stations resumed, apparently.

'You see, Miss Ingram?' he said kindly. 'Everyone is simply delighted you could join us for the festivities.'

Her eyes narrowed at his patronising tone, but before

she could respond, Porter appeared and in a low porten-
tous voice informed Lady Deverill that Cook and Mrs Bun-
ting, the housekeeper, were not in agreement about whether
punch or cider should be served with dinner.

'Goodness. Are they still at it? Do make Miss Ingram
comfortable, Nicholas. I shall return anon.'

Left alone with Miss Ingram, Nicholas was suddenly at
a loss and he said the first thing that came to mind.

'That colour suits you. Even when you are in the full
flush of war, Miss Ingram.'

Her eyes narrowed to slits of flaming gold. 'What *precisely* did you tell them about me, Lord Deverill?'

'You are a distant cousin of my father's and I came
across you stranded by the weather at a nearby hostelry,
your luggage lost in the snow, and so suggested you spend
the holidays here.'

Some of the fire went out of her eyes. 'That is margin-
ally reasonable. But I find your sister's and your mother's
attitude even more surprising, then.'

'Surprising?'

'They are being nice to me without appearing to pity
me.'

'Why is that surprising? They are nice people. Ah, I
see. You thought anyone related to me must be a monster.'

'Not at all. Rupert is a very nice boy. It seems your family deals in extremes.'

He could tell by the jut of her chin that she wished to
goad him, and for once her arrow flew wide.

'It's Christmas Eve, Miss Ingram. Why don't we declare
a truce until the festivities are over?'

The same flicker of unsettled confusion that he'd noticed
when she'd entered the room was back. 'A truce?'

'A lowering of arms. A temporary cessation of hostilities…'

'I know what a truce is.' She glowered. 'I am not quite
certain what it would entail in our instance.'

'You shall be nice to me and I to you until the day after Christmas.'

'Nice or polite?'

'Nice. I have a feeling your version of polite might be painful.'

She ignored that dig, but a hint of a smile shivered at the corners of her mouth. 'Are you capable? Of being nice?'

'Judging by this conversation, I've a head start on you, Miss Ingram.'

'I am not being *not* nice. I am merely wondering what your agenda is.'

'Surviving this holiday without bloodshed.'

Her mouth wavered further and finally curved into a smile. With a peculiar sense of shock, he realised she had dimples. Two half-moon indentations beside her mouth that made her look for a moment like a mischievous pixie.

'Very well, Lord Deverill. I accept your offer of a temporary truce. In any case it feels wrong to fight with you while I'm wearing your sister's finery.'

'It looks far better on you than on her.'

She rolled her eyes. 'There's a difference between *nice* and outright blarney. There's no call for false flattery in any case. While I'm your mother's guest I assure you I shan't misbehave.'

Pity. He almost said it aloud, but managed to keep that unnecessary thought to himself. Instead he said, 'Excellent, then I feel safe enough to offer you a glass of mulled wine without worrying it shall be flung in my face.'

Chapter Six

It had been ten years since Bella had celebrated...*really* celebrated Christmas.

Mrs Bartleby's version of Christmas Eve was to eat a great deal, drink more and then suffer loudly until the New Year. Christmas Eve at Hadley Hall might be very different from the parsonage at Lower Ottington in scope, but not in spirit.

She'd expected Hadley Hall to be dour and ominous, like its master, but she had to admit that she'd been wrong about both. The house was not merely full of light and warmth, but his mother was lovely and, like Philomena, the other two of Lord Deverill's five sisters who were present were interesting and unassumingly warm women.

The eldest, Lady Carruthers, was married to a shy but pleasant man and had two boys, twins of sixteen or seventeen who looked and acted very like their studious father, and a daughter of around ten who bounced around the room with all the energy of a rogue firework. The next sister, Mrs Symmonds-Pike, was a tall, plump woman and married to a tall, plump man with bluff good humour who'd accepted philosophically when Bella informed him she did not play whist. They had a son around the age of the twins who had flushed hotly and mumbled something incoherent when she had been introduced.

Other than facing Lord Deverill in her new finery, she'd rather worried about Mrs Banister, but she made no mention of having met Bella and, after the necessary introductions, she showed every sign of acting as though Bella didn't exist, which suited Bella just fine.

Once Lady Deverill returned she settled at the pianoforte and the festivities began. There was a great deal of music as Lady Deverill went thoroughly against her easygoing nature by insisting that everyone take an active part in singing Christmas carols.

The Christmas dinner was held early just as Bella remembered at the parsonage and, though she could not remember ever seeing such a feast, it wasn't the formal horror she had dreaded. There was a great deal of laughter and mulled wine and people talking across the table in utter disregard for convention.

She was seated between Philomena and Lady Carruthers, who they called Demmie, and as they asked her no intrusive questions, Bella soon lost her unaccustomed shyness and was taking part in their spirited discussion of the latest novels.

After the dinner they retired once more to the large drawing room and to her surprise the men joined them rather than lingering over their port. The husbands and the Banisters went to the card table and were soon deep in a game of whist, while Demmie and Philly drew Bella to a long table where coloured paper and ribbons were heaped alongside decorations waiting to be hung about the house.

The youngest child, Emily, had been escorted to the nursery directly after dinner, but the boys went with Lord Deverill to the far side of the long room where a billiard table was set up and were soon crowing and groaning as they made or muddled their shots. She saw Rupert cast a longing look in their direction, but settle back into his card game.

'Poor Rupert,' Philly sighed, as if reading her thoughts. 'I do hope he cuts the leading strings one day.'

Bella refrained from saying he almost had and was about to make a less contentious comment when Lady Deverill gave a gasp and stood.

'I have had an excellent idea!'

Lord Deverill's sigh fell into the silence that followed this dramatic announcement.

'The last time you had an excellent idea, Mama, our picnic ended up being swept away by a biblical deluge. Should we be worried?'

'Hush, you silly boy,' his loving mother replied. 'Surely it has occurred to everyone here that no one from the village will dare venture out in this snow for the next few days. That means this shall be the first Christmastide in years without mummers or wassailing.'

'How horribly dreadful, Mama,' Nicholas murmured as he came to lean on the long table beside Philly. His mother shot him a quelling look.

'Well, I think it *is* dreadful, Nicholas. But it needn't be. If we cannot depend on entertainment from without, we shall have to create our own. We shall *all* be mummers.'

'Nonsense, Anne,' announced Mrs Banister in repressive tones as she dealt cards for a new round of whist. 'I refuse to be so vulgar.'

'Thank God for small mercies,' Nicholas muttered and Bella pressed her lips together firmly.

'Don't be a sourpuss, Nicky,' Philly said, elbowing him indelicately in the ribs. Their mother eyed her daughters with a martial eye. 'Philomena, I shall need your help making the lists. You, too, Demmie. Come along, now.' They gave a collective sigh, but rose good naturedly and followed their mother towards the writing table.

'The general and her officers. We're doomed.' Nicholas laughed and Bella realised she had been left alone with him.

The pleasantly fuzzy effects of the large meal and mulled wine cleared a little, but she clung to their tails, determined not to break their truce.

'Is it so terrible?' Bella asked him. 'I thought the mummers merely put on a play.'

'You've never seen mummers?' Nicholas asked in surprise.

'When I was a child in our village, but I don't remember much other than that they wore rather terrifying masks and went about hitting each other with wooden swords and spearing unconvincing dragons. I always felt rather sorry for the poor dragon.'

'Well then, you are more than welcome to take his role and fight back. If I remember correctly, Mama brought a dragon's costume from London a couple years ago. A very dashing affair. You definitely have the figure for it.' His gaze skimmed over her and she felt a flush rising through her.

She spoke hurriedly, forgetting all about their truce. 'And who will you be? Beelzebub?'

As his gaze rose to hers and narrowed, she wished she'd kept quiet, but to her surprise he smiled.

'Careful, puss, your claws are showing.'

'You started it.'

'I paid you a compliment.'

'Was that what it was? Clearly you need more practice.'

'What shall I start with? The way your hair catches the deepest colours of the fire? The way flecks of jade appear in your molten honey eyes when you laugh? Or your dimples? I could wax lyrical about them if you like…' His voice was as deep and smooth as that molten honey and it joined the heat slithering through her, pooling at some point deep inside her.

'Stop it,' she snapped in alarm, wishing she hadn't drunk so much mulled wine. He, too, seemed a little flustered, but he shrugged.

'Well, that was the shortest truce in history.'

'I apologise,' she said stiffly, setting down the ribbons she had been plaiting. 'If you don't mind, I shall retire. Pray thank your mama for a lovely evening. Perhaps the snow will melt overnight and you shall be soon rid of me.'

She hurried out before anyone noticed her withdrawal and had reached the stairs when Lord Deverill spoke behind her.

'Do you know what a barometer is, Miss Ingram?'

She turned, surprised he'd followed her. He looked as he used to when they'd faced each other across the battlefield in Bath—his eyes narrowed and coldly taunting. It was hard to imagine those same eyes had just been taunting her in a completely novel and definitely un-frigid manner.

'I… It is an instrument used on ships to predict the weather, correct?'

'Close enough. We have two at Hadley Hall. One inside, one outside.'

'And so?'

'I have made something of a study of them. The level of mercury in them has been falling all afternoon. Do you know what that means?'

'That you've opened the gates of hell and will soon toss me to Hades, Lord Devil?' she asked politely, determined not to show him how unsettled she was. She almost preferred his anger to his charm. But he surprised her yet again, laughter lighting the fugitive mischief in his dark eyes.

'Tossing does have its appeal,' he replied musingly, sending heat flaring up her cheeks at the *double entendre*. 'But falling mercury means we shall likely see a storm tonight. I sincerely doubt the roads will improve enough for you to escape so soon. Now why don't you come back and enjoy the music and practise lowering your drawbridge for a change. You're as prickly as a porcupine wrapped in brambles.'

'You're a fine one to call me pri—'

'Ooh. Are you about to kiss?'

This question came in a high-pitched hiss above them and they both turned in surprise. The banister that curved up on either side of the wide stairs had acquired a new embellishment—the youthful face of the youngest of the Hadley clan poked out from between the posts.

'Emily! What the devil are you doing up at this hour?' Lord Deverill demanded.

The face detached from between the posts and then re-appeared above the rail.

'I've come to spy. Were you about to kiss?'

She pointed and Bella glanced up to see that a clump of mistletoe hung from a hook in the ceiling above them. It was absurd, but a flush of embarrassed heat rushed up from her chest. Lord Deverill looked discomfited as well, moving away from the offending greenery.

'Go back to bed, you unnatural child.'

'Not on Christmas Eve. It is too bad of you. And hypo-critical, too.' She broke the word into two parts, as if she'd been practising it in her mind and was only now testing it out in the open.

'Why hypocritical?' Bella couldn't resist asking.

'Because as a boy Uncle Nick would always slip down-stairs at night when they had Christmas guests. Mama told me so. She *tried* to make him behave, but he wouldn't.'

Bella tried hard to keep her mouth flat. 'I feel for your poor mama.'

The girl grinned, revealing a missing canine tooth.

'And I feel for *you*, Emily,' Lord Deverill intervened, 'if your *poor mama* finds you hanging over the balustrade in your nightwear. You've had your minced pie, now go to sleep. You're tired.'

'Am not,' said Emily, but yawned widely. 'I want to see you kiss.'

'We are *not* going to kiss. We were having a discussion. Until you rudely interrupted.'

'You were arguing. Mama and Papa always kiss after they argue.'

'Oh, for heaven's sake. Upstairs!'

Emily gave a disgusted huff. 'Oh, very well, but remember you promised to take me to the pond early tomorrow morning, Uncle Nick. Do you skate, Miss Ingram?' The question, which sounded almost like an accusation, caught Bella off guard.

'Yes, but...'

'Oh, good. My brothers are useless and lazy and will not go. But if you come and Uncle Nick *happens* to fall through the ice you can run and call for help and I shall watch where he fell in so I can point them to his frozen, lifeless body.'

With that macabre image hanging over them Emily danced upstairs.

'One day...' Nicholas grumbled, glaring after his niece. Bella couldn't help it, she giggled. His gaze switched to her, still glowering, but she could tell he was firmly repressing a smile.

'It *was* funny,' she insisted and he gave in and smiled. She wished he hadn't. It chipped away at her hard-earned defences. She felt the same warmth, like the mulled wine, coursing through her. She was now absurdly aware she was standing beneath the mistletoe.

'It isn't that bad, is it?' he murmured, coming closer.

'What?' she replied, at a loss again.

'Spending Christmas here rather than with your aunt and cousin in Bath?'

She shook her head. From inside the room someone had begun playing on the pianoforte again and others were joining in—she could hear laughter and singing.

'You enjoyed yourself with Philly and Demmie at dinner, didn't you?' His voice, soothing and warm, was un-ravelling a tightly tied knot inside her.

She nodded.

'And you liked the mulled wine?'

'It was very nice.'

'Nice?' He laughed a little, moving even closer. 'Come have some more, then. Just one more cup before you retire from the lists.'

She smiled despite herself. 'Didn't your mother teach you it isn't polite to be smug?'

'Didn't your mother teach you it is dangerous to stand beneath the mistletoe?' His retort caught her by surprise and she looked up again before she could think better of it.

She told herself this was merely another game for him. It meant nothing to him. All she had to do was laugh and step away.

She did neither.

His eyes narrowed, turning dark and slumberous. His gaze moved over her features, possessing them without a touch. Her skin tingled in response—her eyelids, her cheeks, her jaw, her lips...

Then he leaned in, his fingers just brushing the line of her jaw. Her lips parted without prompting. The first contact was light, a gentle settling of his lips against hers, his breath warm, tinged with cinnamon and cloves, turning the tingle into a surge of sparks like the machines at fairs that set your hair on end. A strange noise gathered inside her chest, between a whimper and a moan. She tried to stop it, tried to stop her hand from resting against his chest, and she failed on both fronts. She could feel his heartbeat...or hers. Fast and hard.

When his lips moved over hers, still light, it was like some fabric deep inside her was being rent in two, almost painful. It swept away the world and left her exposed to a storm deep inside her. She wanted...

Then he was a yard away, adjusting his coat.

'We should join the others,' he said, his voice rubbing against her sensitised skin. She wanted to run upstairs, but that was cowardly. As she passed through the drawing room door his words followed her inside.

'Merry Christmas, Bella.'

Chapter Seven

'Wake up.'

Bella shot out of her confused dream about being pushed off a cliff by a dark figure and stared into Emily's grey eyes.

'Skating!' Emily announced gaily and Bella resisted an urge to groan and shove her head under the pillow.

'I doubt your uncle is awake…' she mumbled, but Emily merely bounced on the side of the bed.

'Of course he's awake. Uncle Nick is usually in the study with his fusty books and toys at the crack of dawn. He said you wouldn't want to come and not to bother you, but I think you *would* like to come, wouldn't you? And you needn't worry about the ice. Henry, the groom, has been down there already and said it's as thick as it's been in years. Do say you'll come. No one else except Uncle Nick wishes to.'

She sounded so forlorn that Bella's heart pricked. She knew what it was like to be an only child in a house of adults. She'd loved her parents dearly, but she'd always wished she'd had brothers and sisters to play and argue and go exploring and skating with.

'Oh, do come,' Emily said. 'Uncle Nick is fun, but if you come, he is sure to stay longer on the pond.'

Bella wasn't at all certain of that, but she'd enjoyed watching Emily order Lord Deverill about and wouldn't mind seeing her do so again. And despite herself she wondered what it would be like to put skates on once more.

'I'm afraid I don't have any…'

'Skates? There's Mama's pair and she's never even used them and…' she pointed to a long wine-coloured pile of fabric she'd dumped on the end of the bed '…I brought a warm coat for you and gloves because Sue said—'

Bella gave in to the inevitable and interrupted the girl's relentless flow. 'Very well, Emily. You win. I shall come down as soon as I dress.'

Emily clearly didn't trust her. She was waiting outside her room, bouncing from foot to foot.

'Come along before everyone wakes and finishes all the minced pies and cider!'

Bella wasn't quite certain anyone else would be waking early after last night's festivities and certainly not that they would be indulging in minced pies and cider for breakfast, but she allowed herself to be dragged along, a tingling excitement in her stomach.

She must have been sixteen the last time she'd skated. Her last winter at Lower Ottington before her parents died. She would likely end up flat on her behind at best or with a broken leg at worst. She felt a sudden qualm. She really did not wish to make a fool of herself in front of Lord Deverill, but it was too late to retreat.

The world outside was still and blindingly white under a sky so blue it hurt her eyes. It was also freezing. The trees were all cloaked in snow and various bluish-white shapes and lumps hinted at walls, benches, bushes and what might have been a sundial or a fountain. Bella had a sudden urge to fling herself on to this perfect world like a dog set loose.

A narrow path had been cleared through this quiet beauty and through an open arched gate. Emily gave a whoop and ran, the skates dangling from her hand clacking against each other. Bella followed, her boots crunching on the packed snow, her lovely borrowed coat brushing against the high walls of snow on either side of her.

There was no wind, but the air bit at her cheeks and poked needles in her lungs. A bubble of that puppy-like joy grew and rose inside her. With each step she felt she was shrinking, slipping back into childhood, on her way to the village pond where the children gathered with their makeshift skates, the boys with sticks and a rock to chase across the ice. Suddenly she missed Lower Ottington with a fierceness that made her chest ache.

Emily had already reached the pond and strapped on her skates and she pushed away on to the ice, wobbling and laughing as she stumbled towards the man who glided to a stop beside her.

Bella ought to have known Lord Devil would skate well. He had a natural grace of motion she'd noticed when they'd seen him riding through town and though she had not often seen him dance, he waltzed with the calm ease of a man with several sisters and even more mistresses.

She settled on a wooden bench that had been brushed free of snow and strapped on her skates. Once ready, she took a deep breath and stood, wavering at the sudden increase in height. The thick snow held her firmly, and as she trudged the last yard to the ice her confidence blossomed. It might have been ten years since she'd skated, but she'd been good and fast. Surely it wouldn't be too hard...

She had no clear idea how she ended up on her back. One moment she was settling her skate on the glistening ice and the next she was staring at a single feather of a cloud directly above her.

She heard Emily's squawk of alarm and then a dark vision appeared above her.

'Are you hurt?' asked Lord Deverill.

'I think I landed on my pride and broke it.'

The concern in his dark grey eyes fled, replaced by a more familiar mocking smile. 'It would take more than a featherweight like you to break that. Here.'

He held out his hand as she sat up and for a moment she was so tempted to pull him off balance. His eyes narrowed. His smile widened. He looked distinctively like Lord Devil and far too handsome.

'Now, now, don't give in to temptation, Bella. Remember our truce?'

She sighed and allowed him to help her up. The motion propelled her forward and she clung to his coat, hoping against hope they wouldn't both end up in a pile together. His arm slipped around her, his legs parting to give him more balance as he held her against him, steadying them both.

'I thought you said you could skate,' Emily called out as she whisked past them, reminding Bella of their audience.

'I used to,' she murmured, her cheeks in full burn. 'It's been ten years, though.'

'Slowly then,' he said, his voice a subterranean rumble against her. Her hands tightened further on his coat, her whole body clenched in a surge of what felt like alarm, only worse. He seemed in no hurry to let her go any more than she was to be let go. Her front was burning hot while her backside was still aching and cold from her fall. She wanted to snuggle deeper, tuck her cheek against his shoulder and have him glide her away with him. She wanted… She unclenched her hands, pressed them against his chest… His very firm chest…

No.

'I'm quite all right now. Thank you, Lord Deverill.'

He didn't answer immediately, but then his arm loosened and he shifted back. The cold slipped between them and she concentrated on her skates. She let them take her weight, moved a little, pushed forward, balanced again, pushed forward again. A shiver of anticipation joined the confusing muddle of sensations inside her. It was a feeling she remembered from childhood—from the nights before her birthdays, from the arrival in the lending library of a book she had long awaited, and then from overcoming the stiff resistance of the cover as she opened it, revealing a whole new, wonderful world...

She moved faster. For a moment, as she approached the snowy bank at the end of the pond, her legs lost their memory. But a firm hand clasped her arm, steadying her and turning her lightly. She looked up in thanks and for a moment her mind blanked as well. Just so had he looked when she'd stepped off the carriage two days ago—intent, dangerous—and yet he seemed different now. Not angry, just...dangerous.

'Thank you,' she said breathlessly, 'I can manage now, I think. I shall start my next turn earlier.'

He let her go, his hand sliding against hers, and she pulled away, the same alarm as before slithering through her.

But soon alarm was overtaken by the pleasure of the ice. This time her legs shifted and turned, the skates scraping as she completed the turn and set out again, ever faster, laughing with delight at her success. Emily clapped in enthusiasm and came to skate a circle around her.

'Aren't you happy you came with us?'

Bella laughed. 'Yes, you little heathen. But if you laugh when next I fall, I shall put snow down your neck!'

Emily gasped with delight. 'Did you hear that, Uncle Nick? She's threatened me with violence.'

'Very sensible,' her uncle replied. 'I think she's being restrained, but then she doesn't know you yet.'

Emily laughed and quickly skated off.

'You're actually not bad at this,' he observed, moving alongside her with annoying ease.

She tried another turn and managed not to upend herself. 'I used to love skating on the village pond.'

'Why did you stop?'

She didn't particularly wish to talk about her past, but it felt impolite not to answer. 'My father was a vicar and he and my mother often visited the sick. When I was sixteen they caught the fever and died and so I was sent to live with my mother's sister, Mrs Bartleby.'

'Ah.'

There was a wealth of meaning in that one syllable and she glanced up at his profile. 'What does that "ah" mean?'

He took her arm and guided her neatly through a turn before she skated off the pond and then he left his hand there, somehow communicating his rhythm to her so that her skating became more…fluid, more like her long-ago memories.

'I was wondering how you ended up as your cousin's rather ferocious guardian angel.'

Ferocious did not sound very complimentary, but she let it slide.

'Mrs Bartleby had been widowed not long before I arrived,' she tried to explain. 'She was always poorly, and Violet…'

'Ran wild and did what she wanted.'

Bella tried to pull her arm away, but he held firm. 'Sorry. I shan't say another word. In fact, let's forget all about your cousin and concentrate on recovering your impressive skating skills.'

'Hardly impressive… Nicholas!' she squawked as he propelled her into a rapid turn, not even noticing she'd used his Christian name. She was quite certain her feet would fly out from under her, but instead they angled into the turn, completing it without a wobble. He grinned.

'You evil, evil man!' she breathed and he laughed.

'You did that very well. I dare say you were one of those girls like Emily who insisted on showing off on the ice.'

'That is a far better description of you than of me, Lord

Deverill,' she said primly. 'And it isn't true in the least. I forgot everyone else when I was skating.'

He shifted, suddenly skating backwards alongside her so that he could see her face.

'I see…'

'Is that another version of "ah!"?' she mocked.

'It is. I can see you, head in the clouds as you day-dreamed back and forth across the ice…' His voice trailed off, his gaze moving over her face as the colour she could not hide swept over her. She felt suddenly…naked, stripped of her defences and yet not in danger. Not the kind of danger that woke her at night, that kept her mind jumping from worry to machination and back to worry. This danger was different, unfamiliar, and…and fierce. She swallowed.

And noticed a rather more immediate danger a little too late. She grabbed for his coat, but the end of the pond came swiftly and all she succeeded in doing was going down with him as his skates struck the snow.

At least she landed *on* him.

The snow went up in a puff around them, dusting her face and his hair. Behind them she heard a squeal of laughter and a whoosh as Emily turned and skated off.

'Damned little weasel,' he muttered and Bella blinked, ready to take offence until she realised he'd meant his niece.

She ought to untangle herself. She could feel his legs and chest beneath hers, hard and tense, and the warm, firm band of his arm around her waist. She felt… Good was not the right word. She felt…right. Except that it was hard to breathe because every breath made her chest brush and press against the hard expanse of his, making her insides squirm and tingle in a most uncomfortable manner. She tried to slide off him, but his arm tightened and he made a strange sound, between a gasp and a moan. She stilled.

'Oh, no, are you hurt?'

He shook his head, his hand splaying against her back, holding her against him even more firmly.

'I'm too heavy,' she said and he shook his head again, but said nothing. He'd lost his hat and snowflakes clung to the dark strands of his hair like stardust on the silk of night. He looked beautiful, like an angel fallen to earth, his grey eyes stormy, his mouth tense and yet soft. He had a beautiful mouth—strong, definite lines that were as beautiful when he mocked as when he smiled. It was horribly unfair.

The tingling that had been plaguing her gathered into a surge several times stronger than the one that had assaulted her under the mistletoe and the memory of their almost-kiss blazed into life. It scorched her from the inside, spiralling through her, lighting fires and clenching muscles along the way. She couldn't seem to look away from his mouth.

He made that sound again and she could not help answering with something between a whimper and a moan of surrender. As if that was a signal he'd been waiting for, he finally moved, his hand skimming up her back, slipping under her hood. The soft leather glove was cold against her fevered skin, but she was too far gone to care except to wish it was his hand and not a glove that stroked her cheekbone, her ear, then slipped into her hair, easing her head towards his.

She offered not a smidgen of resistance.

His lips were both cold and warm, warmer than hers, his breath soothing and coaxing as his mouth brushed over hers. He stopped there as he had beneath the mistletoe, mouths touching, heartbeats crashing against each other.

Then he did something awful. His tongue traced the line of her upper lip. Then he did something even worse. He canted her head a little and gently caught her throbbing lower lip with his teeth, caressing it with his tongue.

She wanted to move against him, slip her hands under his coat, feel…

But more than anything, she wanted to kiss him. She had no clear idea how to kiss a man, but somehow she did. Her mouth opening against his, her tongue seeking and finding the contours of his lips. His hand tightened in her hair, his breathing quickening, his leg bending so she sank deeper between his legs. She'd never felt anything like this, like him, even *she* felt utterly new. Her tongue brushed his and another whimper unfurled in her lungs and she tossed her tentative exploration to the wind as the kiss turned fierce, demanding, erasing everything else from the universe but the two of them.

'There's no mistletoe here,' Emily called out with another passing whoosh that sent shards of ice on to the exposed backs of Bella's legs. That woke her.

She rolled off, scrambling to her feet. She heard his grunt behind her, but she was already shooting away across the ice, clumps of crushed snow flying off her damp coat.

When he joined them he seemed just as usual. He threatened awful revenge on his niece for laughing at their fall and after a while Bella's nerves calmed and her good sense returned. Her pride, too. She didn't want him to see how flustered she had been. He probably kissed women for breakfast. It was nothing to him. He had merely taken advantage of what had been dropped, literally, into his lap.

It wasn't so for her. She had never felt anything as powerful as that brushing of flesh on flesh, the pressure of his hand in her hair, his body under hers... She called herself to order.

Though some clouds had gathered once more in the pristine blue skies, it was not snowing. It was entirely possible that by tomorrow she would be on her way back to Bath. Meanwhile she was damned if she would give him the satisfaction of regarding her as another easy conquest.

Chapter Eight

Nicholas and Porter watched as the head groom handed the reins of the snow-flecked mare to a stable boy and stamped snow from his boots. The pristine sky of the early morning was gone and already the low clouds were shedding all over the snowbound inner courtyard.

'That bad, Henry?' asked Nicholas.

'As bad as I've seen it since 1808, my lord. I didn't even try to make it to the village. There'll be no carriages on those roads until there's some thaw. And there'll be no wassailers or mummers coming from the village this Christmastide.'

'We'll survive,' Nicholas said absently, turning to Porter. 'Make a note to send them their pay once we break free from winter's grasp. How are we for stores?'

'No worries there, sir. But her ladyship will be sore disappointed. Very fond of the mummers, she is. So will the maids below stairs.'

'Well, you can tell them an even greater treat awaits them. Her ladyship has decided to try her hand at mummery.' An idea occurred to him. 'Why don't you ask if anyone below stairs wishes to take part?'

Porter's face lit with pleasure and he hurried off while Nicholas went to inform the thorn in his backside that she was well and truly stuck at Hadley Hall. He ought to be as upset as she was likely to be at the news. He *was* upset. Just not quite for the same reasons as a few days ago.

It was all because of that damned kiss. What had he been thinking?

Well, that was easy: he hadn't. He'd managed to pull away from that strange moment under the mistletoe, but when she'd landed on top of him by the pond, his body, already far more curious than advisable, had lit like a Vauxhall fireworks tower shooting sparks through every nerve. All his senses had concentrated on her weight pressing down on him, on her curves muffled by all the unfortunate layers between them. And on her mouth, the lips parted, flushed from cold and exertion.

Why a mouth should suddenly have appeared as precious as a religious icon to a zealot, he had no idea. At that moment all he could think, if it was a thought at all, was—I have to kiss her. Now. Or perish trying.

And then she'd kissed him and eliminated whatever remained of his conscious mind. He'd never in his life lost himself like that… If he'd been drowning he would have sunk to the bottom of the ocean without a fight. To say he'd not been himself would be an understatement. He hadn't been anyone at all. Anything at all. Nothing but sensations.

When she'd pushed away he'd lain there, winded and shocked, as he'd registered the pressure of the broken reeds under the snow beneath him, the cold slither of melting ice against his neck and the first glimmerings of shock that he'd kissed her in full view of Emily.

He winced for the hundredth time since he'd dragged himself back to his feet. He couldn't seem to shake the sensations of shock, embarrassment and something very much like fear.

Perhaps he *had* hit his head when he'd fallen…

He entered his study and closed the door. Across the room the curtains were drawn, but his mind saw through them and down to the pond, bringing forth an image of Bella turning on the ice, winter sunlight shimmering in the deep golden-yellow-brown eyes, catching the reddish lights in her auburn hair.

Oh, hell.

How long now since you've wanted to bed her? a snide little voice piped up. Rubbed you the wrong way from the start, didn't she? Well, now you know why. Why you trailed after Rupert for weeks like a damned penniless tutor.

Don't be an idiot, he replied, stalking towards his desk. I was trying to stop him from making the mistake of his life.

Aren't you a good Samaritan! Mr Snide tittered. So it had nothing to do with the pleasure of crossing swords with Miss Golden Eyes?

Pleasure? It was hardly pleasure having to kick my heels in that damned provincial town full of aching fuddy-duddies. I never would have had to stay there that long if Bella Ingram hadn't kept interfering in my plans to untangle Rupert. I'd never met a woman I disliked more.

Aha! pounced Mr Snide. Never wasted so much time disliking a woman before, did you? And it wasn't Violet Bartleby who got your goat, was it? No, you chose to cross swords with her cousin.

That's because Bella is the dangerous one, Nicholas snapped, backed to the wall by his worse self.

And that, said Mr Snide, digging his finger into Nicholas's chest, is the first truth you've offered today.

Go to hell, Nicholas snarled.

A tap on the door penetrated his self-flagellation and he called out rather more curtly than necessary, 'What?'

There was a moment's silence and then the door opened. Two hours had passed since their return to the house, but his raw insides still gave a kick of resistance. He ought to have known it would be her.

He rose, bracing himself. She wore another of his sister's dresses, the rose-pink a fine foil for her hair and the warm cream of her skin. Her brows were pinched together like ominous wings, but her voice was hesitant.

'I'm sorry to bother you, Lord Deverill, but the maid just told me… Is it true? Are the roads still impassable?'

He cleared his throat. 'I'm afraid so. The snow is lying in drifts several feet high along the roads. Our groom couldn't make it twenty yards past the gates on our sturdiest mount. I'm afraid you are stranded here for a few more days.'

He wished he could fathom what she was thinking. When she wore that cool, blank mask he could not tell if she was angry or upset or merely bored.

'Is that so awful a prospect?' he asked, rather more brusquely than he'd intended, and she shook her head swiftly.

Then, just as swiftly, she nodded.

'Yes. I don't belong here. And these expensive dresses only make it worse.' Her voice was curt, as if she was reprimanding a schoolboy. Remorse entered his stewing cauldron of discomfort.

'You seem to be fitting in very well.'

'Your family…well, most of them…are being kind and polite, but we know better.'

She rolled her shoulders as if preparing to enter the jousting field and he wished she would…relax.

Fine words when he was as tense as a topsail. He went to the hob where he always kept a kettle of tea ready while he worked. It was time he shook off this strange confusion and remember he was thirty-five and the head of the chaotic Hadley tribe and that it had been he who'd forced Bella into this strange situation. He could have, and should have, sent her back to Bath that very night. But he hadn't.

And now that he knew why, he was all the more accountable for her discomfort.

'Come sit down for a moment.'

'It isn't proper. What might your family and the servants think?'

She sounded absurdly prim, like she often had in Bath. He sighed.

'Both my family and the servants know I had something of a reputation when I was younger, but even if I had not put all that behind me, that part of me would never cross the front steps of Hadley Hall.'

Her gaze flickered up with a fugitive smile. 'So the gardens are fair game?'

He couldn't help smiling. 'Why don't you let that twisty solicitor's mind of yours rest for a moment and sit down? Here.'

'Another command obeyed,' she muttered as she took the cup and settled on the armchair opposite him. He laughed, some of his tension unravelling. It was easier to deal with her when she was prickling like a hedgehog.

'How can I make it easier?' he asked. It was the wrong thing to say apparently. She set down her cup and sniffed. With some shock he realised she was about to cry.

'Bella? What did I say?'

'Nothing,' she snapped, brushing a hand over her eyes. 'I am merely tired. I didn't sleep well.'

Neither had he, he almost said. Instead he asked, 'Is there something wrong with your room?'

'No. It is the loveliest room I've ever seen. And, no, no one has been unpleasant to me. Philomena and Emily and your mother have all been everything that is welcoming and...' She dragged the tumble of words to a halt. She was squeezing her hands together so tightly her knuckles shone white. He wanted to take her hands and untangle them, soothe the tension he didn't understand, make her smile...

Double hell.

'Then what's wrong?' he prompted.

'*I'm* wrong,' she whispered and cleared her throat. 'I

apologise. I'm being foolish. It is merely… It's my first real Christmas in years and years. I'd forgotten…'

'Is it all coming back?'

She nodded.

'You miss your parents.'

She nodded again.

He handed her his handkerchief and she pressed it to her eyes like a blindfold, as if that could blank out the past, the pain. The present.

'I am not usually so…emotional.' Her words were muffled and he smiled.

'If you'd told me that a week ago I would have said you are understating the matter,' he said. 'But I rather think I was very wrong about you.'

'Stop being *nice* to me.' This accusation was even more muffled. 'I liked you better when you were hateful.'

'That's not nice.'

'*I'm* not nice.'

'We can't conduct this whole conversation with you hiding behind my handkerchief, you know.'

'I'm not hiding.'

'Do you know why hedgehogs roll into a prickly ball? Because they have a soft underbelly.'

She folded his handkerchief, her reddened eyes glaring at him.

'I am not a soft-bellied hedgehog, and I am not hiding, and I am not nice, and I cannot stay here. I want to go—' The words ended on a strange little gasp, her eyes widening, losing focus. Her lips moved and she swallowed and he could almost see the word move away from her.

Home.

Suddenly he could see it all.

There was no home. Only a corner in someone else's world, contingent upon her loyalty and her service. She'd done her best to be a good niece and cousin, but he could almost feel her loss of balance now she'd been plucked from her little world.

She shook herself and let out a long breath, looking down at the handkerchief twisting in her hands.

'The sooner I return, the better.' She spoke calmly, very like Miss Ingram. Except now he heard a hundred shades behind those words.

'In a few days the roads will open,' he said soothingly. 'Meanwhile all you are required to do is to eat a lot, drink a little and take part in my mother's likely disastrous attempt to recreate the mummers' play. We're a family that is sociable in small bursts, but otherwise each of us has their little burrow in this rambling house where we can recover our strength. This study is mine. My mother's is the conservatory. What you need is your own hedgehog's burrow. I'll have Porter arrange a parlour near your room and you can line it with sweetmeats and books from the library or from Philly's collection of novels which I'm certain she'll be happy to share. We'll still expect you to come out occasionally, though, Bella. Hedgehogs do, you know,' he warned and won a small smile. It felt like a great achievement, somehow.

Her gaze moved around the room, as if seeing it for the first time, and she rose and went to where a long mahogany board was affixed to the wall, its border decorated with mother of pearl in swirling shapes like puffs of wind. At its centre was a round glass-covered dial out of which rose a long glass tube.

'Is this your barometer?' she asked and he rose as well, accepting this change of topic.

'Yes, it's an aneroid barometer. It was made especially for me by Mr Cetti in London.'

'It's beautiful.'

'I'm afraid he was rather disappointed I did not choose one of his elaborate designs. He insisted on the wind decorations, though.'

'They're so delicate.' She traced her finger over one mother-of-pearl swirl and he shoved his hands into his pockets. She moved towards the glass cabinets with the instruments he'd collected over the years and he followed, rather like a schoolboy whose room was under inspection by the school prefect.

'And what's this?' She pointed to a stand with two poles between which was strung a small toy child on a swing.

'That's an electrical swing. Once it's connected to an electroscope,' he pointed to the apparatus on the shelf above, 'the swing becomes magnetised and is repelled by either of these magnets. That makes it swing back and forth. It is merely a toy. My father bought it for me.'

He felt her quick glance on him, but then she looked away, rising on tiptoe to get a better look.

'It's extraordinary. Did he enjoy natural history as well?'

It was a tame question, but he felt strangely unmasked by it. He shrugged. 'Yes. When I was a boy he would take me to lectures at the Royal Institute. I still go when I'm in London.'

She sighed. 'How wonderful. I'm envious. There aren't such things in Bath. I dare say you didn't argue as much when you were young.'

He smiled. 'I'll have you know I was a very well-behaved little boy. I only rebelled when... Later. What of you?' he asked. 'Did you rebel?'

She smiled at the change of subject and shrugged. 'I didn't have much chance to do so. My father and I did love arguing, though. Especially about history. Like who really won the Trojan War and whether the Romans stole all their gods from the Greeks. I was only just beginning my own little rebellion when the fever took them.' Sadness darkened her eyes, but before he could say something foolish, she shook herself and smiled. 'It seems so long ago.

Everything changed when I went to live in Bath. Do you miss your father?'

He shifted his weight. He ought to put her off, remind her that though he was sorry for her current predicament, that gave her no right to pry, but after her own honesty it felt unfair not to respond in kind.

'Yes. He never quite understood why I felt the need to run wild and explore the world and that strained our relations. When I returned we became close again, though never quite as close as before. I was too young then to realise he was more worried than disapproving. If I could go back…'

He felt a brief brush against his arm, but then she was moving away, her gaze on the contents of the cabinets. He followed, feeling both more uncomfortable and yet more comfortable than he could remember in a long while.

At the end of the cabinets she went to the doorway, but turned towards him and smiled.

'Thank you, Lord Deverill. You've been very kind and patient. I shall try to be less troublesome.'

When the door closed behind her he tried to imagine precisely what a less troublesome Bella Ingram implied. It was a bad sign that none of the possibilities he could conjure were in any way reassuring.

Chapter Nine

I shall try to be less troublesome.

Bella paused halfway up the stairs, cringing. What an inane thing to say. Hadley Hall was having a very unwanted effect on her. Thus far it had made her behave outrageously, reveal things she had not allowed herself to think of for years and almost burst into tears in front of the bane of her recent existence.

If she was to remain here a few more days, she had best take herself in hand and…

'Ah! Excellent. Do come here, my dear, and hold this confounded thing down before it utterly defeats me.'

Bella turned at Lady Deverill's breathless exhortation. Her hostess stood to the side of the great staircase, holding one end of a long garland of greenery made of boughs of fir and holly intertwined with a long golden ribbon.

'Hurry, I am losing the battle here…'

Bella hurried back down the stairs and took hold of the unwinding branches. Lady Deverill gave a sigh of relief.

'I noticed it was unravelling and made the mistake of trying to tackle it alone. It is like wrestling one of those monstrous snakes from those horrid Greek tales Nicholas insists on reading. Or is it a hydra?'

'The hydra was a many-headed serpent that guarded the gate of hell,' Bella replied, though uncertain if she was required to answer.

'Goodness. The Greeks seemed to have quite a few animals in hell which is rather peculiar, as animals cannot sin, can they? Here—hold this ribbon, too.'

Bella added the ribbon to her collection of greenery.

'I am not certain whether they can, Lady Deverill.'

'I thought Nicholas mentioned you were a vicar's daughter. Don't they know these things?'

'I'm afraid my father was not much for sermons at home. He, like your son, preferred the Greeks.'

Lady Deverill cast her a sweet smile. 'You loved him.'

Bella's face flared in sudden burning heat. It took her stumbling mind a moment longer to realise the statement referred to her father.

'Very much, Lady Deverill.'

'Pray let us make away with titles, my dear. You shall call me Anne. A plain name, I know, but as my other names are even plainer, it shall have to do.'

'I cannot call you Anne,' Bella replied, horrified.

'Nonsense. And I shall call you Bella. What a pretty name. I'm quite envious. I always wished for a pretty name while growing up. That is why I named my daughters so prettily. Are you also fond of the Greeks, Bella?'

Bella moved along the twisting serpent to hold the ribbon for Lady Deverill.

'I'm afraid I am, Lady… Anne,' she amended at a minatory look from her hostess. 'I find it wonderful how they distilled all their deepest ideas about life into such colourful and exuberant tales.'

'Hmmm. Bloodthirsty, too.'

'Yes, but I imagine all those dramatics must have been necessary back then when so few people could read and write and when stories were the only way to pass along the…the flavour of a people and their sense of right and wrong. And in the end what they mostly caution us about is hubris, our human tendency to think ourselves above others and above nature, and that is always a good lesson.'

Lady Deverill snipped off an edge of ribbon with a pair of sewing scissors. 'Do you think my son suffers from hubris?'

Again Bella was swamped by a tide of confused, embarrassed heat. She turned her shoulder a little to Lady Deverill, bending over the knot she was completing.

'It is hardly for me to say, Lady Deverill.'

'No, no, none of that milk-and-water-miss nonsense. My son says you've a sharp mind and a will of iron. That is quite a compliment, as very few dare oppose him. What he does not achieve on the strength of his title and funds, he's learned to secure by charm. Perhaps if I had more sons I would not be so concerned, but I've nothing to compare him to, you see.'

Bella nodded, hoping this particular diversion would lead away from uncomfortable waters. But Lady Deverill's digressions didn't prevent her from returning to the high road, for she continued, 'So, does he suffer from hubris, Bella?'

Bella brushed fir needles from her hands.

'I… I don't know your son well, Lady… Anne. It is true he can be very opinionated and when he believes in something he can be rather single minded in achieving it. But hubris implies one is so caught up in oneself that one fails to see others. From what I have seen of Lord Deverill since my arrival, that is not at all the case. He is very good with the younger Hadleys. It isn't merely kindness… He sees them and they feel that, which is why they are so drawn to him. I don't think anyone truly lost to vanity and hubris would be capable of that.'

Lady Deverill smiled and gave a little sigh. 'Yes, that is true. He was always so good with animals, too. When I worried about him I reminded myself of that.'

'Were you worried about him?' Bella asked, succumbing to curiosity.

'Not as a boy. He was always happy and warm-hearted, though he had a very serious streak just like his papa. But when he was about Rupert's age something happened that... well, it drove him to extremes. He left home and went travelling, very much against our will, and he lived quite a wild life. At least that is what was gossiped and gossip, as you know, is only magnified over great distances.

'I dare say Barnaby and I did not manage our concern and disappointment well and further put up his back with our moralising letters demanding that he return to the predictable safety of Hadley Hall. In the end he did return, but even after dear Barnaby passed away three years ago, Nicholas has never shown any sign of settling down in earnest. It is almost as if he considers matters of the heart beneath him.' She sighed and tucked the edge of a branch into the garland, adding, 'Or beyond him.'

Bella very much wished to ask what precisely had happened to Lord Deverill all those years ago to have effected such a change. But perhaps this, too, was also a magnified tale—this time by a mother trying to excuse her son's innate aloofness. A week ago Bella would have been certain this was the case. But now... In a matter of days her inner compass, once so certain about true north, was lurching about like a drunken piglet.

'Why have you told me all this? I'm quite certain Nicho...your son would not approve of you sharing such confidences with me.'

'Your certainty is not in the least misplaced, Miss Ingram,' said a voice behind Bella. She froze, a clump of ribbon ends crushed in her hand. She had not even heard the study door open. 'What game are you playing now, Mama?' Lord Deverill's question was icy cold. Her hackles rose in response.

'Your mother was merely making conversation, Lord Deverill.'

'Polite chit-chat,' he mocked and his mother clucked her tongue.

'You are being far too sensitive, Nicholas. Pray do not snap at dear Bella. She has been most helpful and a fine listener. Such a rare trait nowadays among you young people.'

'Thank you, Mama. Are there any other critiques you wish to deliver?'

'Oh, nothing else at the moment, Nicholas dear. Now if you will excuse me, it is time for…'

Bella did not hear what it was time for. Lady Deverill melted away up the stairs and Bella was left facing a very different Lord Deverill from the one she'd just left in the study. She shifted warily towards the stairs, but Nicholas was there first.

'One moment, Miss Ingram. I don't know what my mother decided to divulge to you, but I want to make it clear I would not appreciate you repeating any of her imprudent confidences outside these walls.'

'Oh, and here I was about to rush upstairs and dash off a quick exposé to the gossip columns. You are, as always, ahead of yourself, my lord. Your mother's disclosures would hardly be worthy of two lines below the advertisements.'

'I heard what she said about my parents' disappointment.'

Bella's antagonism receded a little. Under the anger there was hurt and…confusion. 'I think it was far more a case of concern than disappointment. She said nothing hurtful, I promise. I have no notion why she told me anything at all, but sometimes one needs to talk to someone…outside. Perhaps it being Christmas, without your father…' She let the words fall away. He said nothing and she inched a little closer to the stairs.

'I really ought to go… I am meeting your sisters at four o'clock to prepare the mummers' costumes… Philomena said the servants brought down trunks of costumes to the conservatory.' She'd made it to the bottom stair and he hadn't moved, his hands still shoved deep in his pockets, but his expression had lost its glittering edge and there was even a hint of amusement about his mouth at her less than subtle attempt to escape.

'Four o'clock?'

She nodded.

'In the conservatory?'

'Yes, why?'

'I think I shall come see if I can find those dragon's trousers for you. If I'm to be Beelzebub, I might need a stealthy ally of your calibre. You'll be quite useful prying incriminating admissions from my enemies.'

She turned her back on the infuriating man and stalked upstairs. She could feel his gaze on her. No doubt he was thoroughly enjoying her embarrassment.

Chapter Ten

Hadley Hall's Great Mummers Show of 1818
New Year's Eve
All Welcome

That was announced by a sign in big bold red letters painted by Emily and the twins and strung up along the conservatory wall behind the makeshift stage. Bella had been put to work sorting and preparing costumes extracted from three large wooden trunks.

They were bursting not only with all manner of masquerade costumes, but with clothes of bygone days: brocade coats and vests, wigs, frilled collars, and a pair of high-heeled men's shoes in a shade of pink not even a demimonde would be caught dead in. And one devil's costume which was immediately assigned to Nicholas.

'I told you how it would be,' Bella murmured, not without some satisfaction.

'You're a spiteful little hedgehog,' he muttered, eyeing the long black cloak his mother had handed him. 'I was hoping for something a little more…diabolical. This will make me look like the villain from a second-rate Covent Garden pantomime.'

She poked her finger through a moth hole in the cape. 'Third-rate.'

'I'll wear it on the condition you sign on as the dragon. The devil has the privilege of choosing his allies.'

'How fortuitous you should suggest that,' chimed in his mother. 'Look what I found. It is already too small for the twins and rather too large yet for Emily. You shall make a marvellous dragon…dragoness…? What does one call the female of that species, Nicholas?'

'Dangerous, Mama. Now show us the costume. I want to see what my minion shall look like.'

Lady Deverill held out a shimmer of green and gold and Bella stared in awe at a long, almost transparent cape of fine green gauze embroidered with golden scales and ending in a gold fringe. Lady Deverill shoved it into Bella's hands and continued rooting about the pile of fabrics, emerging again with a triumphant 'aha!' This time she held aloft a set of green silk trousers and a laced blouse with long pointy sleeves.

'I cannot wear that!' Bella said, shocked to her very core.

'Of course you can, my dear. It is all part of the play. And pray consider, when next shall you have an excuse to wear trousers? I quite envy you, but I am to play the winter queen and she would look rather peculiar in breeches.' Lady Deverill didn't wait for her reply, towing her towards the parlour that had been set aside for the women to try their costumes. As the door closed, she heard Nicholas's laughter trailing behind her.

Nicholas was still smiling when the door opened and his mother ushered Bella back into the conservatory. His sisters *oohed* and *ahhed* and Emily swirled her pink princess's skirts in delight as she commanded Bella to take good care of the costume as she planned to wear it as soon as she was tall enough.

Nicholas just stood, once again poleaxed by his treacherous body. The trousers were made of fine silk and clung to her legs, making a faint swishing sound that skittered along his nerves as his mother propelled her forward. She might not be tall, but her proportions were...delectable.

The blouse, too, was fitted close to the chest and, as it had been designed for the twins, it was just a little too tight about her bodice. The only parts of her body adequately covered by the fabric were her hands where the green silk hung over them like claws, but that didn't help him at all. And the absolute worst was that his mother had taken down Bella's hair and placed an embroidered gold braid about her brow, leaving long auburn waves to fall about her shoulders.

'Like a dragon's mane, don't you think?' asked Lady Deverill, clearly very pleased with herself.

Nicholas didn't correct his mother that as far as he knew dragons were not supposed to have manes. He was far too occupied with Bella. She stood stock still as the Hadley women examined and exclaimed, her cheeks hot with colour, her eyes wide. Then, as if he'd compelled her, she turned to look at him. And once again his stomach dropped, his skin tightened, while his heart flopped about like a landed fish.

In a long-forgotten corner of his mind he remembered reacting like this almost twenty years ago. Back then he'd been a blind young fool who mistook his first serious bout of lust with love. Since then he and lust had become better acquainted.

This wasn't lust. Well, it was, but in the same way that a glass of water and an ocean were water. The glass was a nice manageable amount, you could drink it and move on. This...whatever *this* was...had no manageable boundaries, no discernible shape, and it seemed to extend beyond his known horizons.

Four days ago he'd thought he hated this woman. Two days ago he'd realised he wanted to bed her. And now a single glance from her told him he was somehow already tethered to her.

He didn't want her to feel lost, or hurt. He wanted to push aside his well-meaning family, take her hands, anchor her gaze in his and tell her everything would be all right.

These were uncharted seas and he was far gone over the edge of the known map.

Chapter Eleven

It was agreed by all occupants of Hadley Hall, other than Aunt Agatha, that the play was a resounding success.

It was also an utter disaster. Most everyone forgot their lines, fumbled with the notes they'd been given by Lady Deverill, tripped over their costumes, or began giggling at the height of the drama.

It was simply marvellous.

Bella could not remember the last time she had so much fun. The days that had passed between Christmas Day and New Year's Eve had swept by far too fast and yet had been richer and fuller than much of her life since she'd left the vicarage at Lower Ottington.

Even when she was squirming with discomfort, she felt…marvellous. Alive. She wasn't quite certain who Bella Ingram was any longer, but she was certainly a far happier person than the one who had resided in Bath all those years.

After Bella's first shock at seeing her costume, she thought she made a very dashing dragon. The trousers were a trifle tight and she managed to trip twice on the fringed cape in her attempt to vanquish Rupert's St George, but she loved the feel of the silk against her skin and the way it slipped between her legs. Trousers were very freeing.

The only moment she was thoroughly jarred out of the merriment was towards the end of the play when the dragon had to swear fealty to Lord Deverill's Beelzebub. Lady Deverill's directions, changed at the last moment, had her go down on one knee before the lord of darkness and pledge herself to his cause.

On her knee, her eyes on his polished boots, she'd felt the urge to look up as she spoke her elaborate oath, the one part of her role she'd managed to learn by heart.

It was a long way up, her eyes travelling the length of muscled thighs, the shirt that hung loose, but did nothing to mask the hard muscles of his chest, the shadowed line of his jaw… Then she found herself speared on the stygian darkness of his eyes that flickered with the light of the candles as he gazed down at her.

She forgot everything: her lines, her audience, herself. All she saw was Nicholas. Lord Devil. Come to claim her.

Except she was already his. There was no denying or escaping it any longer. This man had turned her world upside down and her heart inside out. She'd fought him and the pull he had on her by convincing herself he was selfish and cruel, but ever since he'd brought her to Hadley Hall she had to let all those comfortable lies go. She had never before in her life felt that someone saw her so clearly, for good and for ill. It was a devastating combination and it had completely seduced her mind just as his touch had seduced her body.

Worst of all, he'd made her care. Seeing him happy made her insides melt, her mouth curve into a smile without even noticing. And when sometimes she noticed that same melancholy that had caught him in his study settle on him she wished it was her right to take his hand.

She'd felt all that working against her these few long, long days, but she'd not allowed herself to admit the truth. Until now.

She looked up at him and let the knife fall.

So this was love.

Perhaps he'd thought she'd forgotten her lines like the

others. He reached out, touched her head briefly, his fingers gentle against her loose hair.

'I pledge myself to you for all eternity,' he murmured above her and something deep inside her cracked open, spilling liquid fire through her veins. Yes. Those were the words her heart was singing. She swallowed and somehow managed to speak them.

'I pledge myself to you…for all eternity. My lord.'

He was supposed to smile in triumph. At least that was what the directions had said. But he didn't smile. He held out his hand and she placed hers in it. He raised her slowly and she stood dumb before him, hardly noticing that Emily's princess had hopped into the tableau, trailing yards of pink tulle, calling in a warbling voice for St George to save her from the forces of evil.

It was only when her train tangled with St George's wooden sword and Emily and Rupert went down in a clang of fake armour that Bella woke from her stupor and the remainder of the play continued in cheerful chaos until Lady Deverill hushed them all and pointed to the clock where the long hand hovered at ten minutes to midnight.

In a flurry of activity, glasses of hot punch were handed out just in time for silence to reveal the final ticks of the clock.

The whole house seemed to reverberate with the first gong. Then a warm hand closed on hers. She did not look up to see who it was, didn't need to. No one could see their clasped hands among the black and green folds of their cloaks. There were others among the family holding hands or arms and she cautioned herself this might be nothing more than the Hadley warmth she'd come to value so.

Right now all that mattered was that the man she loved was holding her hand as the old became the new. Right now her heart was full and for the first time in so many, many years she felt whole. Whatever happened from here, whatever the New Year brought, it could not take away this gift.

When the twelve gongs fell away, family and guests and servants began exchanging blessings for the New Year. Bella pulled her hand away, but for a moment he caught her wrist, his words almost lost amid the cheer around them.

'I wish you all the happiness you deserve, Bella Ingram.'

Chapter Twelve

The knock on the door fell unto the New Year's revels like plague bells. Everyone fell absolutely silent. The clock managed three ticks and two tocks before the knocking began again. Emily squealed.

'It is just after midnight on New Year's Eve! The first footer has arrived!'

'Impossible!' Lady Deverill cried, 'The snow…'

But Emily was already raring down the hall. The rest tumbled after her, pulling Bella in their enthusiastic wake. First footers were not common in Lower Ottington, but she knew there were those who believed that it was good luck to have a dark-haired man bearing gifts be the first to cross one's threshold in the new year.

The sight that met their eyes as Porter swung open the door was certainly dramatic. A great bear of a man stood on the steps, bathed in candlelight. Bella's memory shot back a little over a week ago to Nicholas standing in the inn door as she stepped out of the carriage, snow falling between them. So much had happened since then.

'I bring New Year's blessings to ye all!' boomed the man, holding up a rush basket covered in a cloth under which a bottle and loaf of bread peeked out.

'Samuel Plunkett,' cried Lady Deverill in delight. 'We are beyond delighted to see you, but you must have known we did not expect you to risk yourself in this weather. Mrs Plunkett shall have my hide.'

His laugh boomed round the hall as a beaming Porter rushed to hand him a glass of hot punch.

'It was she who packed the basket, your ladyship. And the snow's been melting on the lower roads all day. Another day or so and we'll be wondering what the hubbub was about. And a happy New Year to you, my lord.'

Nicholas shook his hand warmly and Mr Plunkett was soon led to the drawing room to partake in the midnight festivities. Bella hung back, feeling strangely breathless, the man's word's echoing in her head.

Another day or so and we'll be wondering what the hubbub was about.

As the pianoforte and singing started up in the drawing room, Bella took a step back and another. Without thought her feet led her back to the conservatory. It was dark now except for one candelabra beginning to sputter and the stage area was a muddle of discarded costumes and paraphernalia, all except for the devil's throne which glinted faintly. Bella moved towards it.

Another day or so...

Ten years ago her life had changed in a matter of days. That week of illness and loss had felt eternal, but had been nothing more than a tiny fraction of her life.

Now, in a week, her life had changed again.

She couldn't return to Bath, to her life before. She just couldn't.

She did not know where she would go, or how, but she knew she could not go back. Violet was a grown woman, no longer her little cousin whom she truly had tried to love and care for in recompense for her aunt taking her in. Violet didn't really need Bella. No one did.

She took a deep breath, pressing her hand to her heart.

So, heartache was real.

The music filtered through the walls. Bella closed her eyes and tried to remember everything that had happened to her in this week, to fix it in her mind so she could take it with her and keep it close.

For a moment as a hand rested on her arm she didn't think it strange, it seemed part of her memories.

'Come dance,' Nicholas murmured and she nodded and let him turn her, his hand on her waist. She opened her eyes, but the candles were all spent and there was only the glimmer of moonlight on the snow outside and the rim of golden light like a fan beneath the now-closed door. Nicholas was dark on dark, his eyes like cut obsidian.

She placed her hand on his shoulder and let him guide her. These last days she had kept hoping he'd take advantage of the mistletoe hung about the house, but he'd not touched her other than in the play. It made no odds. Her body knew him—his scent, the brush of his legs against hers, the hard warmth of muscle under her hand. But she wanted so much more—she wanted to touch *him*. Feel his skin against hers, to be tangled with him as she unravelled, to feel his hands in her hair, on her hips...

She closed her eyes on her fantasies. Be content. You are dancing with the man you love. Creating another memory to take with you.

She smiled and his step faltered for a moment, his arm tightening.

'Happy New Year, Bella.'

'Happy New Year, Nicholas. Thank you.'

'For what?'

'For this week. The best of my life.' Suddenly the ache was too extreme, it cut upwards through her, like a great spear. How could she leave? 'Mr Plunkett said the roads are opening. That means I should leave.'

Nicholas didn't answer as they continued dancing in slow, gentle movements, theirs bodies coming closer with each turn. Then he stopped, his hand low on her back, his breath warm on her temple.

'Is that what it means?'

She nodded, her hair snagging on the fine stubble of his cheek. She raised her head and with a daring utterly unlike her she brushed her lips over that rough surface, setting all the bells ringing again.

How could she leave?

'Mama celebrates Epiphany, too, you know. That's another week of this.'

Another week of *this*.

She wanted to cry. 'It wouldn't be right. I have no excuse to remain.' She tightened her hand on his coat. 'And I'm not returning to Bath. I'm going to London.'

He stilled. 'London?'

'Yes. I cannot return to my aunt's. I shall seek my fortune in London. Like Dick Whittington.'

He raised her lightly by her waist and set her down on the devil's table where the dragon had signed its oath of fealty.

'You'll need a cat,' he murmured, tucking her hair behind her ear.

'I'll need a position. Perhaps I shall work on the stage. I rather enjoyed the costumes.'

He didn't say anything, but his hands were doing a great deal of talking. They traced her face in the dark, shaping the line of her cheekbone, the hollow beneath her jaw, lingering on the sensitive skin behind her ear. Then he bent and brushed his mouth over hers.

She wanted to cry. No memory could suffice. She wanted *more*.

'I could meet you, Nicholas,' she whispered against his lips. 'If you wished. Somewhere in town. No one need know.'

His mouth stilled on hers. He seemed to be reverberating, like a plucked string. Then he drew back, very slowly.

'Meet? As in assignation?' he asked, and she nodded.

'Just so I understand, Bella. Are you offering to become my mistress?'

She set her shoulders. 'Yes.'

It seemed a very long time until he answered.

'I accept. I have some conditions, though.'

She drew a deep shaky breath and stopped herself from saying: Whatever your conditions, I'll agree.

'Such as?'

'Such as you remain here until Epiphany, you come skating with me again before the ice cracks, you dance with me in the dark…you kiss me… That condition is especially important, Bella.'

She made a sound between a sigh and sob of relief and wrapped her arms around his neck and kissed him, holding nothing back.

He pulled her towards him, pressing her legs apart to make room for him, his hands on her bottom as he pulled her against the hard heat of his erection. A thrill of hunger coursed through her and she angled her hips to feel him fully. Yes, *this* was what she wanted.

Her hands tugged his shirt from his waistband, splaying on the warm smooth skin of his back. His body shuddered against hers and he buried his face against the curve of her neck, his teeth scraping the sensitive skin there before suckling it gently, sending another wave of naked need through her body.

'There is one more condition, sweetheart.' His voice was almost harsh, demanding.

'Any…anything,' she stuttered, too desperate to negotiate.

'Anything?' It wasn't a question, it was a demand, and she answered it without hesitation.

'Anything.'

He finally kissed her back. He wasn't careful, or gentle, or coaxing. This kiss was weeks of fury and frustration and need and all the confusion she'd felt and not understood. It turned her inside out, melted her and rebuilt her around a new core that now included Nicholas beside her at her very centre. She kissed him without worry or thought of the future. She kissed him with all the love she'd discovered in her, like magic released from a long-locked box. She stopped short of speaking the words, afraid they would awaken his conscience and push him away. But everything else, she gave.

They finally drew apart, their breathing harsh and uneven in the darkness. They remained there for a long moment in silence, then he smoothed her hair and replaced the golden headband, slipped her off the table and led her back to the others. No one appeared to notice their arrival any more than they remarked on their absence.

The rest of the festivities were a warm blur. Bella could later recall dancing with the first footer, laughing as he swirled her around, and then with Rupert and Lord Carruthers and finally, blissfully, with Nicholas.

And after the music stopped she helped Lady Deverill serve more punch and she played spillikins with Emily and the twins on the carpets until Emily fell asleep with her head on Bella's lap. Finally, they all staggered up the stairs at dawn. Her last memory before sleep took her was of Nicholas, dressed as Beelzebub, looking down at her as she pledged herself to him for eternity.

Chapter Thirteen

Epiphany

'The snow is melting fast.'

Bella's voice was wistful as she brushed a clump of soggy snow from the branch of a fir tree. It landed on the path, splashing her boots, and was swiftly swallowed by a puddle on the dark flagstones. Nicholas stood watching her, enjoying the contrast between her vivid hair and cape amid the mostly bare trees. She wore the same wine-coloured cape as the time they had gone skating and she'd knocked him off his feet in more ways than one. That image sprung to mind—only this time she was spread out on the snow instead of him, her cape and hair bright against the white world, waiting…

It was a fine image, but rather out of tune with the fast-melting snow.

He looked up at the sky, but it was a damnably cheerful blue. Epiphany had come far too fast for his purposes. The last few days had been the happiest in his memory, a good part of it because Bella was happy. Ever since he'd agreed to her offer to be his mistress she'd been freer, happier, so much more herself.

They had not spoken of it again, but he knew she thought of their agreement as often as he did. Which made his lie all the more uncomfortable, because at some point very soon he had to tell her he had no intention of having an affair with her. That what he had in mind was far more permanent.

She turned away from the tree and came towards him.

'Nicholas, may I ask you a question?'

'Of course.'

She opened her mouth, closed it, shook her head. 'No, you shall be angry at me for asking.'

He took a step closer. 'What if I promise not to be angry?'

'You were when your mother spoke of it.'

'Spoke of...?'

'In the hallway while I was helping her...'

'Ah. I remember.'

'See? You're angry already.'

'No. Wary. What do you want to know? Whether there was any truth to the gossip?'

'I'm not concerned about the gossip. I wondered what happened to drive you away from Hadley Hall when you love it so.'

Nicholas's hackles dropped entirely. There was concern in her voice, as if it mattered what had happened to that young Nicholas. If he'd learned anything in these recent days, it was that Bella had a heart as soft as its shell was hard. And the more he intentionally chipped away at her shell, the more the warmth she could not truly hide chipped away at his. If at the beginning of this Christmas miracle he'd been terrified of feeling too much for her, now he was terrified of her not feeling enough.

He held out his arm, not because the wet path was truly treacherous, but because he needed any excuse he could find to get close to her. She placed her hand on his arm without hesitation, as if it was the most natural thing in the world, and the ache in his chest deepened into pleasure. Did she even notice how much she had come to trust him? Sometimes he thought she was aware of how important she had become to him and sometimes he thought she was as unsuspecting as a child. It was damnable that he had to tread so carefully when more and more he wanted to just stand up in the middle of breakfast and make it clear to everyone that he…

He drew a deep breath, tightened his hold on her hand and answered her question.

'I ran away because I was a young fool and I imagined myself in love with someone when all she wanted was my money and title. Just like Rupert.'

She stopped abruptly, her eyes wide.

'Oh.'

'Yes, oh.'

'So that was why you were so upset about Rupert and Violet. I did think—' She cut herself off and he sighed.

'That I was rather overly dramatic about the whole affair? Possibly. Probably. It brought back rather embarrassing memories.'

'Who…? Are you still in love with her?'

'Good God, no. That was fifteen years ago and my youthful passion didn't last the year. My mortification and anger lasted a hell of a lot longer. I didn't trust my judgement for years after that. Like Rupert I thought she was the sum of all virtues. And it didn't help that her mother was a good friend of my own mother who I had always looked up to. It hurt almost as much to discover that she had taken an active hand in driving me into her daughter's trap.'

'That must have been *horrid* for you.'

'Well, I don't want to exaggerate it, but it wasn't very nice. On the positive side it knocked me out of my complacent, trusting stupidity and ensured I learned a bit about the world. And very luckily I discovered the truth before I offered for her, otherwise I would have been a great deal more miserable. That is the sum of my Great Secret. Not very exciting, is it? Were you hoping for something more dramatic?'

'No, I wasn't and you must not belittle it. I can understand why you mistrust anything romantic and certainly why you hated us so. I dare say you thought I was just like that silly girl's mama, manoeuvring poor Rupert into Violet's net.'

He shook his head, not at all certain what to say. He knew what he *wanted* to say. That he no longer thought that love was a load of bunk or lust dressed in fancy feathers. That he knew it was real and could reach deep into your core and not let go.

Love had changed him in a manner he'd never known was possible, made him want to open himself to feeling, needing, trusting... *She* had changed him by opening his heart like a boarded-up house with the windows thrown open to light and air and life.

Now that he knew what bedevilled him, he understood why his desire for Bella burned a thousand times brighter than his rather foolish youthful escapades. At the root of it all he'd come to trust Bella and that magical fuel set the flames blazing.

Sometimes like now when she looked at him with that honest concern he felt she *must* care for him. That he could not possibly be alone in this. But then the scar on the foolish boy he'd been would twinge and burn and he'd remind himself that it was *always* possible to be tricked. Not that he thought she was trying to trick him, but he did worry at least three dozen times a day that she might not come to care for him as he did for her.

'I didn't mean to be intrusive,' she said hesitantly at his silence. 'I'm sorry, Nicholas.'

He shook his head. 'No, don't be. I'm glad I told you. I should be the one apologising. I know I behaved badly in Bath. If I could go back...'

She squeezed his arm. 'I behaved just as badly. I was every bit the shrew you thought me.'

'I thought you a hedgehog, not a shrew. And if we are

putting cards on the table, though I was not intelligent enough at the time to admit it, part of me thoroughly enjoyed crossing swords with you. I can't account for my insistence of dragging myself back into the ring time and again despite losing every round.'

'You most certainly did not lose *every* round,' she said, her cheeks pink.

'Every round. In fact, my self-esteem was so badly bruised it might never recover. If you are truly contrite, you should offer to make amends.'

Her dimples wavered into existence. 'Though I would argue your self-esteem appears in very good form, I will not have it said I shirk my debts. How precisely does one make amends for damages to one's esteem?'

'One nurtures it back to health, Miss Ingram. A kiss here, a compliment there. In fact, a kiss right here would do as a fine first step.'

Her lips parted, her tongue just grazing the swell of her lower lip in a wholly involuntary and utterly intoxicating manner that made him want to sink to his knees and make an utter fool of himself right there. God in heaven, he wanted her so damn much…

'Here…?' Her voice was husky, as raw as his insides.
Yes, here, anywhere, everywhere. For ever.

He called on what remained of his calm good sense and nodded. 'Here. No one can see us from the house. I'd offer to find some mistletoe to string up in the branches above us, but my injury is acting up and without some immediate… nurturing I'm afraid I might not have the strength to make it to the house. I might perish on these snowy banks.'

Her dimples finally made an appearance. 'That would be a very poor way to repay you for your hospitality, Lord Deverill. I shall just have to imagine the mistletoe.'

She moved closer, placing her hand on his chest, her lashes lowering for a moment and when they rose her eyes

were dark, smoky with need. Without thought his arms
went around her, drawing her even closer. Whatever she
felt, she felt this heat between them. He was not wrong
about that. It might not be all he wanted from her, but it
was a damn good start.

She leaned back a little in the confines of his arms and
to his surprise she slipped off her gloves and tucked them
into the pocket of his coat. Then she slipped her bare hands
up, over his chest, his shoulders, one hand slipping between
the collar of his coat and his nape, her fingers cool against
his heated skin. He felt a groan struggle against the chains
of his control, heat thudding into his loins even at this almost innocent touch. Her other hand touched his jaw, his
cheek. He did make a sound, but it was lost as she rose on
tiptoe and touched her mouth to his.

For a moment they stood there like a frozen statue,
though there was nothing frozen about them. His pulse
was racing, his erection already pressing against her, their
breaths uneven as they clung to the edge of the cliff. Then
she moaned, a long, almost despairing sound, and kissed
him into oblivion.

He slipped one hand under her cape, wishing it was the
middle of summer and there was no one within ten miles
of them so he could strip her and lay her down on her cape
and taste and kiss his way over every inch of her. One day,
one day *soon* that was precisely what he could do. Make
her his and give himself to her.

After the kiss they remained locked together, their
breathing harsh in the quiet of the trees as they waited out
the crest of frustration. Then he placed a gentle kiss on her
cheek, resting there for a moment.

'That is much, much better, for the moment. But I foresee a need for many more applications of this remedy. Now
we'd best return to the house. It's time to prepare for the
highlight of Christmastide.'

'There have been so many highlights,' she murmured. 'I don't think I can envision anything higher or lighter.'

He laughed and took her arm as they made their way up the path. When they reached the garden gate he stopped her for a moment.

'Remember when I said I had another condition, Bella? On New Year's Eve?'

She nodded warily. 'What is it?'

'I shall tell you. Tonight. Now come, you should gather your forces for the plum pudding surprise.'

'That sounds ominous. What is a plum pudding surprise and why does it require gathered forces?'

'That is the surprise.'

Bella dressed with more care than usual for dinner. She knew this magical time was drawing to an end, but when before she'd reached almost timidly for the treats set out before her, now she was seeking them out and grabbing them before the clock struck midnight on her dream.

The days since she'd admitted to herself that she loved Nicholas had been even more precious than those that had come before. Freed from the worst of winter's chokehold, the Hadleys rushed to atone for all that had been missed, and as she lay in bed every night she would remember everything that had happened, securing the smallest gesture and event in her memory so that she could revisit this most wonderful time of her life for years to come.

The Christmastide acts of charity that were squeezed between New Years and epiphany. The gifts of minced pies and sacks of wheat and clothes brought to the villagers and the needy. A visit from the mummers was arranged and, though the Hadleys were clearly of the opinion that their effort didn't nearly compare to the original, they applauded loudly and Lord Deverill was very generous with both refreshments and coin. The wassailers came through as well and they all gathered and sang in the courtyard under a slowly sinking winter sun.

Just this morning they had gone to the Epiphany eve celebrations at the village church. While Bella had helped Lady Deverill give gifts to the children, she'd watched the man she loved hold congress with the yeoman and farmers and shopkeepers over three impressive silver bowls of hot spiced punch. It reminded her so much of Lower Ottington, she felt as if time had stitched together her lost past and her precious present into one joyous fabric.

The only thing missing was her future and every night as she sank into sleep she allowed herself a few moments to imagine what it would be like when she left Hadley Hall and became his mistress. She no longer doubted that would happen. He made no attempt to hide his desire for her and, while it baffled her, it gave her such joy and courage to face what was to come.

Courage enough even to ask him the question that had bothered her so and then courage enough to kiss him with all the love that was bursting from her it was a wonder she didn't just shatter into a million pieces and be blown away by the wind. She was so happy she felt giddy, utterly unlike herself. She knew there would come a time when Nicholas would likely tire of her and she would deal with that as she had dealt with other blows, but for now Nicholas was a part of her life and the thought of making a new way for herself filled her with hope.

Her giddiness stayed with her as she went down to join the others that evening. When dinner was cleared, its place was taken by the punch and Cook's traditional Epiphany eve cakes. Emily gave a squeal of excitement when her slice was placed before her and proceeded to squash it into a shapeless mush and then groan aloud.

'Nothing! Who has the bean?'

The others set to work, dissecting their slices one by one. Bella laughed and searched hers as well, rather sorry Cook would have to see the massacre of her fine work. There was a clinking and they all turned to Nicholas who'd touched his fork to his wine glass. He held up a single, simple little brown bean.

Emily groaned. 'Unfair! You're already the king and you can always buy yourself gifts. I was going to ask for a new saddle.'

'Hush now, Emily,' said her mama as she split the remains of her cake between the ravenous twins. 'Let Nick tell us what he chooses.'

'You'll have a new saddle, muffin,' he promised Emily. 'But I'm not asking for a gift, I'm invoking the old tradition.'

'What's the old tradition?' asked Bella, confused but amused by another Hadley variation on already half-forgotten traditions.

Emily bounced in her chair and burst out in delight, 'Uncle Nick is going to choose a queen!'

A strange silence fell on the table and, quite as if time itself had slowed to a turtle's crawl, all faces swivelled towards Bella.

She froze.

When Nicholas spoke his voice sounded like portent.

'That is my final condition, Bella.'

'What?' she said, her voice high and reedy.

'You accepted it, remember? One final condition. This is it. That you become my queen, or rather…that you become my countess. Not quite as grand, but it's all I can offer, I'm afraid.'

She shook her head, confused, terrified, pressing back against an avalanche of hope and heat. He could not mean it. She'd offered to be his mistress. Why would he do this…? With his whole family looking on…? Surely he must realise…?

'Bella…' Something in his voice penetrated the cacophony inside her. Uncertainty… Fear? *Hurt?*

She didn't understand what was happening, but she didn't want to hear that in his voice. She held out her hand and he took it and let out a long, careful breath that was drowned out by the cheers around the table. He drew her to her feet as the others pushed back their chairs and surrounded them, showering them with congratulations. Bella smiled through them, that part of her that wasn't frozen in shock surrendering wholly to what she was more and more convinced must be one of her dreams gone wild or a punch-induced hallucination.

It was only when Lady Deverill enveloped her in a hug scented with lavender and lilies that something cracked inside Bella. Nicholas must have felt her hand shake in his, or felt the change in her breathing. He said something over her head and led her out of the room to his study. When he closed the door behind him she walked blindly into the centre of the room and stopped, waiting for reality to return.

'I shouldn't have done that, should I?' he asked abruptly. 'Not like that. I thought… It seemed… Bella. *Say* something.'

'Why would you do that?' she managed to say, shock catching her. 'Do you know what they are thinking?'

'Of course I know what they are thinking. They are thinking I just proposed to you. I don't know what *you* are thinking.'

She shook her head. 'I don't understand. I said I would be your mistress. You said you agreed.'

'I did. I meant it. I want you to be my mistress. My lover. My wife. My companion. Not to mention the chief thorn in my side.' The words were tossed at her like shards of ice. 'I thought… I hoped you wished it, too. That night in the conservatory… And today… I thought… I told myself you would not offer yourself to me if you did not care. That you could not kiss me like that if you didn't… Apparently I was fooling myself.'

'But you *must* know I cannot marry you, Nicholas.'

His face was stony now, but she stumbled on.

'Even if…even if you did wish to wed me, though I cannot understand why… It is all wrong. You would not let Rupert marry my cousin and her father is higher born than mine. Your family believes I am a relation of your father's, but such a lie would soon come to light. They would be furious and…and your mother would be miserable. I could not do that to them, not when they have been so kind and welcoming. I don't even understand why you think you wish to marry me. I told you I would be your mistress until you tired of me. You needn't marry me at all…'

Her tumble of words ran dry and he drew a deep breath.

'I disagree. I'm afraid that is precisely what I do *need* to do. I've been happier these past two weeks than I can ever remember. In agony trying to keep my hands off you, but happy. Taking you as a mistress, stealing furtive meetings with you and having to keep you hidden from my family, from the world… That isn't what I want. I want you here, with me. I want you to *want* to be here with me, Bella.' He took a step towards her and she took a step back.

'No. This makes no sense. You wouldn't even have thought of it if you hadn't been the one to find that bean.'

His laugh was short and sharp and unamused. 'Did you honestly think I left that poor bean up to chance? I arranged it with Cook.'

'Oh.'

'Yes, *oh*. It was a damn fool idea. I realise that now. Cowardly, too, but I hoped… I know you are worried about my family, but I thought if you saw how they have come to care for you… How much you do belong here… I should have waited, not pushed you into a corner and ruined everything. My only excuse is that for the past two months you've addled my mind, Bella. Ever since I met you I've lost control over my mind, my body, and my heart. You're like my own personal Pandora's box.'

Strangely his angry words steadied the ground beneath her, clearing the fog of confusion a little. She still didn't know what to do, but she knew she loved Nicholas. And miracle of miracles, it seemed he truly cared for her, too.

Her heart soared and plummeted at the same time. Joy— hopeful and radiant and utterly foolish, flapped about towards the clouds, cooing and burbling. But there was also another part of her that made its first appearance. She was now responsible for Nicholas as well. If he thought himself in love with her, it was up to her to ensure he did not make a mistake he would regret.

'Damn it, Bella, say something.' The words burst from him and he took another step towards her. She held up her hand, stopping him.

'I must speak to your mother.'

For a moment he stared at her, then laughter washed over his face like sunshine escaping a cloud.

'My mother? How old do you think I am?'

'Not old enough not to make mistakes. You were wrong about me once; you might be again.'

'And discussing me with my mother might clarify matters?'

It did sound ridiculous, but she couldn't help it. She nodded. He went to the door and opened it, still laughing.

'Go to it, then. I'll even be *adult* enough not to eavesdrop on what promises to be a fascinating conversation. I'll give you, say, half an hour?'

She didn't rise to any of those taunts. Not even when she passed by him and his hand patted her bottom quite as if he already had every right to do so.

Chapter Fourteen

She ought to have known any conversation with Lady Deverill would not proceed along the dramatic lines that plagued her imagination as she made her way to her parlour. Her hostess patted the sofa beside her, inviting her to sit with a quiet gentleness that made Bella's throat burn.

Bella approached but did not sit. She couldn't.

'There is something I must tell you, Lady Deverill. I am here under false pretences. I am not a relation of the Hadleys.'

Lady Deverill's left brow rose, but she smiled invitingly. 'Do sit down, Bella dear, and tell me all about these false pretences.'

Bella sat at the furthest edge of the sofa, but Lady Deverill reached over and patted her tightly clasped hands and just like that the words began tumbling out of Bella. She told her everything: about Violet and Rupert, about the battle she and Lord Deverill had waged, the foiled elopement, her own modest circumstances… It all swept out of her like a flood through a dam made of dandelion fluff. When she was done, she sagged back against the back of the sofa, out of breath and as red as a holly berry.

'Well,' announced Lady Deverill, 'that was quite a confession. And wholly unnecessary.'

'Unnecessary?'

'My dear child, I knew within ten minutes of my son's very garbled explanation of your arrival that something serious was afoot. I also know every last cousin of my late husband's sparse family tree. He was an only child of an only child of an only child. Nicholas's miraculous delivery, on Christmas Day, of a hitherto unknown cousin conveniently located within hailing distance in the midst of a snowstorm…' she trailed off. Bella didn't know whether to be mortified or to fall into helpless giggles. Her ladyship nodded and continued.

'And then there was the peculiar argument he had with my sister Agatha. I might appear muddleheaded at times—' Bella interrupted with a confused denial, but it was waved down and Lady Deverill continued. 'That is kind of you, my dear, but it is quite true. In any case, though I might appear muddleheaded, my understanding of my children is unmatched. The next day I took Nicholas aside and wrung the truth from him.'

Bella couldn't help smiling. She wished she could have been a fly on that wall.

'Precisely,' nodded Lady Deverill. 'I was also made aware that his opinion of you was, to say the least, mixed. I was left wondering how a young woman could possibly possess the skills of Machiavelli, Napoleon, Richelieu and Circe all at once. In any case, I decided to take you aside and see for myself.'

'The garland by the stairs,' Bella said, and her ladyship smiled.

'Indeed. Once I was satisfied my son was clearly, and, I would add, wilfully, mistaken about you, I was naturally left wondering why. For him to be so grossly mistaken about someone… I found that most curious. And when Emily told me about the incident at the pond…'

'She told you?' Bella's voice had a distinct squeak to it and her cheeks were now so hot they hurt.

'Naturally. Emily tells me everything. That is the benefit of being a grandmama. The last piece in my puzzle fell neatly into place. Everything since then only confirmed to me that my son, very reluctantly, mind you, had fallen in love in earnest for the first time in his life. Watching the two of you together has given me great joy, Bella.'

Bella's heart was pounding so hard she felt it might crack something. She pressed a hand to her chest. Why Lady Deverill's conclusion should matter so much, she did not know. But it did.

'But I know I cannot truly be what you want for him, Lady Deverill. Surely you would wish him to marry someone more…'

'More what?' Lady Deverill prompted.

'More accomplished, more well born, more beautiful… Just *more.*'

Lady Deverill patted her hand.

'You are precisely what I want for him. You are intelligent and strong and, most importantly, you see him, the man, not his title or even his unfortunately good looks. He needs someone who can stand firm, but also be gentle. I could not have asked for a better match for him. Hush, now, don't cry, my dear. Or rather do. Come here and have a good cry. You have earned it fairly.'

She put her arms around Bella who did as she was told and cried as if she hadn't cried in years, which she hadn't. When the storm passed they rang for tea and talked of nothing in particular until the housekeeper knocked on the parlour door to discuss menus for the week.

Bella returned to her room and once she'd done her best to erase the signs of her utter collapse, she went to find Nicholas.

Despite Lady Deverill's kindness, she was worried. It was one thing to be accepted by his loving family, but they were so accustomed to privilege they might not even realise how viciously society could turn on him for making such a mésalliance.

She would tell him that she cared for him, she decided, but that she thought it best he take his time to consider whether his and his family's interests were best served by marrying her.

That was best. She did not want him to regret this as a moment of midwinter madness.

He was seated in his study, his hands clasped on his desk, but he did not appear to be working. He rose, yet remained behind the desk, a wary look in his eyes.

'You were gone an awfully long time. That usually doesn't bode well. I was beginning to think you might have made your escape.' His voice was clipped, hard, but all she could hear were all the shades she'd come to recognise since she fallen in love with him—worry, need, uncertainty.

She shut the door and leaned back against it.

'I love you so much, Nicholas.'

She clapped a hand over her mouth. That was *not* what she'd meant to say at all. His eyes narrowed and he came around the desk. She held up her hands. 'No, I mean, I *do*, but what I meant to say is that you should take your time, not rush…' He'd reached her by now and leaned one hand on the door behind her. She bunched her hands into fists and pressed them together, trying to gather her scattering resolve. 'I couldn't bear it if you regretted this, Nicholas. I would rather walk away than watch you come to hate me.'

He considered her for a moment. 'You do realise this is all pointless, love. You already pledged yourself to me.'

'I didn't yet. I said I would think about it…'

'No. You went down on your knee and pledged yourself to me for all eternity.'

She swallowed, remembering that moment again. It would likely haunt her all her life. 'I… That was a line. In a play.'

'No, you meant it. And so did I.'

'You…you were giving me my lines.'

He shook his head.

'No. You knew your little speech perfectly. You were scared to say it. So I said it first. I doubt I've much talent as a playwright, but I'm rather proud of that scene, sweetheart.'

Her heart hiccupped. *'What?'*

'Didn't you guess? Mama was very happy for my help in writing the silly play and I was very happy to take you up on your offer to play Beelzebub to your wicked dragon. My version was rather far from the original, but then I had an agenda, you see. I had this image. You, on your knees, before me, telling me that you're mine. Primitive, I admit, but very…' he traced a finger down her neck, along the line of her bodice, giving it a little tug in the middle and making her nerves bloom all along her breasts '…alluring.'

'Nicholas…' she breathed out the word, but couldn't manage anything else. Tension seemed to seep back into him as well, the shadow beneath his cheekbones darkening.

'And then when you looked up at me, I knew those words were far more than a device. They were true. That was why I spoke them first. I meant what I said. I'm yours, Bella. For always. If you leave, I'm afraid you'll have to put up with me following you about and making a nuisance of myself, reminding you that you pledged yourself as well. And in that moment I felt you meant every word. I felt…loved. It might have been a delusion on my part, but I don't think so. I can't believe those were just empty words, sweetheart. I won't.'

She thought she'd got rid of all her tears, but two more slipped out. He brushed them away and kissed her cheek very gently.

'You're so brave for others. Trust yourself to be brave for yourself, love.'

'I want to,' she sobbed. 'I *did* mean it. I think I was in love with you before I even came here. I'm such a fool.'

He laughed, pulling her against him. 'You're *my* fool. And I'm yours. You see? We need each other to balance out our folly. I thought I hated the very sight of you. No one had made me as angry or as frustrated in my whole life. And I was too big an idiot to even question why. But not so much of an idiot as not to grab that chance to bring you here and keep you. I was watching my barometer like a mother hovers over her newborn babe and every time it told me more snow was coming... Suffice it to say that I've never been happier to be snowbound with my very annoying family. The gods of winter themselves conspired with me, love. It wouldn't do to turn up your nose at this Christmas miracle. Bad luck, you know. The pond might never freeze again.'

'That...that would be a pity.'

'It would, wouldn't it? Because you clearly need more practice.'

'I am doing very well for someone who hadn't skated in a decade.'

'I wasn't talking about skating. I meant practice knocking me on my back into the snow. There's an art to it and though you proved very precocious, there could be some improvements. Such as...'

As he spoke his hands were moving her against him, as if he could hear the strains of a waltz, or as if they were skating. Slow, languid slides of his hands on her hips, up her waist to brush the swell of her breasts and down again. He might be talking of snow, but all she felt was fire.

'Such as?' she prompted, giving in to her baser instincts and letting her own hands roam, her body shape itself to his.

'Such as you let down your beautiful hair so that it falls about us like warm honey and when you slide your leg between mine you stay there and keep me nice and warm and hard against you, then you kiss me like you kissed me on New Year's Eve, like you kissed me this afternoon, and like you are about to kiss me now—without fear, without worry, without thought. With all your heart.'

Bella looked up at the man she loved and did as she was told.

* * * * *

A KISS AT
THE WINTER BALL

Joanna Johnson

For everyone who'd like a Viscount
in their stocking this year, Merry Christmas!

Author's Note

I'll admit it: before I saw it on a TV program last Christmas,
I'd never given much thought to where Regency
households got their festive turkeys. Apparently the best
birds were raised in Norfolk and then walked all the way
down to London on foot, a journey taking around three
months, and the costs involved made them an expensive
luxury only the wealthiest could afford. Some farmers even
went so far as to fashion little boots for their flock to protect
their feet during the long walk, which (if you ignore what
fate the poor turkeys were marching towards) is almost too
adorable. It got me thinking—how could I include this odd
little historical snippet into my story for this anthology?

Enter Maria Bartlett.

Determined Maria dreams of a more exciting future than
sewing and arranging flowers, wishing instead to help run
her family's farms despite constant disapproval. When an
opportunity to prove herself finally comes, she seizes it
with both hands, not realizing a resulting chance meeting
with charming Alexander, Viscount Stanford, will change
her life forever. For his part, Alex doesn't suspect what will
come next, either—merely curious as to why a mysterious
young woman is trying to cross his land at night with only a
flock of turkeys for company... A glittering yuletide party has
unexpected consequences, and both Maria and Alex will
have to be honest about their feelings if they're to
have a merry Christmas together!

Chapter One

Gathering her cloak more tightly around her, Maria Bartlett squinted again at the brooding clouds above. They'd followed her all the way from the inn she'd left in such a hurry that morning and for the first time since her escape an edge of doubt nudged her otherwise unshakable determination.

That looks like snow. If it starts to fall it'll take us even longer to reach Atherby.

Maria set her jaw, although her travelling companions remained unmoved by the increasingly bitter December chill. They seemed content to go wherever they were guided and being late for an important appointment clearly hadn't crossed their minds, placidly walking onwards without a care for any delay the events of the past few days had caused.

Hardly surprising, I suppose. Turkeys aren't particularly known for their timekeeping.

There were only twenty of them now, the rest of the three-hundred-strong flock that had left Norfolk in September already claimed by their wealthy new owners. Walking the birds down from Thetford to London was a time-consuming endeavour, but the Christmas season yielded the year's biggest profits, Papa's farm growing richer with every journey, and for a decade Maria had watched enviously as her older brother, Carew, was dispatched to supervise the expedition south.

No amount of pleading could ever persuade her father to let her go too, however—as a gentleman's daughter her place was at home, honing her accomplishments, practising the piano and sewing neat buttonholes until she had thought the boredom would drive her mad. To help manage the farm and estate like the men had been her burning desire since childhood, when as a determinedly tomboyish girl she'd watched their bustle and purpose and ached to join in…but it wasn't to be.

Listening to conversations between Papa and Carew and surreptitiously reading the business newssheets was as close as she was allowed to get, but Maria treasured any opportunity to learn, longing for the day when she might be given the chance to prove she was capable of far more than just sitting prettily in a parlour. One year had followed the next, though, with no change to the dull, repetitive path laid out before her, until finally fate had intervened.

'Back in line, please.'

Maria held a long stick in one hand and used it now to usher a stray turkey back on to the track they followed over yet another field. The wind whistled into her ears and tugged at the auburn curls leaping free from her bonnet, her wild hair the perfect metaphor for the woman beneath. Both were reluctant to be restrained, rebelling against any attempt to contain them, although Maria's usual spirit was momentarily dimmed by a glimmer of guilt.

I hope Carew is better soon…and that Mr Cartwright doesn't get into trouble for letting me slip away.

Papa had only allowed her to take over the final few miles of the journey on the understanding one of his own trusted tenants shadowed her like a hawk. Carew's twisted ankle had spelled the end of his own involvement, forcing him to stay behind at the Crown Inn, only a two days' walk from London, and he hadn't seemed especially pleased to see his younger sister arrive to step into his place. The road was no place for a lady, even one not allowed to move a single pace without an escort, but the letter Papa had sent down from Norfolk with her soon soothed Carew's worries.

Maria would be in no danger with Cartwright at her side, their father was certain, and the experience would surely cure her baffling desire to take on a man's role. As soon as she saw the true hardship of such work she'd gladly run back to the safety of the feminine sphere where she belonged, at last ceasing her constant requests for more involvement in a world a woman couldn't possibly understand. A short, sharp shock would do it, or so Mr Bartlett wrongly imagined. The letter only made her more determined and it was at the very moment she saw it lying discarded on her brother's bureau that she had made up her mind.

Clearly if I want respect I'll have to earn it. And there's only one way to do that...

The clouds were building ominously. The sun would begin to set soon, Maria realised uneasily, and then even the already dim light would vanish, leaving her to stumble across unfamiliar fields with nothing to guide her. Herding the turkeys before her during the day was one thing, keeping them together in the darkness was quite another, and apprehension knotted in her stomach.

'It should only have taken a day to walk to Atherby,' she confided in the nearest bird, waddling solemnly at her side. 'I hadn't intended on staying out overnight, especially with snow in the air. I'd thought we'd be there by now and I could take rooms at some inn, to wait in comfort until Cartwright and the rest caught up with us and saw I coped very well alone.'

It was the only way she could think of to prove to her father that she wasn't made of glass and, even with anxiety circling, Maria couldn't bring herself to regret her hasty plan. If she could only show him that she was just as capable as Carew of action and hard work, then surely Papa would include her more, instead of dismissing her just because society forced her into a corset. If other women enjoyed a life of leisure then Maria was happy for them, but she didn't, and it was with a renewed sense of purpose that she ushered her charges through a narrow open gate.

A bank of trees reared up before them, partially concealing what lay beyond, and Maria paused for a moment. Atherby was in that direction—if she cut through the trees she might be able to get there more quickly than if she stuck to the path. There could even be a chance she'd reach the village before darkness fell and the idea of a soft bed rather than a night spent huddled in a hedgerow was enough to help her make her choice.

'Come on. This way.'

The turkeys did as they were bid and Maria followed behind, still chased by the chill wind. It stirred the bare branches above her head and snatched at any unwary curls, but she lowered her head against it, pressing onwards without thinking until a voice at her back made her jump.

'Are you lost?'

She spun round, heart thumping. A man stood a few steps away, partially camouflaged against the darkening undergrowth by his green coat, and he held up a hand as she turned.

'Sorry. I didn't mean to startle you.'

'No? Well, you managed it regardless!'

Maria pressed a palm to her chest. For a split-second she was afraid, but the fright drained away as she took in the unexpected figure in front of her, her heart executing a strange flip for a very different reason than fear.

He was handsome: more so because of the friendly openness of his face rather than just its features. There were good-humoured lines etched beside his blue eyes and his mouth seemed to fall naturally into an upward curve, so immediately engaging that Maria could hardly look away. The hair beneath his stylish hat was dark and by the cut and quality of his equally fashionable coat she could tell he was clearly no fieldhand.

In all likelihood he was a gentleman farmer like Papa, the familiarity helping her to shrug off the last of her concern. She'd known similar individuals her whole life and they held no worries for her, reminding her so strongly of the men back home that any lingering doubts disappeared at once.

'Why else would you be lurking about the woods, if not to make unsuspecting passers-by jump out of their skins?'

The stranger's eyebrows rose a fraction, but his smile didn't falter, instead seeming to grow a little at the accusation. 'No lurkers here, ma'am. I was trying to avoid Mr Goddard. He's just passed over yonder and I'd rather not speak with him if I can help it. Just as I imagine you might not wish him to see you trespassing, either.'

'Mr who?'

'Goddard. The manager of the Milbrooke estate.'

Maria frowned, trying to ignore the insistent pitter-patter of her pulse at her throat. For all he resembled Norfolk's farmers something about this one seemed different, the ironic tick of his lips inviting hers to lift in return. 'Is that where I am? The Milbrooke estate?'

'That's right. Didn't you know?'

'No.' Maria shook her head, suddenly wishing her untidy hair didn't waft about *quite* so freely as she moved. 'I didn't.'

'Aha. So you *are* lost.'

Sudden worry gnawed at her as she realised he was right. Somewhere after her flit from the Crown Inn she must have lost her way and now she was stranded, unsure how to go forward and determined not to go back, and it

was only when the newcomer came carefully closer that
Maria realised she'd been biting her lip.

'Can I help? Where are you headed?'

'Atherby. I'd hoped to be there by now, but...'

She waved helplessly at the growing gloom all around
them, anxiety nipping a little harder. By rights she ought
to have been more alarmed by being alone with a strange
man, but instead his presence felt more reassuring than
threatening. Perhaps it was the deep, measured voice or the
way he approached with respectful caution, making sure
not to stand too near. Either way the rapid skip of Maria's
heart was still not one of apprehension, the clean line of
his jaw momentarily distracting her from her predicament.

She watched his mouth turn down at the corners, still
intrigued by the pleasing shape of his lips. 'Atherby? I'm
afraid you won't get there before dark. It's another few
miles yet, right on the other side of this estate. It will take
quite some time to walk there.'

Maria clenched her teeth on a groan. She must have
taken a wrong turning. The desire to kick herself was
strong, but she *just* managed to restrain it, aware a pair of
bright blue eyes rested on her.

'How unfortunate.' Maria tried to offer a resigned smile
although her mouth felt unusually difficult to control. That
sapphire scrutiny pinned her to the spot and made her
strangely self-aware, conscious of every tiny movement she
made. 'Is there somewhere nearby I might find shelter, just
for one night? I'd continue on first thing in the morning.'

The man regarded her closely. It wasn't anything quite
as rude as a stare, but his study was a curious one, as if
trying to read something in her face, and Maria felt a blush
warm her freezing cheeks. It could only have lasted for half
a moment, one beat that seemed to stretch out far longer,
but then the stranger released her with a brisk nod.

'I'm certain Milbrooke Hall would never turn away a

lady in distress. The owner is known to be a good deal more friendly than his estate manager.'

Still a little rattled by that one powerful look Maria hesitated. 'Milbrooke Hall? That sounds very grand. I couldn't possibly intrude somewhere like that.'

'I doubt the Viscount would consider it an intrusion. He'd be far more concerned about the prospect of a woman travelling alone in the cold and dark.'

Her new acquaintance certainly sounded sure and Maria felt herself relenting, a fresh gust of icy wind around her ankles making a very persuasive point. This man clearly knew the Viscount well—he *had* to be a gentleman tenant on the estate, perhaps running a few farms of his own under his noble landlord in much the same way her own papa made his fortune. He certainly seemed familiar with the landscape, now gesturing encouragingly towards the edge of the trees.

'Come. I can show you…' he paused to run an amused eye over the turkeys scratching around his boots '…*and* your friends the way.'

Maria swallowed. *I suppose I don't really have much choice.*

Her options were severely limited. Either follow a stranger or brave a night in the freezing woods, trying to prevent her birds from disappearing into the darkness. Neither was a road her father would be happy with her taking, she thought wryly, but now wasn't the time to be timid. If she was to win any respect she had to be brave: her life would only change if she was the one to change it…and besides…

He really is handsome. The kind look in those blue eyes…

Kicking the rogue thought back where it came from, Maria gathered her courage. 'Are you certain? I wouldn't want to be an inconvenience.'

'Not at all, ma'am. It would be my pleasure.'

* * *

Alex watched the woman beside him out of the corner of his eye as they walked together through the darkening field, her navy cloak almost making her a shadow herself.

Well. I can't say this is how I thought my evening stroll would end.

She drove the turkeys before her with ease, one hand clutching a stick she used as a makeshift crook. If not for her obviously expensive clothes she might have been a shepherdess, the stark contrast between her appearance and behaviour piquing his interest more with every step. He hadn't expected to meet anyone else out in the woods, especially in such bitter cold, and he found himself instinctively wanting to know more about the woman who had turned to him with such a look of challenge on her face that he'd known immediately she had no idea who he was.

With her fresh, windswept complexion and fiery hair, his first impression of her had been as a dryad, a wild, beautiful creature that lived in fairy-tale forests and defied any attempts to tame it. It was a ridiculously romantic notion and he'd dismissed it at once, although he couldn't *completely* shake the image. Wandering about in the dusk just wasn't something elegant young ladies *did*—and certainly not with a flock of turkeys in tow, the strangest escort he'd ever seen for a woman on her own.

Augusta most definitely wouldn't behave so rashly. I know that much for a fact.

The very idea of his refined intended in a similar situation was so preposterous Alex could have laughed out loud. Respectable, graceful Miss Augusta DeVere would never stoop so low as to allow mud to touch her expensive hems, unlike the mystery beside him. As a knight's daughter she knew her role and played it well, just as Alex was ever conscious of the duties his own position placed like a gilded collar around his neck.

Not that they had much else in common apart from an understanding of obligation, he thought now, attempting to ignore how well his new acquaintance kept up with his long stride. He was pleasant to Augusta and she was polite in return, but both knew there was no love to be found in their union. Objecting to it had never been an option. A man of his station needed a wife to continue his line and so one had been selected, something as irrelevant as feelings never entering into it.

His parents had been matched the same way and although thirty years and three children had left them with a measure of fondness for each other, any regard that had developed was very much by the by. Marriage was a necessity for a man of his standing and so he would do it, something he accepted as part of the role he'd been born into. He would be kind to Augusta and do his best to be an agreeable husband, although he would be lying if he pretended the prospect of a life lived by her side was anything other than a duty he was sure she saw the same way.

It was a sobering thought and Alex frowned briefly. Their engagement was to be formally announced in just four days' time, at a Christmas ball hosted by his parents for that very reason. Once the word was out there would be no turning back, but that wasn't a possibility. He and Augusta would be married and his family name would carry on for another generation, and there was nothing else to be said on the subject than that—even if the stranger next to him *did* capture his imagination in a way the serene Miss DeVere never had, her direct green gaze and proud chin hinting at a spiritedness he couldn't deny he liked.

The wind flipped the edge of her cloak, giving him a glimpse of its costly lining alongside another flicker of curiosity. How was it she was so finely dressed and yet herded animals like a lad fresh from the fields? It didn't make sense and Alex couldn't help his interest growing, stirred at first by the fairness of her face and stoked higher by the secrets behind it.

'Excuse my presumption, but you don't look much like a farm girl. How is it you find yourself in this position? Ushering turkeys across the countryside without anyone to help?'

The woman didn't reply at once and Alex felt the novel sensation of being judged whether deserving of an answer. He'd been right to assume she didn't know who he was—and for the moment he shied away from telling her. Once he revealed himself she'd doubtless retreat behind the wall of respectful silence most people did in his presence and then he would never uncover the truth.

Finally a verdict came from beneath her bonnet.

'No offence to you, sir, as you've been so kind, but I feel that as a *man* you wouldn't understand.'

Alex's mouth lifted into the characteristic curve he was well known for. *Just as I thought. No idea at all.* There was no way she'd speak to him like that if she knew his position and he struggled to keep the amusement from his voice.

'I may only be a man, but I'd still like to try.'

'If you insist.' She paused to gently guide a wayward turkey back into line, its black feathers making it almost invisible in the gathering dusk. 'I'm attempting to persuade my father to allow me to help him and my brother in the running of our estate. He thinks that a young lady shouldn't— no, *can't*—manage such things and is determined I stay at home being idle while the men attend to business. I thought that if I managed to drive these Christmas turkeys the rest of the way down from our farm in Norfolk he might realise I'm not entirely useless after all.'

Alex's eyebrows rose beneath the brim of his hat. Of all the things he'd been expecting her to say, it hadn't been that, a desire more fitting for a young boy than an elegant woman, and he couldn't quite keep the surprise from his voice.

'You want to be a *farmer*?'

'Of sorts. More than anything I just want to be *useful*.'

She sounded so decided that Alex tried again to catch a glimpse of the face hidden in shadow. Clearly something unusual lay behind that pretty façade and it intrigued him more than was probably polite, so different from the other young ladies of his circle that he couldn't help but push further.

'But why are you alone? Surely your task would have been easier with help?'

There came a sound suspiciously like a tut. 'I didn't *want* it to be easy. I wanted to prove I'm just as capable as my brother. He sprained his ankle and was forced to rest at an inn, sending word to my father that the rest of the journey would have to be delayed. I begged to take over, just for the last few miles, and Papa finally agreed on the condition I be chaperoned every step of the way.'

Alex's curiosity grew more with every word. 'So you sneaked away by yourself?'

'Just before dawn this morning. I wasn't entirely thoughtless—I left a note explaining where I'd gone and why, asking them not to blame my father's man for my actions. I'd planned to reach Atherby and be waiting for them, but I must have taken a wrong turn… I suppose that explains why they weren't able to catch up with me after I'd left.'

She lapsed into silence and Alex didn't try to break it, a natural pause descending as he led her onwards. There was no awkwardness, only two people caught up in their own thoughts, and it would have surprised him—if he'd stopped to consider it—how markedly *un*awkward he felt in her company. The unaffected way she spoke to him was refreshing, quite different from the usual reverence he seemed to inspire, and as for her hopes for the future…

A singular woman and no mistake.

The fields were in almost total darkness now, the moon hidden behind heavy-bellied clouds, and he didn't know whether to feel glad that the Hall was only a few minutes away. On the one hand it would be pleasant to be out of the cold, his breath hanging in the air and the stranger's likewise as they walked, while on the other, things were more complicated. She was a beguiling mystery and he was aware of the increasing urge to know her better, her face and the slim figure beneath her cloak almost as enticing as her clearly unusual ambitions.

Don't get carried away.

A stern voice at the back of his mind issued a warning and Alex felt a nip of discomfort to know it was right. He was an engaged man—*or very nearly*—and he owed it to Augusta to behave with honour, keeping his head even when temptation whispered for him to turn it.

He cleared his throat, hoping he could manage to sound casual.

'That was a risky strategy, considering how badly it could have gone wrong.'

His puzzling new companion looked across sharply as if suspecting he was lecturing her, saw that he wasn't, and then Alex's chest gave a wrench as her lips twitched into a smile.

'Perhaps. It was a risk worth taking, however, if it meant I might finally be able to live the life I dream of. There comes a time when you have to take control of your own destiny, I think.'

His own mouth moved to smile back—quite without his permission, but he couldn't have stopped it if he'd wanted to. In the dim light her expression was determined, a glint in her eyes that spoke of a mind made up, and the sight made him feel he'd swallowed a lit match. A secret part of him understood what she meant. His position of privilege was also a cage, its constraints tying him for ever to a way of life he hadn't chosen for himself. She wanted to break free of her own binds and he respected it, all the while knowing it was far easier said than done.

'What about you? I imagine you must live somewhere on this estate?'

He managed a nod, almost all the reply he could muster in his concerning state of mind. 'That's right.'

'And you know the Viscount well, it seems. He's an amiable man?'

'He has his moments.'

'Well. I only hope he won't be too inconvenienced by my sudden presence. I may baulk at *some* rules, but I know not to impose upon my betters.'

It was Alex's turn to send a swift glance to the side. 'That's how you would regard him?'

'Of course.' He watched her shrug, slight shoulders moving in the gloom. 'I know the way the world works just as I imagine you do. My papa may be a gentleman, but our family's money was made first through *his* father—and I can't imagine a peer of the Realm welcoming a trades-man's granddaughter to sit at his table. I wouldn't dream of asking a favour without your word of introduction. It wouldn't be right.'

The sudden turn of the path they followed into a side gate saved Alex from having to reply. Instead he went quickly ahead, holding the gate open as the woman herded her flock through it and on to the wide drive beyond, at the end of which a large and handsome house loomed out of the darkness. Candles lit in every window cast an inviting orange glow over a manicured lawn and hinted at the russet brick of the walls, a flight of fine marble steps reaching up to where the front door waited for their approach. It was a sight Alex had seen countless times, but his companion stopped transfixed, gazing up at Milbrooke Hall with such wonder he had to brace himself against another spark.

'It's so beautiful. I'm not sure I dare go any closer.'

She hesitated, the sculpted line of her profile illuminated by the flickering flames, and Alex clenched his jaw. *You're being ridiculous. Get hold of yourself.*

Forcing a laugh, he stepped past her, heading towards the grand steps. 'That can't be true. I think you would dare anything.'

Another smile was his reward for such nonchalance. 'I shall take that as a compliment. Would you knock for me? I can't leave the birds outside alone...'

Sudden realisation flooded her face. 'I've just realised I don't even know your name. I was so distracted when we first met I didn't introduce myself properly.' She dipped an accomplished curtsy, its elegance hardly spoiled by the filthy hem of her cloak. 'My name is Miss Maria Bartlett and I beg forgiveness for my terrible manners.'

Standing above her on the steps, Alex paused.

I suppose there's no avoiding it now, although I doubt she'll be quite so forthcoming once I've told her...

'I'll forgive yours if you'll forgive mine.'

He looked down at her, a slightly bedraggled figure gazing back at him with wide green eyes that were far prettier than he was comfortable with. It would be a real shame if she retreated behind social etiquette after he revealed his name, just as she'd implied she believed necessary...or perhaps not. Perhaps her unconventional behaviour would extend to other areas too, something he found himself hoping as he offered a bow.

'My name is Alexander, Miss Bartlett. Alexander, Viscount Stanford—and this is my house.'

Chapter Two

Standing at the window of the sumptuous bedroom in which she had spent the night, Maria stared despairingly at the view that lay before her.

Heaven help me. What on earth do I do now?

Gleaming in the early morning sun, a pristine blanket of snow stretched out as far as the eye could see, a covering of dazzling white over the Milbrooke lawns. The clouds she'd been so worried about had clearly been busy and Maria's heart sank, the regret already lying heavy in her chest growing as she turned away from the glass. It would be nigh on impossible to walk the turkeys any further while the snow was so deep and yet she had to try, the luxury of choice not one she possessed.

I certainly can't stay here a moment longer than I have to. Not after yesterday...

Her cheeks burned as the events of the previous day came back round again, repeating the same series of mortifying scenes that had kept her awake until the early hours.

My embarrassment at realising he was the Viscount all along...the shame of having to accept his hospitality under such ridiculous circumstances...and then, perhaps worst of all, being obliged to borrow a nightgown, not even having so much as handkerchief of my own with me...

She closed her eyes briefly. Thank goodness she'd managed to conceal the instinctive attraction to Alexander that had leapt up out of nowhere, so misplaced now she knew

the truth. Alexander's face was handsome and his manner
so engaging she'd felt herself warm to him at once—but
he was far above her and now that she knew it any rogue
wonderings would be extinguished at once. She belonged
to a different world, her father a gentleman, but in another
class entirely to the one she'd somehow stumbled into, and
it was necessary for her to leave as soon as she could.

A glance over her shoulder at the frozen beauty beyond,
however, made her mouth twist. Quite how she was going
to make an escape in these conditions—her second flight
in two days—she wasn't yet sure, a soft knock at the door
interrupting her quest for an answer.

'Beg pardon, ma'am.'

The handle turned and a maid appeared, bobbing a respectful curtsy at Maria's uncertain smile. She looked to
be carrying the gown Maria had worn yesterday, the hem
now clean of mud, although the warm shawl draped over
her arm was unfamiliar.

'His Lordship bade me to help you dress. He's stepped
out for a short while, but he asks if you'd do him the honour of speaking with him after breakfast.'

Maria felt herself stiffen. The prospect of meeting Alexander again did something odd to her stomach, but she
stubbornly set it aside, submitting to the maid's attentions
as her mind strayed to the man unwittingly responsible
for her unease.

*Of course I have to speak with him. He was kind enough
to let me stay in his house and that deserves my heartfelt
thanks, even if I'll struggle to look him in the eye.*

The maid turned her with a gentle touch and Maria
moved obediently, still thinking hard. She would go down
to breakfast, meet with the Viscount and then decide how
exactly she was going to leave. The turkeys wouldn't sell
themselves, after all. She had a mission to complete and
she wasn't going to forget it, no matter how much the image

of Alexander's irresistible smile lingered as she tried to strengthen her resolve.

Breakfast, a quick thank-you and then on my way. That's my plan and I'm sticking to it.

By the time she had finished eating, however, Alexander still hadn't returned, and Maria's unease began to build again as she sat at his luxuriously linen-swathed table. Such idleness encouraged her to dwell on things she shouldn't and she got to her feet, determined to outrun the thoughts that tried to creep in. Checking on her turkeys in their temporary lodging would provide a good distraction, she decided, and with resolute strides she crossed the room to tug on the bellpull that hung beside the fire.

An obliging footman showed her the way to the yard, which was just as well. Milbrooke Hall seemed even bigger in daylight and Maria couldn't help but stare as she was led through one resplendent room to the next, marvelling at the tapestries and paintings that hung from every wall and furniture that wouldn't have been out of place in a palace.

In the entrance hall great boughs of greenery had been hung in readiness for Christmas, their fresh scent mingling with spiced pomanders set above each door, and when Maria eventually emerged into the cold she was dizzy from the colour and luxury crowding in from all sides. The slap of stinging air to her face was almost a relief, goose pimples rising as she huddled deeper into her borrowed shawl and staggered unsteadily across the snowbound cobbles towards the stable Alexander had generously provided for the night.

She unbolted the door and stepped inside, relishing the comparative warmth of being out of the wind. The smell of hay hung in the air and she smiled to see the turkeys scratching about contentedly, a scene so reminiscent of home that she felt a sudden pang of guilt join the jumble of sensations already causing havoc.

I hope Carew isn't too worried. I'll write him a note as soon as I meet Cartwright in Atherby.

Her brother wouldn't understand, she knew for certain. He had always been able to come and go as he wished, never constrained by anyone else's views on what was deemed proper, and he would be both anxious and angry that she had taken such a drastic step. She'd have to weather yet another of his scoldings when they were reunited and Maria was just about to sigh when a shadow fell between her and the open stable door behind.

'Sorry. I really must stop sneaking up on you.'

The deep voice sent a jolt through her, setting her heart beating with instant speed. It wasn't necessary for her to see who had spoken for the words to have such an effect and she hesitated, trying to rein in the immediate heat that roared into her cheeks before turning around.

'Good morning, Your Lordship.'

She sank into a curtsy and came up a little awkwardly, praying her agitation wasn't as obvious as it felt. Alexander's eyes were just as blue as she remembered and Maria cursed inwardly to know her face must be on fire as he looked down at her, so handsome that she could hardly meet his gaze. By his windswept hair he must have only just returned and she found herself wondering where he had been, everything about the Viscount far more interesting than it should be.

'I hope you slept well? You must have been tired from your exertion yesterday.'

'Yes, thank you,' Maria lied, her mouth feeling curiously dry. Whether it was being in the presence of nobility or her appreciation for the height of his cheekbones she wasn't sure, only certain that *something* was making it very difficult to think. 'I'm quite refreshed. I'll be leaving shortly so as not to inconvenience you any further.'

'Ah. If that was your plan, I fear I have bad news.' Alexander's brow furrowed, the action doing nothing to dim the striking set of his features. 'I've just been on reconnaissance and I'm afraid to report the snow comes up to *here* in places.'

He cut his hand along one thigh, Maria unable to stop herself from following with her eyes. His breeches were indeed damp from wading through the drifts, but it wasn't that which caused her gaze to linger there far longer than it should. The shape of his legs beneath the clinging material was enticing and she felt her innards knot, such a dangerous train of thought something she ought to put a stop to at once.

He is a viscount, Maria, and even if he wasn't—what kind of wanton spends her time staring at a man's legs?

Alexander was still talking and with great effort Maria pulled herself back into line, only belatedly registering what he was saying.

'It's treacherous out there and I'm certain your birds wouldn't get through. If you can stand my company a few days longer, I'd invite you to stay here until the snow has melted enough for you to travel on safely.'

Her already tangled insides gave a lurch. 'Stay here? Until the snow has gone? No, Your Lordship. I couldn't possibly impose upon you for that long.'

She shook her head, hoping he'd understand without needing to be told why. Even the most determined gossip would struggle to make scandal from Alexander offering her shelter for a few hours when the alternative was sleeping out in the snow, but the longer she spent beneath his roof the more suspect it would appear to anybody looking in.

An unmarried, unchaperoned woman was a dangerous thing for a single man to harbour in his home, although in the next moment her certainty wavered. If the snow was as deep as he said, then he was right. There was no way the turkeys could manage the walk to Atherby and she couldn't very well leave them at Milbrooke Hall alone. If they stayed she would have to likewise, and besides…was one even *allowed* to defy the eldest son of an earl?

Her indecision must have been obvious. One dark, aristocratic eyebrow raised good humouredly and a flash of that heart-stopping smile made it suddenly impossible to concentrate on anything else but his alluring lips.

'That's two Your Lordships in five minutes. I'm not sure I like this sudden deference. You weren't quite so reserved yesterday.'

Maria winced. 'If I'd known who you were, I never would have spoken so freely.'

She heard a quiet laugh, one note that stirred the hairs on the nape of her neck. 'I confess that was my intention in concealing my name. So often people clam up when they know my title—it was refreshing to have an uninhibited conversation for once.'

'I can generally be relied upon for that. My father often despairs of it.'

'That comes as no surprise. You mentioned how much your desires clash.'

Another wave of embarrassment washed over her. 'There were many things I said yesterday that I shouldn't.'

'And yet I'd like to hear more. It's not every day I meet a lady with your aspirations.'

She looked up from the straw-strewn ground. If she wasn't very much mistaken, he sounded genuinely interested, his eyes fixed on hers, and the openness she saw there something it would be difficult to fake. Even if he hadn't already been handsome that friendliness would have made him so, his natural charm drawing her in without even trying.

'You don't disapprove?'

'Why should I?'

'I often find men hold very decided views as to how women should behave. If you'll excuse my saying so.'

He shrugged a broad shoulder, the coat covering it still damp with snow. 'You can say whatever you like. As I said, I enjoyed your candour yesterday. I'd hoped for more of the same today.'

A mixture of surprise and scepticism prevented her from replying. Her mother would have turned pale if she'd overheard this particular conversation, her unruly daughter once again speaking out of turn following the lifelong habit no amount of reprimands could cure. Mrs Bartlett had often feared it would prevent the finding of a suitable husband for her youngest child: very few men wanted a wife with her own ideas, after all, and even fewer would accept one so quick to voice them.

However…

The Viscount professed to *like* the informality that so exasperated her family, Maria mused. Alexander spoke to her as an equal and seemed to want the same in return, a marked departure from the respect most important men demanded. Even her own loving father expected complete and unquestioning compliance and it had driven a wedge between them ever since she was a child. Her host wanted none of that, however, and she found some of the tension leave her, helpless to resist the little voice that whispered for her to smile back at that waiting, captivating face.

As long as I keep my head everything will be fine, she assured herself, with the uncanny sensation that she didn't entirely believe her own words. *After all, when I leave I shall never see him again and surely this far from home there can be little chance of damage to my reputation. How hazardous can spending a few more days in such agreeable company truly be?*

Alex followed the procession of different thoughts through Maria's expression, wondering whether he ought to be quite so invested in the outcome. In truth, he'd struggled to get much rest the previous night, the image of his guest's open-mouthed horror at the revelation of his name flashing every time he closed his eyes. She'd looked mortified and the desire to make amends was strong—far more so than it should be, he admitted with an internal grimace. The effect she'd already had on him was not to be encouraged and yet he felt it still, the heady combination of her fair face and rebellious nature drawing him in like a moth to a flame.

I had no choice but to offer her a place to stay. There was no chance she'd be able to reach Atherby in all this snow, especially not with her flock, and only the most suspicious minds would see anything untoward in her remaining at Milbrooke a little longer.

Miss Bartlett's hesitation to accept was understandable, but Alex reasoned the real risk of scandal was small. His servants could be trusted to guard their tongues and the snow made it unlikely any visitors would come to stumble across things they might misinterpret. If questions were raised, he could always claim a maid was in constant attendance as a chaperon, leaving no obstacle for him to extend a charitable helping hand that had *nothing whatsoever* to do with the fact she was such an interesting young woman.

His argument was rational, but some slight discomfort lingered, its flames fanned when Maria cast him a quick glance.

'I'm in your debt, Your Lordship. If it's candour you require in return, I'll answer anything you want to know.'

The wind renewed its howling around the stable, whistling through a crack in the door, and Maria folded her arms as she waited for his request. She looked so obliging he was tempted to indulge the curiosity that had harried him since the first moment they'd met, but Alex forced it back in favour of a much less risky direction.

'I would have thought my first question was obvious,' he

ventured, frowning solemnly at the turkeys picking through the straw. 'It's the same thing anyone would want to know. I must ask you… Do they all have names?'

Maria hesitated—and then her laugh was like the peal of a bell, ringing out high and just as sweet. 'That's what you would ask me? When you might pose any question in the world?'

At Alex's nod she spread her hands in defeat. 'No. A cardinal rule of farming. Never name any animal you don't intend to keep. It encourages sentiment and there's little room for that in business—' She broke off for a moment, then lowered her voice. 'Besides… I'm not sure I could tell them apart. Not that I'd ever hurt their feelings by saying so.'

The gleam of humour in her eye was like a magnet and Alex felt its enticing pull, only just in time managing to check the urge to lean closer.

'Did your father teach you that?'

He had the impression she repressed an unladylike snort. 'Absolutely not. Everything I learned was despite his presence, not thanks to it. He'd be far happier if I stayed at home, sewing quietly, where my mother could keep a watchful eye on me.'

Alex almost gave a grunt of his own at the familiar picture she painted. 'My parents were much the same with my sisters before they wed. They, too, were kept close and cosseted but, unlike you, they didn't seem to mind it.'

He watched Maria sigh. 'No. I've often wished I could be satisfied with my lot. My friends have found contentment in their places and I'm glad of their happiness…unfortunately the same serenity just seems to elude me.'

She sounded close to wistful and Alex saw a shadow cross her face, a fleeting darkness he understood all too well. It was the conflict between what one was *expected* to do and what one *wanted*, a battle that he had to quell inside himself more and more of late, and he spoke without thinking as if from one troubled soul to another.

'Wondering if you might prefer something different isn't necessarily a bad thing. Surely everyone feels that way at times.'

'My father would disagree. I believe he wishes he'd been given a more agreeable daughter rather than some boyish aberration with ideas above her station.'

She smiled—a lovely thing that raised her rosy cheeks in the most distracting way imaginable—but he could tell she was only half joking. There was a ghost of regret in her voice and it stirred something in his chest, a strange sensation growing there he didn't know how to name.

'You are nothing of the kind. Your ambition is a credit to you and I'll freely admit I admire it.'

He hadn't meant for his opinion to come out quite so warmly and he could hardly blame Maria for the sudden uncertainty with which she looked away from him. Apparently his mouth was determined to run wild and he wrested back control before he could stray any further from the safest path, seizing on her shivering as the safest way out.

'Will you come back to the Hall? I think you must be freezing by now.'

'Thank you. I must write to my brother to inform him of your generous hospitality. He'll have feared the worst when my father's men couldn't find me.'

Maria stepped past him as he held open the door and he heard her sharp intake of breath at the biting wind outside. It wasn't far to the house, but the snow was deep and he saw she wore only a pair of flimsy shoes more suited to dry paths than wading through icy drifts. It would be easy for her to slip and, firmly bolting the door behind them, he held out his arm.

'Allow me. I don't want you to lose your footing.'

A perilously pretty blush lit her face and Alexander bit

down on the tip of his tongue in a reminder not to stare. With her fiery mane and decided chin she would have tempted a saint, let alone a mere man trying to remember his duty lay elsewhere—but any such thought fled as her little hand crept into the crook of his elbow and Alexander could think of nothing but the soft weight of her palm.

The thrill that licked through him was nothing he'd felt before and he almost stumbled, distantly grateful he might blame his clumsiness on the snow. He'd danced with more women than he could count, a parade of the richest and most beautiful ladies of the *ton* passing through his hands without leaving any impression at all, and yet it was the feather-light touch of a farmer's daughter that made his heart feel it might leap from his chest.

Maria walked carefully beside him, her rosy face hidden now by a stray swathe of curls teased out by the wind, and he found he had quite forgotten how to speak as her slender fingers robbed him of all rationality.

I've never had this reaction to Augusta.

He tightened his jaw against the rogue thought although all the denial in the world couldn't make it untrue. Augusta had never had the same baffling effect on him as Maria had managed in less than a single day, his soon-to-be fiancée's presence generally leaving him unmoved. Alex had no doubt she felt the same about him and it had always seemed so simple, a dutiful, straightforward match uncomplicated by anything as messy as feelings. He hadn't expected to ever feel anything close to love…but with Miss Bartlett on his arm he was overcome with the sudden realisation he might just have been missing out.

His throat felt far too tight. It was a ludicrous situation. Maria had only appeared the previous night and yet his mind was running away with him, a flight of fancy inspired by his weakness for a pretty face. Her unorthodox ambitions had roused his curiosity, but that was as far as it went, anything else too stupid to be entertained for as much as a moment.

The gentle grip of her fingers, however, would not let him rest. Their progress across the frozen yard was torturously slow and in desperation Alexander seized on the first thing that came to mind, feeling as if he was trying to keep his head above water against a growing flood.

'So you feel you know everything you need to about farming? Enough to make your dream a reality?'

Thankfully Maria's attention was on the precarious ground, leaving only her profile to tempt his disloyal gaze.

'I believe so. From the moment I learned to read I devoured my father's reports and newssheets and I followed him about the farm so frequently he often forbade me from leaving the house. I understand the rotation of crops and rearing of animals and I've a good head for figures…again, something that was *not* to be encouraged. If it wouldn't help me secure a good husband, what was the point?'

She hesitated, perhaps regretting the touch of bitterness that had crept into her voice. 'I apologise, Your Lordship. I shouldn't criticise…'

The slight furrow of her brow was like a physical touch to Alexander's skin. Even that small trace of unhappiness in her face was more than he liked and he moved before he could stop himself, bringing his hand up to cover the small one laid softly on his arm and feeling his stomach turn over at those delicate fingers under his.

'If that's how you feel, you should say so. And please stop calling me *Your Lordship*. I'd much prefer you call me Alexander.'

As soon as the words were out he knew he shouldn't have spoken them, but a strange kind of sorcery still seemed to have charge of his tongue. It was the particular kind of magic only a pair of fine green eyes could weave and his breath caught as he watched her answering nod.

'If you insist. You must set the terms in your own house—but if that's the case it only seems fair you call me Maria.'

Alex dipped his chin in what he hoped she might take as approval, although in truth his mind was far more busily engaged. Why had he done that, knocking down the first barrier between them as if he had any right to indulge his dangerous fancy? He knew how to behave and yet he seemed intent on doing the opposite…something that made him frown as he guided Maria the last few steps to Milbrooke's kitchen door, the withdrawal of her hand from his arm leaving behind the most curious sense of loss.

Chapter Three

Maria craned her neck upwards, the portraits adorning the walls of the long, oak-panelled gallery peering back at her as she walked. Several generations smiled down and she studied every one, tracing the shadow of Alexander in each painted face. The bright blue eyes seemed to be as much a family inheritance as Milbrooke Hall itself, although the dark hair appeared a much more recent addition to the line, perhaps courtesy of Alexander's handsome, raven-tressed grandmother, who from her picture might almost have been a Spanish princess. Whoever turned out to be responsible for the current Viscount's looks, however, had a lot to answer for and Maria was quick to turn away from the final portrait hanging at the very end of the gallery.

Even when rendered in oils Alexander's direct, open gaze had the power to make her heart beat faster and she was reminded, yet again, why it was so essential to avoid the real thing. He'd been kind to offer her shelter, but her feelings strayed far beyond gratitude and, if she wasn't careful, they might just spin out of control completely.

Nobody has ever shown such interest in what I want from my life.

The scene out in the stable had replayed so often in her head since that precious moment the previous day and it came again as she moved to the gallery window. Fresh snow had fallen overnight and Alexander's man had only just been able to reach Atherby with her letter, handing it to

Cartwright who had apparently been much relieved to learn that she was safe and to send on her small bag of clothes. All that remained was for the drifts to thaw enough for her to lead her flock the rest of the way and then she'd be gone, Alexander nothing more to her than a fading memory of a man she could never hope to have.

It was chilly by the lead-paned window and she drew back from a cold draught, wishing she could escape disagreeable thoughts as easily. Impressive as the gallery was, it wasn't particularly warm and Maria rubbed her arms as she wondered where Alexander might have hidden his library.

A cup of tea and a book will distract me from things I shouldn't be thinking. Surely it shouldn't be too difficult to find either of those things close by.

Her enticing host had disappeared soon after breakfast that morning and she hadn't seen him since, something the resultant pang of disappointment proved was a good thing. The less time she spent with Alexander the better—the feelings he inspired were unladylike, her scandalous appreciation of the shape of his thighs beneath damp breeches still firmly imprinted on her mind alongside the thrill she'd felt on placing her hand into the crook of his arm. It had been so strong beneath her fingertips, so solid and radiating reassuring warmth despite the heavy snow…

Muttering under her breath at her own deplorable weakness, Maria set off in search of a cosy sanctuary where, hopefully, she might regain her sanity. A library would be perfect and she headed for the second floor, descending one of the many ornate staircases. The Hall was so sprawling it seemed to go on for ever, one room leading to another in a rabbit warren of grandeur so confusing Maria wished she had a map, and her irritation with herself grew as the next door she opened revealed nothing more promising than an empty guest bedroom.

Is this what happens when you find yourself attracted to a man? All sense of direction abandons you completely, even when you know full well there's no chance of your feelings being returned?

Maria retraced her steps back on to the landing, closing the door behind her, perhaps a little too firmly. Why did the first man she'd ever met who seemed willing to take her seriously have to be a *viscount*? Even if he hadn't been so pleasing to look at, his respectful curiosity would have won her favour, his handsome face only half of his appeal. She'd known comely men before who had spoiled the effect as soon as they opened their mouths, the same old staid opinions spilling out that hadn't changed since the Ark. Alexander, however, clearly possessed a more open mind and if he hadn't been set so high above her she might even have told him so.

But he is above me and that's that. The best thing to do is carry on avoiding him as much as possible and add no more fuel to the fire.

Another door stood across the landing and she reached rather pessimistically for the handle. Doubtless it would be yet another disused space, she thought as she turned it, another false step in her quest for some peace of mind...

Her heart recognised the figure at the other end of the room before her brain did, giving a powerful squeeze that almost made her gasp.

'Your Lord—Alexander. I'm sorry. I didn't know you were in here.'

He straightened up immediately. A handsome billiard table stretched out between them and evidently he'd been about to take a shot when she stumbled in, his mild surprise turning quickly to that bone-melting smile as he dipped a shallow bow.

'Don't apologise. You're welcome to come in.'

Maria hesitated on the threshold. Two rival voices issued instructions: one demanded she make some excuse to turn away while the other encouraged her to enter the cosy room, the fire in the grate and velvet curtains blocking out every draught making it an appealing prospect. It was a fleeting glance at Alexander, however, that provided the strongest motive and, knowing she ought to at least *try* to resist the urge to get closer, she stepped guiltily inside.

'I was looking for the library.'

'Ah. Other side of the house. I can show you if you'd like?'

Alexander made as if to put down his cue and Maria quickly shook her head. 'No, no. Please, finish your game.'

Her already leaping heart skipped faster at his laugh. 'Actually, your interruption is very welcome. I wasn't doing well and now I have an excuse to start again.'

He swept the balls back into the centre of the table, corralling them neatly inside their triangular rack. Watching curiously, Maria found she couldn't take her eyes from his hands, large but with none of the clumsiness so many men seemed to suffer from.

'Would you like to play?'

She looked up quickly, hoping he hadn't noticed her staring. 'I don't know how.'

'That's no matter. I could teach you?'

A touch of heat kindled in Maria's cheeks. Only minutes ago she'd resolved to spend as little time with Viscount Stanford as possible and yet her mouth seemed to have other ideas, answering with no regard whatsoever for what her better judgement might suggest.

'I *do* enjoy learning new things.'

Alexander waved her closer and she felt her legs obey, carrying her around the side of the billiard table before she had time to think. Standing so near him didn't help to slow her racing pulse and it soared higher as he handed her a cue, the very tips of his fingers brushing hers to send a sharp thrill the full length of her arm.

'I'll teach you the rules shortly, but we'll start with the basics. Begin by holding the cue like so.'

With immense dignity Alexander demonstrated the correct technique although Maria was sure she caught a glint of humour in his eye as he flourished his cue. Trying not to smile herself, she followed suit, brandishing her own with perhaps a little too much enthusiasm as Alexander ducked swiftly out of the way.

'Like this?'

'Not quite. More like this…'

He gestured again in what seemed to Maria the exact movement she'd just made, but she nodded solemnly in return.

'Ah, yes. I see. Quite different.'

'Indeed. And then you take your aim—like this.'

With one skilful thrust he sent the white ball neatly across the table. 'There. As simple as that.'

He straightened up, acknowledging Maria's admiration with a modest bow. It only took a moment to reset the table and then he stood back, waving her forward with an encouraging smile so delightful that it made her insides twist.

'Now you try.'

Attempting to ignore the brazen whisper that would have preferred to keep watching Alexander, Maria approached the table. He'd made it look easy enough; but looks could be deceiving, she found, her first wild jab sending the balls flying not only across the green baize surface, but a couple of them hurtling over the side, where they bounced noisily away as if to deliberately draw more attention to her failure.

'Simple, you said?'

She stood up, any embarrassment chased away by Alexander's genuine laugh. The lines at his eyes creased endearingly and for a half-second she wondered how it was he put her so at ease, inviting her to share the joke rather than feel the victim of it.

'Perhaps you could try again with a fraction less exuberance.' He gathered himself, although a ghost of amusement lingered as he collected up the runaways. 'Your stance could be improved, too, and would make control much easier.'

Maria was about to make some reply—probably one far too pert—when Alexander came a step closer, the sudden proximity stealing the words from her mouth.

'Would you permit me? It would be much simpler to show you rather than explain.'

Maria nodded, not trusting herself to speak. At this distance she could see every detail of Alexander's face, from the tiny scar above one eye to the faintest shadow of stubble his close shave had left behind. The subtle scent of woodsmoke and expensive soap drifted from him, a combination so intoxicating it made Maria's head spin—but then he moved behind her and her legs turned to water at the gentlest of touches on the small of her back, and she could focus on nothing else but the sudden sensation of his fingertips brushing her spine.

'If you stand square to the table, instead of at an angle, you might find that helps.'

Very carefully Alexander guided her forward, Maria going along like a puppet whose strings had been cut. The intimacy of a man's hand hovering close to her waist was nothing she hadn't already experienced at respectable dances, but somehow this was different, Alexander's light touch more rousing than any heated palm. Unable to see him, her other senses grew sharper, every nerve standing to attention in delicious anticipation of what he might do next.

The question was soon answered.

He leaned over her shoulder, Maria's skin singing as his murmur stirred a stray ringlet. 'You could hold your cue more firmly. You'll have more control if you tighten your grip.'

Mutely she tried to obey, although her body seemed to have gone on strike. All it was interested in was how near Alexander stood, his chest pressing lightly against her back and her spine wanting to curve closer, to close the gap between them and revel in whatever lay secreted beneath his shirt. Her already shallow breathing hitched at the thought and desperately she tried to regain control, the wayward desires flooding through her, threatening to make her cast caution to the wind.

But it seemed the situation was against her. Trapped between Alexander and the table, Maria swallowed a sharp breath as his hand came up to rest over hers, his fingers guiding hers into position around the cue.

'No, no. Like this.'

With her heart flailing against her ribs she allowed him to draw back her arm and take the shot, hardly noticing whether this time was more successful. The whole world seemed to have shrunk to fit into the palm of Alexander's hand, warm and wonderful against the back of hers and so gentle despite its strength that she almost closed her eyes to better savour the moment she knew would soon have to break.

What are you doing? Control yourself this instant!

The frantic little squeak at the back of her mind tried to jolt her back to reality, but Maria scarcely heard it. The edge of the billiard table dug into her thighs, another distraction that should have pulled her up short, although that discomfort was immediately borne away by Alexander's lips close to her ear.

'An excellent shot. You're a very quick learner.'

His voice was low—and so charged with *something* that Maria turned automatically, moving on instinct she wasn't fast enough to curb. Twisting to look at him brought them face to face and a shiver rippled through her at the shadow she saw in Alexander's eyes.

He gazed down at her, green meeting blue with a crackle of static she felt in the very depths of her stomach. His hand had grazed her waist as she turned and the skin there blazed like wildfire, so hot she was dimly surprised it didn't scorch the fabric of her gown. Where only minutes before they had been laughing, any humour had abruptly died, replaced by tension that stretched between them now as clear and brittle as glass.

Either it hadn't occurred to him to take a step back or he had decided not to. Whatever the reason, they were so close Maria could have kissed him without taking a single step, that dangerously enticing mouth for once not shaped into anything resembling a smile. Instead it was a straight line, so serious she felt another shudder climb her spine, but it was intensity, not displeasure that set it so firmly, and as she watched his stare travel from her eyes to her mouth and back again her blood began to heat in her veins.

He wants to kiss me. And if he tries, I'm going to let him.

Once, many years ago when he was only a child, Alex had come perilously close to tumbling down a well on one of the farms on the estate. Only just in time a stable lad had lurched forward to grab him, but he could still recall the sensation of teetering on a precipice, time seeming to slow while fate decided which way he would fall. In a strange way he felt the same thing now, looking down into Maria's upturned face and wondering—in the last corner of his mind that wasn't completely saturated with the burning desire to bend his head and claim her lips—whether he possessed the strength to turn away.

One hand still lingered dangerously close to her waist and the urge to reach out was like a physical ache, his arm itching to snake around that narrow curve. Her eyes were wide and a dusky pink suffused each cheek, but she hadn't tried to pull away, some measure of his own desire reflected back at him to hint that an advance might not be unwelcome...if only he dared to take the chance...

Remember you're not free to behave like this.

The truth swam up from the depths of his foggy mind, unwanted yet insistent, and at once his conscience gave an unpleasant stab. It wouldn't be fair to Augusta to act on his yearning, nor, indeed, to Maria, whose softly parted lips were a temptation beyond all endurance.

She doesn't know you're all but engaged. If you had any honour at all, you wouldn't lead a respectable young woman on like this.

The realisation came like a flash of lightning throwing everything into stark black and white. As much as Miss Bartlett roused him, made him feel things he had never felt before with her strong opinions and flaming hair, *he could not have her.* By her reaction she was just as attracted to him as he was to her—but it wasn't to be and with a lead weight settling in his chest he was just about to explain himself when the sound of a door opening sent Maria fleeing from his hold.

He turned to see who had interrupted at such an unfortunate moment, his frustration growing as Mr Goddard stepped into the room. The estate manager wasn't his favourite person and to see him now was something Alex could have done without, keenly aware of Maria pretending to study one of the bookcases that lined the room as if her burning face wouldn't give away her discomfort.

'Goddard?'

'Your Lordship.' The other man bowed, his dark eyes narrowing slightly as he saw they weren't alone. 'I'm sorry. I wasn't aware you had a guest.'

Alex forced a poor approximation of his usual smile. 'I have indeed. Allow me to introduce Miss Bartlett.'

At the sound of her name Maria looked up from the book she had selected from the shelf, apparently taking care not to turn in Alex's direction. 'Good afternoon. Mr Goddard, I believe?'

'That's correct. Good afternoon, ma'am.'

Out of the corner of his eye Alex watched her elegant curtsy in response, but made himself turn his attention instead to the estate manager.

'Did you want to see me about something?'

'Only a few details concerning the upcoming ball. I can return later, however, when you're not otherwise occupied.'

Alex nodded as carelessly as he was able, although the mention of his parents' Christmas ball made him feel suddenly cold. Only two more days and he and Augusta would be bound together for the rest of their lives, just as he'd been about to explain to Maria before the unwanted interruption had snatched away the chance. Now he'd have to find another moment to tell her—having to delay the inevitable only making the prospect worse.

Goddard was evidently waiting for a proper response and Alex tried—for what must have been the thousandth time—to check his instinctive dislike. He'd never been able to warm to the man even after a decade of service, Goddard too cool and smooth to inspire much fondness. His family had served as Milbrooke's estate managers for generations, however, and it would be considered a slight to terminate his employment, leaving Alex little choice but to endure his presence around the Hall, as stern and unbending a man as any he'd ever met.

'Yes. I'll meet with you later this afternoon. We can discuss the ball then.'

The untimely reminder of Augusta stirred something at the back of Alex's mind. Hadn't he caught Goddard watching her once or twice, with far more animation in his sharp eyes than had ever been there before? It wasn't a crime to look at a beautiful woman, Alex supposed—something he was glad of, uncomfortably aware that he, too, would be strung up on the gallows if it was against the law. Maria tempted him to stare far more than Augusta ever had and he almost didn't hear Goddard's quiet step as he left the room, closing the door behind him with a definitive click.

Left alone now with Maria, Alex busied himself putting the abandoned cues back in their rack. He was stalling for time, trying to think how to break what could easily turn into an awkward silence, but she beat him to it.

'You're having a ball?'

Her tone was determinedly pleasant, like one making polite conversation with an aged relative, and Alex wanted to groan aloud at the difference from only a few minutes ago. *Then* she'd seemed at ease, laughing with him as though they'd known each other all their lives, but that had been before he'd lost his head and pushed too far, and now all he could do was try to muster some forced cheeriness of his own.

'Yes—or rather, my parents are hosting one here. It's to be held in two days.'

'To celebrate Christmas?'

'That's one reason.'

The truth balanced on the tip of his tongue. He'd have to tell her now. There was no alternative, Goddard's intrusion only making that fact doubly clear, yet he found himself reluctant to voice it.

But why? What do you think you have to lose?

Maria had only known him a few days, he reasoned uncomfortably. A woman like her must garner attention wherever she went, surely never wanting for admirers, and it would be foolish to expect her to have developed the same curiously strong feelings that he had fallen prey to so quickly. Whatever just passed between them had been a momentary flicker of mutual attraction and nothing more, although he couldn't ignore the tightness of his throat as he tried to speak.

'The other is to announce my engagement.'

For one long beat Maria didn't move and Alex realised how intently he watched for her reaction. *Something* passed over her face, as quick and unfathomable as smoke, but then she came towards him, reaching out to touch his arm for a half-second that sent splinters into his chest.

'Your engagement. Many congratulations.'

'Thank you.' He dipped his head, wondering what that nameless look had *meant*. 'It has been intended since I was a child. Neither myself nor the lady were particularly involved in planning the match.'

There was no reason for him to have added that unromantic little snippet, but if Maria thought it odd she didn't let it show.

'Of course. A man of your standing must wed sensibly. With so much at stake it's no wonder your parents were careful.'

It was a more generous response than he deserved, the ghost of warmth left behind by that little hand the only comfort he could find. A haze of shame washed over him to think he had almost behaved so dishonourably to both Augusta and Maria, two women who could not have been more different in both nature and the effect they had on his heart, and he almost winced at how earnestly he wished he could turn back the clock.

To when, though? Before you almost kissed Maria—or further still, when you might have had a chance at marrying someone other than Miss DeVere?

It was a horrible question and he elbowed it aside as hard as he could, although he couldn't pretend he didn't know the answer. It taunted him even as he looked down at Maria, her auburn curls characteristically springing free from their ribbon to fall in a cascade of copper down her back.

'I'd like it very much if you were to attend. You'll still be here regardless and I would far rather you did than stay in your room the whole time.'

She glanced up at him. 'I couldn't. I have no place at a gathering hosted by an earl...'

'You have every right to be there. As my friend you would be one of the most honoured guests.' Alex swallowed, unsure for a second if he trusted himself to carry on. 'If, of course, you'd permit me to think of you as such.'

Maria's sandy eyelashes swept down, shielding her olive eyes from his scrutiny, and he had no way of knowing what might have passed through them before she looked up again once more. 'You won my friendship the first moment you warned me Mr Goddard was in that field. It would be a privilege to be included in your celebrations.'

The full lips moved into a smile so lovely it made the sun seem dim in comparison, but Alex could have sworn it took her some effort to achieve. If he didn't know better, he might suspect she wasn't quite as happy for him as she wanted him to believe...but he had no chance to dwell on the thrilling possibility.

'Is that the time? I ought to go to change. If you'll excuse me.'

His bow was rewarded with a neat curtsy and then she was gone, leaving the room with speed Alex might have found suspicious if his mind hadn't been otherwise engaged. As it was, the sight of her narrow waist was the only thing he could focus on—that, and the desire to kick himself as he watched her walk away.

Chapter Four

Curled in an armchair beside her bedroom fire, Maria tried again to continue with her book. It had been the thickest one she could find, hoping it would distract her from the hurricane trapped inside her head, but her eyes refused to focus and after rereading the same page three times she had to admit defeat. While the image of Alexander's intent face as it had been the previous afternoon still lingered, she could think of nothing else…apart, of course, from the revelation soon after that had made her heart shudder to a halt.

Laying the book aside, Maria pulled her shawl more tightly around her shoulders. The fact that Alexander was engaged was none of her business, yet her stomach had plummeted at the news, with her only just in time managing to wipe the disappointment from her face to offer some painful congratulations. The unconcealed hunger with which he'd looked down at her as they stood beside the billiard table had given her hope, even if only for the most fleeting of moments, that something might be building between them, but that hope was shattered almost at once and she wondered now how she could ever have been so foolish as to indulge it.

Of course a man like Alexander would already be spoken for. With his position it was no surprise his parents had planned his marriage while he was still in the nursery, able to take their pick of the best-bred young ladies in the county as a match for their heir. Doubtless his wife-to-be was a flawless example of femininity, sure to be refined and graceful and demure—in short, everything Maria knew she was not and for the first time in her life she wondered if her mother's ceaseless striving for perfection might have had a point after all before reaching for the poker.

'Useless to think like that,' she muttered as she leaned over the side of her chair to stir up the already glowing coals. 'Even if I was the very pinnacle of womanhood, a farmer's daughter still couldn't match with nobility and that's the undeniable truth. I had no right to expect anything of Alexander and I should be glad of such a clear reminder not to make a fool of myself any further for a man I could never have had.'

The fire crackled as if in agreement and Maria dropped the poker back into its stand, retreating again into the warm hollow of her chair. Long shadows moved against the opposite wall and for a moment she watched them dance, lost in unhappy thought until a knock at the door cut through the silence.

'Come in.'

The maid assigned to attend her for the duration of her stay appeared round the doorframe and Maria made herself dredge up a smile.

'Nancy. Did you want me for something?'

'Yes, ma'am. Or rather, His Lordship did.'

At once Maria's pulse stepped up a pace. 'His Lordship?'

She made to uncoil herself from the armchair, but stopped as Nancy came fully into the room. While she stood half out on the landing, what the maid was holding had been concealed by the door, but now she was in full view Maria frowned.

'I think there's been a mistake. That isn't mine.'

'No mistake, ma'am.' The maid shook her head with the smallest trace of a smile. 'His Lordship sent it with his compliments. Said he realised far too late it was bad manners to invite a lady to a ball knowing she had nothing suitable to wear and asked you forgive the oversight.'

Maria couldn't immediately think of a reply as she watched Nancy cross to the bed and lay the dress she carried out on the counterpane. It gleamed there like a river of emeralds, the Christmas-green silk glowing in the firelight and drawing Maria towards it without her even having realised she'd got to her feet.

Staring down at the gown stretched in splendour before her, she felt her mind run blank. It looked to be roughly her size and its colour the one her mother declared most became her, the contrast of rich green against her copper hair admittedly flattering. It highlighted the streaks of gold in her eyes and lent warmth to her pale complexion, although at present she was so flushed she resembled a poppy more than anything else.

'But…' She turned to the maid, still unable to bully her brain into anything more coherent. 'How…?'

'His youngest sister, ma'am. Lady Aurelia as was, now the Duchess of Carmodale. She'd often come to stay with His Lordship before she wed and he was much in the habit of buying her gifts as an indulgent older brother. I understand he bought this dress at her insistence, but she changed her mind before so much as trying it on.'

Gently, as if afraid it might rear up and bite her, Maria traced a fingertip over the bodice. The silk there was the smoothest she'd ever felt, so delicate she feared even her light touch might leave a mark and she drew back again in bewilderment.

'I couldn't possibly wear this. A gown this fine must have cost a fortune.'

'His Lordship seemed most earnest. He said if you didn't wear this dress it would only continue to hang in a wardrobe gathering dust and that you would be doing him a good turn in seeing it used.'

Maria looked again at the exquisitely embroidered neckline and hem, tiny seed pearls winking back at her as though they shared a secret.

Was it proper to accept such a gift from a man she'd only known for a few days—and then to wear it to his engagement ball, of all places? Somehow it didn't seem quite right, the more doubtful part of her wondered, and yet there could be no mistaking the innocence of Alexander's intentions.

He wanted to spare her the shame of attending a gentry ball in one of her entirely unsuitable travelling dresses, a testament to his kindness that he'd had such forethought where many other men wouldn't have considered it for a moment. It was evidence of the good nature she already held in dangerously high esteem, as if more proof was needed, although she tried to push that into the background as she cautiously ran a hand over one shining sleeve.

'I could try it on at the very least. Surely there could be nothing wrong in that?'

'Nothing at all, ma'am. I'd be glad to help you.'

At Maria's hesitant nod Nancy came forward. Together they swapped her sensible dress of sprigged muslin for the luxury of emerald silk, neither speaking until the gown was in place and the maid stood back a pace to regard her with frank admiration.

'I don't know when I've ever seen a lady look so well in a dress. It might have been made with you in mind all along.'

Maria cast her a small smile. 'You're being too kind, I suspect. I'd be glad of a longer mirror, though, to see for myself. The one on my washstand is only big enough to see my face and I know what that looks like well enough.'

'There's a full-length glass in what was Lady Aurelia's room, ma'am. If you'd come with me?'

She followed Nancy out of the guest bedroom and along the landing to the family wing, her beautiful skirts rustling with every step. One of the many closed doors they passed by must be Alexander's, she thought as the maid led her onwards, and she couldn't help but wonder which it might be. Any of them could be his, the place where he laid his dark head each night, perhaps wearing nothing but his shirt as he readied himself for bed…

The image was far more thrilling than it should have been and Maria bit the inside of her lip in a warning to do better.

He's all but engaged—and I am not the kind of woman who imposes on another's intended. No matter how tempting he might be.

Nancy seemed to be slowing down. Evidently their destination was somewhere towards the end of the corridor and Maria was just about to give thanks for the distraction when the sound of a different door opening brought the maid up short.

'Your Lordship. I was just taking Miss Bartlett to the mirror in Lady Aurelia's room.'

Maria watched the back of Nancy's white cap bob respectfully, for one heartbeat unable to look higher to meet Alexander's eye. She hadn't seen him since that terrible, delightful moment in the billiard room, when he'd stared down at her like a starving man stumbled into a banquet before Mr Goddard's intrusion had broken the spell. Perhaps he'd been avoiding her just as she'd been attempting to avoid him—but there was no escaping him now. Standing face to face on the landing and dressed in finery that only a rare man would think to give, Maria felt herself shiver as she saw his sapphire gaze instinctively rake over her from head to foot before he managed to take back control.

'So I see.'

Alexander's smile was as friendly as ever, although Maria could have sworn she sensed a new stiffness in the broad set of his shoulders.

'Thank you, Nancy. I can escort Miss Bartlett from here.'

At once the maid dropped a curtsy and turned away, retreating down the corridor the way they'd come, and Maria watched her go with the feeling a shield had been removed. Now there was nothing to stand between her and Alexander, the immediate effect he had on her calling her closer, but she tried not to listen as she smoothed down her skirts, not yet trusting herself to look fully into his face.

'Alexander. This dress… I hardly know what to say. Your generosity—'

'Say nothing of that. I only hope you weren't offended.'

Out of the corner of her eye she saw him run a hand through his already somewhat tousled hair. 'I realised it was unlikely you'd have a ballgown in your luggage and, knowing what I do of your priorities, I thought it unlikely you'd think of such a thing until it was too late. My aim was to prevent any embarrassment for you, not cause more.'

Maria shook her head, pretending to be absorbed in studying her delicately stitched hem. 'I wasn't offended. In truth, you were right. It hadn't occurred to me that I had nothing suitable. My mind has been engaged elsewhere since you invited me.'

Instantly she bit back a groan. She'd just as good as admitted how she'd spent the last twenty-four hours, fixating on the events of the billiard room until she was dizzy, those few minutes when she'd swung so wildly from elation to dismay the only thing passing through her mind. She'd be mortified if Alexander guessed her train of thought and Maria prayed fervently that he wouldn't understand what she had meant, that slip of the tongue enough to bring fresh colour to her already heated cheeks.

Fortunately, it seemed her prayer was granted.

'As I thought. What interest is some trivial ball when there are turkeys to think of?' His voice bordered on amused, but it would have been impossible for her to take offence. 'I was correct all along to assume a serious lady farmer would care nothing for something so frivolous as a party gown.'

'I'm not so sure of that.'

Again Maria let her gaze wander down the front of the gown. The embroidery sparkled with gold thread, the perfect accompaniment to the Yuletide green of the silk, and again she was struck by Alexander's kindness in giving her such a gift. It spoke of respect for her feelings, something her family back in Norfolk often neglected to consider, and another wave of regret washed over her to think such a man could never be hers.

'Any other dress, possibly—but not this one. I've never seen anything quite like it in my life.'

That's a sentiment I could entirely agree with—albeit with one fairly major adjustment.

It wasn't the dress itself that had made it difficult to breathe at first glimpse of it shimmering down the corridor towards him, Alex thought now as he struggled to control the desire to stare. That honour had gone to the person wearing it, the sight of Maria enveloped in emerald silk so mesmerising it had stolen all the air from his lungs.

The gown whispered around her like a second skin, as supple and delicate as mist, and only a man made of stone could have remained unmoved by the perfect clash of veridian against russet curls. She looked like something from a painting, the light coming in from the landing window illuminating her as if with a heavenly glow, and it seemed the hardest thing in the world to pretend to feel nothing when his heart raced and his hands itched with the urge to reach out and touch.

She was tracing a fingertip over the pearls at her neck and Alex tightened his jaw. If she didn't stop drawing attention to the fragile dip at her throat, he feared he might go mad, every pass of those fingers unconsciously pushing him closer to the edge. He hadn't known a moment's peace since the scene in the billiard room and she was doing nothing to help him now, the passage of a single day nowhere near enough to quell the rising feelings for his guest he knew he had to fight.

'I have some slight reservations, however.'

Maria peeped up at him, a glint of dry humour only just visible, but a relief all the same. He'd tortured himself wondering how she would conduct herself towards him after his unforgivable behaviour, but it seemed he needn't have worried. For all her unusual attributes it appeared she still possessed the well-bred talent of glossing over awkward incidents and Alex could have kissed her for sparing him the contempt he knew he deserved.

But then, you could have kissed her anyway, couldn't you?

'Reservations? Of what kind?'

She gave a smile that could have brought a city to its knees—or, at the very least, turned Alex's knees to water. 'A dress this beautiful deserves a real lady to wear it. I shall have to endeavour to become far *more* sophisticated and far *less* improper by the night of the ball if I'm to be worthy of it.'

The arch little twinkle was too much. With his self-control already strained Alex felt himself weaken further beneath the arc of her lips, so pretty his own moved before he could consider their wisdom.

'You're more than worthy just as you are. There isn't a single thing you ever need change and even less that could be an improvement.'

He watched the humour fade from Maria's expression, replaced at once by uncertainty that made his stomach drop down to his boots. A hint of dusky pink rushed into each cheek, accursedly making her even prettier than she was already, and Alex only just had time to wonder how on earth he could possibly salvage yet another unfortunate situation before she took a short step back.

'I— Thank you. How kind of you to say so.'

Even as she spoke she was moving away and Alex had to check the instinct to follow, the desire to be close to her almost overriding all else. Instead he made himself stand still, outwardly calm but inside raging against the carelessness with which he'd allowed the truth to come spilling out.

'I think I ought to go back to my room and change out of this dress. I'd hate to spoil it before the ball.'

'Of course,' Alex managed through gritted teeth. 'I think I'm wanted in the great hall, anyway. Something Goddard said…'

He tailed off, horribly aware he had no idea what he was saying. Maria looked ready to run and he almost wished she would, leaving him alone to drop his head into his hands at his foolishness. Probably she was horrified an engaged— *nearly* engaged—man had spoken to her so tenderly, with intimacy that should surely have been reserved for his intended and his intended alone…

'Ouch!'

Alex started forward at her sudden sharply drawn breath. 'Maria?'

Her hands were at her heavily embellished neckline and it took a second for Alex to understand. Her beautiful but undeniably disobedient hair had caught on the embroidery at her throat as she'd turned to flee, trapping her head at an awkward angle. She couldn't quite look down enough to free herself and he wasn't sure whether it was a blessing or a curse that he would have to step closer to help before she could escape.

'Do you need—?'

She glanced up, only briefly meeting his eye before looking away again with a short nod. Her high colour hadn't abated one bit and Alex took a deep breath, hoping his hands would remain steady as he carefully drew nearer to unpick the tangle.

Maria's eyes were trained firmly on a spot on the wall, saving him from having to see whatever flickered through them. Standing so close to her was a temptation like no other and he steeled himself against the assault on his nerves, every fibre wanting to choose a copper ringlet to wind round one finger and know for certain if it was as soft as he imagined…

It happened quite by accident, although later Alex had to admit how unlikely that sounded. His hands were just far too large for such delicate work. The intricate neckline was so narrow that perhaps it was inevitable his fingertips mistakenly brushed the slim ridge of one collarbone, skin gently touching skin for no more than half a moment, but even that contact enough to set his entire body ablaze. If that was all that happened then he might have been able to find the will to prevent what happened next—but the shudder that ran through Maria at his fingers' feather-light touch was too rousing, too pure and too damned exciting to be ignored.

It wasn't a shudder of disgust or revulsion or anything so heart-wrenchingly savage. Instead, Alex stilled as he saw the hopelessly unconcealed longing in her face before she resolutely turned away from him, determined not to let him see—and yet he couldn't bear to let her go.

As if in a dream he brought a hand up to trace a burning path across the sculpted line of her jaw, tilting her face back towards him as gently as if she had been made of glass. It would have been easy for her to break away and he braced himself to back down immediately if she seemed unsure, but she didn't. Instead, Maria allowed him to cradle one blazing cheek, at last lifting her gaze to meet his in a connection so powerful it sucked the air from the room.

He couldn't have torn himself away if he'd wanted to,

suddenly held prisoner by the unwavering brilliance of that stare. It was the same feeling he'd had in the billiard room, of drowning in the olive perfection of her eyes, only this time there was no hope of pulling himself back from the brink as he bent his head and allowed all rationality to be borne away by helpless need.

Her lips were as soft and sweet as summer berries as they parted under his, drinking in his kiss the way parched earth would the rain, and his arms came round her with the instinctive, unfightable movement of a magnetic pull. Holding her to him, nothing could have made him let go. The exquisite silk of her bodice was crushed against his chest, but neither was aware of anything other than the scalding contact of their mouths as they danced in unchoreographed harmony, giving and taking, until Alex couldn't remember when he'd last taken a breath.

Maria was all there was: the scent of her hair and her tiny, swallowed murmur as his hand trailed down the links of her spine, flattening at the small of her back to steady her against him and keep her safe in the cradle of his arms. He would never drop her or let her crumple to the ground—to stand with her was all he wanted, letting her draw from his strength and make better use of it than he ever could. She was so sharp and daring, and her mind so set on achieving her goals, that as he shivered at the feel of her palm cupping the sensitive nape of his neck he knew she was the only woman he ever would have chosen for himself.

She came to her senses first.

Alex's eyes flew open as Maria pushed him away, her hand shaking, but forceful none the less.

'Alexander… That should *not* have happened.'

Maria backed out of arm's reach, her breathing fast and shallow. There was a trace of the same dazed wonder in her flushed face that Alex was sure she could see in his, although it rapidly gave way to mortified as she pressed a hand to her chest.

He could have sworn he heard the cogs turn inside her head, the full realisation of what had just occurred crowding in on her like a pack of wolves.

'I shouldn't—*we* shouldn't… That was inexcusable. I think—I think I must leave at once.'

Taking another pace backwards, she passed a hand across her forehead as she clearly tried to collect herself. 'I'll send word for Cartwright to come. If you'd allow the birds to remain here a few more days he can take them the rest of the way to Atherby. I think that's for the best.'

She sent a single sharp, desperate glance his way and Alex's chest squeezed to see the naked confusion in it, her heart perhaps mirroring the wild delight and then regret of his own. Running a hand through his hair, he tried to order his thoughts, but they wriggled away from him, as writhing and many-faceted as a bag of snakes.

How could I have allowed that? How could my self-control have failed so spectacularly?

If he'd wanted to hide his head in his hands before, the desire was ten times as great now. She wanted to escape and he could hardly blame her, his ungentlemanly conduct something of which he was already ashamed. He hadn't been able to stop himself and now it was his fault she wanted to abandon her plan to prove her worth to her father, his momentary lapse of judgement possibly having a ripple effect on the rest of her life.

'If that's what you want then I won't stop you, but please reconsider. I know what you set out to achieve, winning your father's approval, and I won't have you forced to forsake that by my lack of self-control. I'm sorry, Maria. I should never—'

She cut him off with a shake of her head. 'I was just as much to blame. I *wanted* you to kiss me.'

Her cheeks flamed like raging wildfire, but she met his eye, the honesty he so respected coming to the fore. 'But it won't happen again. You're to be married and I should know better than to admire a man set so far above my station.'

Alex's mouth twisted in disbelief as he watched her turn away from him, her fingers toying unhappily with the ends of her hair. The desire to make her face him rose up sharply, but he pushed it back, hardly able to credit how badly she'd misread him.

How could she think her social standing was any kind of impediment to the feelings that had begun to grow inside him, only born a few days previously but already strengthening into something so much more?

'Do you truly think that matters to me? That if I *were* free to choose, your background would prevent me from seeking your hand?'

He spread his fingers, grasping at nothing in an attempt to make her understand. 'The strength of your convictions and determination to live as you choose won my respect the first moment I met you, even if your family would seek to convince you to change. Perhaps in rank I'm placed higher than you, but most certainly not in worth.'

He saw her eyes widen, those perfect, kissable lips parting on a reply that refused to spill out, and he found he didn't know what else to say. Probably he'd said too much already—certainly things he never should have spoken out loud. He was going to marry Augusta and Maria would leave Milbrooke as soon as the snow thawed—but in this frozen moment they might have been the only two people in the world and he wondered distantly if Maria felt it, too, as he offered one last try.

'Please stay. I'd like to help you show your father you deserve more than to be some man's ornament.'

She gazed back at him, uncertainty radiating from every

inch of her slight frame. Still cloaked in dazzling green she looked more like a dryad than ever, more suited to a forest glen than some stuffy English manor house—wild and beautiful and not meant to be caged in the way her family intended. If he drove her away now she might never escape that future…something Alex knew, beyond a shadow of a doubt, he couldn't allow.

'I won't impose upon you again. I give you my word.'

Chapter Five

Standing in Milbrooke's grand entrance hall, Maria felt her spirits sink as she reread the letter in her hand. It was only a few sentences, but Carew had managed to make his displeasure plain in every word and for a moment she was too absorbed by it to notice the presence behind her.

'Pardon me, Miss. Could we get past you?'

She started, stepping quickly out of the way of two men carrying a huge bundle of fir boughs between them. Another followed behind, pushing a barrow filled with holly, and she watched all three deposit their burdens beside an already heaped pile of greenery towards the back of the hall. Servants flitted about busily, some twining ivy around the grand pillars either side of the entrance to the ballroom while others wove sprigs of mistletoe into the lowered chandelier, and despite her unhappiness Maria couldn't help but admire the festive splendour beginning to take form for the evening's celebrations.

Just as with the workmen, she was too distracted to realise Alexander had approached until he was directly at her side and an immediate thrill ran through her to find him so close. She gave it no chance to develop into anything more dangerous, however, the resolution she'd come to during the long, restless hours of the night *just* lending her the strength to guard herself from its pull.

She hadn't really slept, staring up at the darkened ceiling as the memory of Alexander's mouth moving over hers came again and again, drawing her into a sea of confusion from which there was no escape. It was almost as if his hand was still on her, his palm scalding against the small of her back to pin her closer than she'd ever been to a man and setting her mind whirling with desire—but it was his pained confession that intruded just as much as their physical entanglement, the recollection of his words a bittersweet agony that sat over her chest now like a basket of rocks.

If he was free to choose his own wife...he implied it might be my hand he sought.

Hidden beneath her bodice, Maria's heart skipped faster and she struggled to keep her rising emotion from showing in her face. Under other circumstances she would have rejoiced that the man she was coming to care for seemed to feel the same way, but in truth it felt more like cruel mockery. Before her very eyes the decorations for his engagement ball were well underway and the sight was like a dagger thrust into her gut, twisting savagely until she wanted to cry out.

Instead she briefly closed her eyes, taking a moment to steady herself. In the silent despair of the night she'd sworn to turn her back on every pang of longing she knew she couldn't indulge, each one a shard of glass that would cut her if she tried to hold on to it.

Doubtless it was for the best that Carew insisted on coming to fetch her the very next day, declaring in his letter the doctor had decided him fit to move. He'd be furious and the onward journey with him would not be pleasant, but there was no alternative and some part of her would have endured anything to avoid having to watch Alexander dance off into the future with his soon-to-be bride.

He still stood beside her now, as tall and eye-catchingly handsome as ever, and she prayed her voice wouldn't betray her as she nodded across to where the heap of foliage was being transformed into banners and wreaths. 'This is all very grand.'

'Isn't it? I'll say one thing for Goddard. He knows how to make a statement.'

Both looked to where the estate manager stood with his arms folded, supervising the chaos with his cool gaze. Every so often he gave a curt order and the maids rushed to obey, although from the set of Alexander's lips Maria had to wonder if such attention to detail was truly appreciated.

'He's very dedicated.'

'That's certainly one word to describe him. I might choose another.'

'You don't like him?'

For the first time since his appearance in the hall Alexander glanced down at her and Maria had to steel herself to keep back a frown. He looked tired, his face drawn despite the now-familiar smile he was careful to wear, and her insides gave a wrench to wonder if his night had been as sleepless as hers.

'Not especially. He's too smooth and more than a touch too sharp with the servants until I put a stop to it. His family has managed the Milbrooke estate for generations, however, and it hardly seems sporting to dismiss him just because I don't care for his manner.'

He spoke lightly enough, probably only one listening for it able to catch the strain in his voice, but to Maria it was plain as day. Clearly Alexander was trying just as hard as she was to affect normalcy, although she had no opportunity to dwell on the idea as his face suddenly changed.

His gaze was directed at something behind her, whatever it was making his already stiff smile all the more rigid, and Maria turned to see what could have had such an immediate effect.

Coming towards them was quite possibly the most beautiful woman Maria had ever seen. Tall and willowy, she seemed to glide across the polished parquet floor, the living embodiment of everything Mrs Bartlett had always taught her daughter a real lady should be. Not a single strand of her well-dressed hair was out of place and it shone like spun gold in the morning light coming through the Hall's open front door, the china blue of her eyes finishing the overall impression of angelic loveliness that made Maria want to stare. The woman returned her gaze with only the smallest flicker of a politely quizzical brow before dropping into a curtsy so elegant it had clearly been honed at court.

'Good morning, Alexander.'

'Augusta.'

Alexander bowed respectfully, Maria following the movement with unfolding comprehension that sent a fist thudding into her stomach. Surely this had to be his intended. Good breeding emanated from her like a tangible force, the exquisite lines of her face calling to mind a classical painting and exuding the natural confidence the upper classes seemed to be born with. Why a man might look to another when he had such a woman already Maria couldn't fathom, keenly aware how unflattering a comparison would be if she were forced to stand beside the one Alexander was now addressing.

'I wasn't aware you were coming here this morning.'

'Mama thought you might need our assistance. Have we arrived at an inconvenient time?'

'Not at all. You know you're always welcome at Milbrooke.'

Alexander spoke gallantly, only the smallest shadow of discomfort in his eye as he turned back to Maria. 'May I introduce Miss Bartlett? She's been a guest at Milbrooke Hall, prevented from travelling onwards while the weather is so inclement. Miss Bartlett, Miss DeVere.'

'A pleasure to meet you.'

'Likewise, I assure you.'

Miss DeVere smiled with a calm civility it seemed it would take a great deal to disrupt, far removed from Alexander's much more carefree air. There appeared to be scant likeness between them, Maria noted uncomfortably, reading the slight air of reserve on both sides that surely nobody could have missed. Alexander had implied it wasn't a love match and he'd clearly been telling the truth, their polite façade only managing to partially conceal the lack of anything underneath as he went on to ask Miss DeVere— with somewhat forced cheerfulness—for her opinion of the decorations.

Too focused on her writhing innards to listen, Maria looked away, suddenly sensing stillness where once there had been movement on the other side of the hall. Glancing across, she realised the reason for the uncanny feeling, although as soon as she'd made the connection she wished she hadn't.

Goddard was standing quite still, his eyes fixed immovably on Miss DeVere, and Maria almost gasped aloud to see what flickered in their usually expressionless depths. It was the same look she'd seen in Alexander mere moments before he'd kissed her, thwarted longing that knew it was doomed even while refusing to die, a passion that could have no happy ending for all that it burned. Goddard's dark eyes held all the fire of Alexander's as well as the hopelessness and, although he turned sharply away the instant he saw Maria watching him, the picture of that haunted stare was already seared deep into her mind.

He's in love with her.

The realisation was like a trickle of cold water down her spine and for a moment she stared unseeing at the ivy-strewn pillars beside the ballroom door, hardly hearing the conversation passing between Alexander and the beautiful woman at his side.

Did Alexander already know of the manager's feelings

towards the one about to become his wife? It seemed unlikely. Men weren't always the most perceptive when it
came to that sort of thing, her mother had advised her more
than once, and surely there was little danger of Goddard
acting on his desires. Doubtless the safest course of action
was to say and do nothing—the situation was none of her
concern, after all—and once Carew came to whisk her
away she'd never set eyes on Alexander or his troublesome
estate manager ever again.

But the thought gave her little comfort, the prospect of
parting from Alexander for ever driving a wedge of ice between her ribs. It stayed there, cold and sharp and gleaming,
as Miss DeVere took his arm and with a murmured word
began to draw him away, Maria watching them go on together while she herself was left entirely alone.

By the time evening fell Alex already wished the day
was over. Augusta had taken up most of his morning and
the Earl and Countess the rest, arriving early to impress the
importance of the occasion on their son as if there was any
danger he might forget. By candlelight the Yuletide decorations seemed even more impressive, but Alex had hardly
noticed them as he descended the grand central staircase
and prepared himself to endure an evening he would have
much rather not.

The heat and noise were overwhelming now as he moved
through the crowded ballroom, pushing past the hoards as
politely as he could while making for the door. The band
was playing and the dancing begun full force, the sound of
thudding feet joining the already deafening buzz of voices
and laughter that made his ears ring. A moment of peace
was what he wanted more than anything—or at least, so he
told himself as he finally stepped out into the much cooler
calm of the entrance hall and took a deep, steadying breath.

He hadn't seen Maria for hours and he wondered uneasily where she could be. He shouldn't still be thinking of her and yet he couldn't seem to find a way to stop the image of her upturned face from coming again and again, her lips parted on a breathless gasp as he'd bent to claim them.

Ever since he'd surrendered to that forbidden passion she hadn't left his mind for as much as a second and it had taken all of his self-control to appear calm during their earlier meeting, when in truth he'd wanted to reach for her all over again, longing to relive what might have been the most perfect moment of his life. The feeling of her mouth on his was still fresh, constant dwelling on it allowing no detail to fade, and only the bleak knowledge that the situation was hopeless kept him from losing his head entirely.

Alex rubbed a tired hand over his face. The bitter irony of pining after another woman at his own engagement ball wasn't lost on him, the spectre of that one heady kiss almost bringing him to his knees. He *should* have been thinking only of Augusta and a spark of guilt flared in his gut, although not quite brightly enough to completely eclipse what rose unstoppably behind it.

Surely the only way I'd find any peace of mind is if it was Maria my parents were welcoming into the family tonight rather than Augusta. I can't imagine any other release from this torment—and yet it's the very thing I know can't come to pass.

A sudden coldness soaked down from his chest despite the fire blazing in the hall's enormous hearth, chilling him as it went. He'd strayed too far in his unhappiness and ought to turn back before thoughts of what might have been drove him past the brink of despair. Imagining Maria as his fiancée was the most agonising temptation and it would do him no good to allow it to take root when there was no hope, the inevitability of his future sitting inside him like a dull ache.

I'd be the worst kind of man if I broke off my understanding with Augusta, throwing her over after an almost life-long acquaintance. She's expecting to become my wife and I have to honour the agreement between our families, even if we both know there's little else but obligation binding us together.

A niggling pain in his palm made Alex look down, only belatedly realising his hand was clenched into a tight fist, and he forced himself to relax his fingers. His rapidly unravelling despondency was threatening to run out of control and he tried again to master it, realising as he tried to distract himself that he couldn't recall when he'd last actually seen the woman soon to become his wife.

Perhaps Augusta's doing the same thing I'd like to: finding a quiet place to hide from what has to come next.

He ought to go in search of her, to present a united front for the hundreds of pairs of eyes that would soon turn on them when the announcement was made and perhaps offer some of the reassurance he would have welcomed himself. Neither one of them had chosen this path and he felt a fresh pang of empathy for her, all but forced into a match she hadn't sought. If she'd taken refuge somewhere it was his duty to find and comfort her, their mutual unease uniting them at last even if his heart belonged so irrevocably to another.

He sighed. Misery covered him like a shroud, but he set out across the hall regardless, heading for the door that would take him to the corridor beyond—

It opened before he reached it, a figure flying out so quickly it was almost a blur, and Alex had to throw out a hand to stop them colliding.

'Maria!'

She pulled up short, although the vivid alarm still clear in her face put him on his guard at once. She was flushed and her eyes slid away from his when he tried to meet her gaze, her hands twisting together with repetitive unease. If it was possible for a person to look more guilty Alex couldn't imagine it, his instinctive pleasure at seeing her swallowed instantly by concern.

'What's the matter? Is something wrong?'

'No, no. Of course not.'

Maria shook her head unconvincingly, the pile of glossy curls on top of it glowing in the candlelight. Between the forest hue of her dress and copper hair she could have been the very spirit of Christmas itself, a thought that flashed through Alex's mind before he could stop it.

'Has someone offended you? I saw Lord Stoatley speaking to you earlier—if he's said something to upset you…'

'No. He was a gentleman in every way.'

'Then what? Why come racing out like a rabbit running from a fox?'

She chanced a short glance up at him, saw how closely he watched her and looked away again at once, her brow creasing with agony that made his concern rise all the more.

'Please, Alexander. Don't press me. I don't know if I ought—'

What she would have said if they hadn't been interrupted at that moment Alex had no way of knowing. As it was the appearance of his mother in the hall made Maria's mouth close with a snap, the Countess's regal bearing infamous for producing respectful silence in most people she encountered.

She stopped a short distance away, close enough for him to catch the appraising look she cast over Maria before bestowing a generous nod that was hastily returned.

'Alexander? Will you come back into the ballroom? Our guests are asking where you are.'

'Yes. I'll come directly.'

His mother inclined her head again, granting Maria a civil smile before gliding back towards the light and din spilling out through the ballroom doors. It was a fleeting encounter, but still it managed to give his worry time to

grow, Maria no less flustered when he tried again to persuade her to speak.

'What is it? Why won't you say?'

Alex examined her face, hunting for clues in the evasive
green eyes so enhanced by the shade of her gown. If things
had been different, he might have rejoiced at an excuse to
stand so close, his heart jumping faster at how easily he
could have reached for her hand...

With some effort he found a shadow of a smile. 'You
heard our hostess. I have to re-join the party—but I'd like
you to come with me. I can't leave you alone in this state.'

Immediately Maria took a step back. 'I couldn't—'

'You could. You're not the only one with a determined
streak.'

He watched her lips part on some argument, too transfixed by their lush pink to hear what they said. He had to
set his feelings for her aside, knowing as he did they could
never amount to anything, but he was still a man of flesh
and blood, and even a viscount wasn't safe from giving in
to temptation one last time.

After this evening he'd have to let her go. She'd return to
Norfolk and he'd never see her again, their final few hours
together already slipping away as unrelentingly as sand in
an hour glass. It would have been far more sensible to take
their conversation outside rather than into the ballroom,
where curious gazes could follow their every move, but his
sense seemed to have all but abandoned him at the prospect
of holding her closer one last, precious time.

'Come and partner me in the next dance. That way you
can't escape again and you have an entire movement to tell
me what's wrong.'

Chapter Six

Maria's heart was beating so hard she feared Alexander might hear it even above the clamour of the packed ballroom as she reluctantly took up her place in the set, the heat and noise immediately suffocating in contrast with the quiet calm of the hall. The lines for dancing were full and two young men opposite looked at her with unconcealed appreciation, although Maria could think of nothing but the hideous moment she knew had to come as the band struck up and the first lively notes cut through the chatter.

He said there'd be no escape, and he was right—but will he wish he'd let me go when I tell him the truth?

Nausea writhed through her. The sight she'd stumbled across in the study flashed before her again, so unexpected and shocking she'd run from it into the very arms of the one person she'd have done anything to avoid. Now she had no choice but to either reveal all or lie and Alexander's sapphire gaze was too intent to be fooled.

He turned it on her now as he surfaced from a low bow and came forward, hand outstretched to take hers, and every nerve in her body seemed to focus on her fingertips brushing against his palm. Even with her gloves a barrier between them Maria had to grit her teeth on a rogue spark that crackled from that one chaste touch, skittering the length of her arm to light a bonfire in the darkest hollow of her chest.

Under cover of the music and sound of stepping feet Alexander muttered into her ear, scattering a brilliant constellation of tingles across her nape at the feel of his breath on her neck.

'So. Now you can't run away—what happened to cause you such alarm?'

He drew back again, retreating in time with the music, but never releasing her from that direct and questioning stare. Clearly he was determined to have the truth and there was little she could do to dissuade him, although a combination of concern and apprehension made her desperately want to try.

They came together, the dance calling for them to circle each other, and Maria seized her chance.

'I don't know that I should tell you. It was something never meant for my eyes and, besides, once a thing is told, it can never be unsaid.'

She watched the rise of his dark brows, a gleam of grim humour present in their furrow. 'That sounds ominous. Keeping secrets now, where once you were so outspoken? Surely not.'

Yet again they parted, Maria glad to turn her back for a beat or two as she rose up on to her toes. The reprieve was short-lived, however, and when she turned around it was to see the dark amusement had disappeared completely from Alexander's waiting face. His mouth had dropped from its customary curve into a straight line, suddenly worlds away from the easy-going man she'd come to think so much of, and her gut clenched at the unfamiliar solemnity in his voice when he murmured to her again.

'Maria. I can see whatever you're thinking pains you. If there's something seriously amiss in my house, I would truly like to know.'

His eye sought hers and didn't let go, the invisible connection no less intense for its subtlety. There was nowhere to hide from it, the bustle of the ballroom growing grey in comparison with the bright blue, and Maria's insides roiled with the knowledge he wouldn't let her go until she spoke.

'I'm afraid you'll be grieved. The very last thing I would want is to play a part in your unhappiness.'

'Your compassion does you credit. I am, however, resolved.'

Tearing herself away from Alexander's stare, Maria scanned the dancers around her. Nobody seemed to be paying much attention. The appreciative young men were now fully absorbed by their partners' charms and any onlookers would have no chance at eavesdropping over the scraping violins and heavy-booted feet. For all the crowds it was the perfect place for a private conversation—if Maria could just get the words to come, her throat tight and dry and the image of what she'd seen flickering before her like a bad dream.

She took a deep breath. The air was hot and cloying, but it steadied her nerves a fraction, giving her just enough strength to go on—as she had to, Alexander leaving no alternative.

'I'd withdrawn to the study to rest for a moment, hoping to be alone. At first I was…until Miss DeVere came in with Mr Goddard. They didn't notice me sitting in the corner and I was about to make my presence known when I saw…when I saw them—'

She broke off, quite unable to proceed. Spinning away from Alexander gave her a moment to think, but then he was there again, the delightful brush of his hand contrasting painfully with the weight pressing against the bodice of her dress.

'Yes? You saw…?'

Maria swallowed hard.

Heaven help me. How to describe what happened next?

The study candles hadn't been lit, the only light coming from the fire dying in the grate, but it had been just enough to prevent any chance of being mistaken. From her hiding place in one of the overstuffed armchairs she had seen the shadowy figures enter the darkened room and the discreet cough she'd been about to make had died in her throat at the intensity in Goddard's face as he turned to Miss DeVere. The other woman had backed away, seeming on the brink of escape—but then tears had sprung up in those beautiful eyes and Alexander's wife-to-be had thrown herself into the manager's arms with all the passion of waves crashing against a cliff and he'd held her to him fiercely as if he never intended to let go.

It was far too intimate a scene to paint in detail, *especially* given her audience, and Maria cast about for the gentlest way to phrase something not gentle at all.

'I… I saw them in an embrace.'

It was fortunate the dance forced them apart again at that very moment. Spared from having to see Alexander's reaction, Maria could hardly remember the steps as she moved away, her pulse skipping at lightning speed when he took possession of her hand once more.

'I see. Please go on.'

One desperate upward glimpse showed his face was carefully impassive, giving no clue as to what was going on behind it, although Maria knew he couldn't possibly be as calm as he looked.

Unhappily she lowered her voice, half hoping Alexander wouldn't be able to hear. 'Miss DeVere was crying—in her defence, it seemed she was attempting to sever whatever connection they must have had, but Mr Goddard was not to be deterred. He said he would never give her up, even after she wed. At first she tried to reason with him, but in the end… In the end I'm afraid she agreed.'

Alexander's head came up sharply, having bent slightly to catch her reluctant mutter. 'Augusta agreed to carry on her dalliance with Goddard even after becoming my wife? You're sure that's what she said?'

Maria nodded miserably, wishing with all her heart she'd stayed put in the ballroom all evening. Alexander's marriage might not have been based on love, but surely no man would be pleased to hear what she'd just told him, guilt for being the bearer of bad news as well as for exposing Miss DeVere's secret rising inside her.

She'd had no option but to tell him, yet she hated herself all the same, torn between protecting Alexander and sympathy for a woman whose life had been mapped out for her with little regard for what she might have wanted for herself.

'There could be no mistaking it. I'm sorry, truly. If I've caused you pain—'

The people around her stopped moving and Maria stumbled to a halt, too distracted to realise the dance had come to an end and in her clumsiness bringing her heel down on the hem of her lustrous gown. Only after freeing herself was she able to snatch a glimpse of Alexander's face—and what she saw there made her heart turn over in her chest.

The smile that she'd come to hold so dear was present once more, his eyes alight with something that made it impossible for her to look away. Far from an unhappy man whose plans for the future had been thrown into disarray he seemed instead invigorated, his shoulders back and the bow he swept her brimming with barely concealed energy.

She had no time to wonder what it meant. Before she could take a single step he had given her fingertips the briefest squeeze, sending a tidal wave of sensation through her with that one tiny touch, and then he was gone, striding from the dance floor towards the hall with such resolve she realised afterwards she should have guessed what he was going to do.

* * *

In the end, the conversation didn't take very long at all. Only fifteen minutes passed between Alex opening the study door and closing it again, and as he leaned against the wall beside it he had to marvel at how quickly things could change.

Less than an hour ago my future was set in stone. Now, however...

His chest rose and fell a little more rapidly than usual, still not completely able to believe what had just transpired. Goddard had certainly looked stunned at Alex's abrupt entrance to the room, leaping away from a flustered Augusta like a scalded cat, but the estate manager's surprise hadn't lasted long. It was to his credit he didn't try to deny his intentions when confronted with them, frankly admitting a love for Miss DeVere in a way that made fresh tears gather in her frightened eyes, and it was in the moment Alex should have disliked him the most that Goddard finally won his respect.

Now Alex pinched the bridge of his nose, attempting to marshal his thoughts. They wouldn't co-operate, too many trying to push forward at once, although he still managed to find room for a jolt of apprehension to see his mother crossing the hall towards him for the second time that night.

He moved away from the wall, intercepting her with as easy a smile as he could manage. 'Coming to collect me again?'

'I wouldn't have to if you didn't keep disappearing.' The Countess looked up at him severely, far too well bred to frown in public, but the rebuke still plain. 'And where is Augusta? Your father is making the announcement soon, yet she's nowhere to be seen.'

Something heavy slid down Alex's gullet. There was no escaping what would have to happen now and the prospect made it difficult to keep his smile in place, its sudden stiffness something his mother thankfully didn't notice as he took her by the arm and began to guide her back towards the ballroom.

'I need to speak to you about that. Father, too. Where is he?'

The Countess studied him, the first glimmer of suspicion sparking in eyes just as blue as her son's. 'Cloistered in a corner with Augusta's parents, suffering her mama to talk endlessly about their summer home in Bath. But what is there to say? For what reason do you need to discuss your engagement when everything is in place at last?'

Alex gritted his teeth, hoping the strain wasn't obvious from the outside. Addressing both sets of parents at once would get the ordeal over with more quickly, but it certainly wouldn't make it any less unpleasant, his own relief tempered by the knowledge of how his shocking news would be received.

'I'll wait until you're both together. I suspect you'll be glad of my father's support.'

His mother's wariness seemed to segue into alarm, but there was nothing she could do as he drew her into the ballroom, for the first time in his life grateful for the curbs rank placed upon behaviour. The Countess would never make a scene in front of her guests and it leaned in his favour, his own thoughts more difficult to hide as he caught sight of a now-familiar green gown emerging from the crowd.

Maria's face was a picture of confusion as she watched him pass, the subtle jerk of his head in a silent request for her to follow prompting a bewildered stare. She granted his wish, however, trailing at a hesitant distance as he led the Countess towards where his father was trapped in a secluded alcove by the DeVeres, although it was clear from the crease between her sandy eyebrows that she didn't understand.

But she will soon enough. I can only hope her reaction will be the one I'm hoping for.

His heart beat rapidly beneath his shirt, but he tried to ignore it, bracing himself for the storm he knew was about break. The best way to proceed was with as little preamble as possible, coming cleanly and directly to the point, and so he took the plunge, leaping off the edge into an abyss he knew only one of the five people watching him would have any reason to expect.

'Lord DeVere… Lady DeVere. Father.'

He bowed to each in turn, aware of his mother's hand tightly gripping his arm and Maria hovering just out of his sight. 'I'm sorry to inform you all that the engagement between Augusta and I will not be taking place. She has expressed her preference for another and so I have released her from any understanding between us, with no injured feelings on either side. I hope you can forgive the inconvenience.'

Nobody moved. The Countess's fingers lay perfectly still in the crook of his elbow and for a moment Alex wondered if the assorted collection of parents had heard his lowered voice until Lady DeVere turned slowly towards him.

'I would like to be quite clear. My daughter has broken off your understanding?'

'We came to the conclusion together. She has no blame to bear and I won't speak a word that could mar her reputation.'

Lady DeVere gazed up at him, the rigid set of her face like a china mask, and Alex hoped she would be merciful. Even if Augusta had meant to cuckold him he still wished her well, all too aware by now that love made its own choices and stopping it was like trying to hold back the tide. Somewhere behind him Maria waited and the urge to look for her was strong, the undeniable desires of his own heart pulling at him even as he tried to navigate one of the most awkward moments of his life.

'I see. Where is Augusta now?'

'In my study. I think she might appreciate a comforting word.'

Lord DeVere stepped forward, his embarrassment clear, but the thought of his daughter in distress overcoming all else. All of society knew him for a doting papa and he almost forgot to bow in his haste, taking his wife's arm and beginning to lead her away before she could make any objection.

'Please excuse us. I think Augusta... I think we will be required.'

Alex gave them his most generous bow in return, watching as they made a swift—but still elegant—break for the door. As long as Augusta had her father's support she would be safe from too harsh a punishment, he thought with relief, although it would be some time before Lady DeVere reconciled herself with having a private gentleman for a son-in-law rather than a viscount. It was an adjustment any parent would find difficult and his own looked no less stunned when he turned to face them again, the very public setting his only saviour from his mother's wrath.

'Alexander!' Her voice was little more than a hiss, delivered between lips stiff with restrained outrage. 'What have you done? You cannot break off a sensible match for something so trivial as Augusta liking somebody else!'

Careful to keep his expression bland, Alex leaned down. 'It was more than just a liking. I wouldn't say so in front of her parents, but it was a far deeper connection—one I have reason to suspect both she and Goddard would have been reluctant to abandon even after the wedding.'

The Countess's mouth sagged open. For the briefest of beats it seemed her infallible decorum had at last abandoned her, but with admirable determination she collected herself almost at once.

'*Goddard?* He's the man? And…after the wedding…?'

She tailed off into horrified silence, looking to her husband as if the Earl could help her understand the unthinkable. When he said nothing, only pulling his greying eyebrows even more tightly together, Alex shook his head.

'Don't be angry with them. I know I'm not. None of us can help where we lose our hearts and I'd do nothing to expose Augusta to scandal.'

'Scandal.' His mother almost moaned the word, her fingers biting into Alex's arm. 'That's exactly what we'll have now there'll be no announcement. Almost our entire acquaintance is here, expecting your father to confirm your match, and when he doesn't they won't hesitate to guess why. What will they say about you? What hideous reason will they conjure to explain why we couldn't persuade anyone to marry our heir? Henry, what are we to do?'

The Earl placed a steadying hand on his wife's shoulder, unease flaring behind his impressive moustache, and the sight of his parents' distress tightened Alex's chest. It was just as well he was prepared for this very moment… but that didn't mean his innards didn't twist at the thought of taking the final step, the idea that had dawned on him the instant Maria revealed Augusta's secret both thrilling and terrifying in where it might lead.

'You needn't worry about that. I think I have a way we might avoid society's speculation.'

His mother peered up at him uncertainly and he tried to appear confident as he turned to look over his shoulder, his heart thumping as he picked out one particular figure in the crowd.

'Miss Bartlett? Would you join us?'

Maria came forward immediately. 'Of course, Your Lordship. Is everything well?'

She studied his face, the worry reflected in hers quickening his already leaping pulse. He could never tire of looking into those green eyes, he knew that without the slightest doubt. Their compassion was captivating and he had no wish to ever be released from their hold.

'I hope it soon will be, if you'd consider helping us with a very delicate matter.'

He could sense his mother's anxious gaze following him as he drew Maria away, one female hand on his arm exchanged for another that had a very different effect on his breathing. Another alcove a short distance away was unoccupied and he headed towards it, the closest thing to privacy he was likely to find in a room filled with the nosiest people imaginable.

Maria didn't say a word, no doubt sensing the nervous energy that Alex was trying his hardest to repress, and when they were sheltered in their secluded bay the look she turned on him was so apprehensive he could have kissed her there and then.

He snatched a breath, willing the dryness of his throat to allow him to speak. The longer he delayed the more time his unease would have to grow, tying his tongue until he couldn't croak out a single sound.

'You may have overheard what just passed between me and my parents. My connection to Miss DeVere is at an end and with that comes certain complications regarding this evening's events.'

He saw her face change, a subtle shift that someone else might not have caught. A hint of renewed tension seemed to have entered it, sharpening her already taut expression, but he didn't allow himself to pause to wonder what it signified.

'To put it bluntly, if no announcement is made, my mother is worried the entirety of the British upper classes will think there's something wrong with me.'

To his relief Maria nodded. 'I understand. Your family's reputation rests heavily on public perception of its heir.'

'Precisely.'

He tried to smile, although he gave up at the reluctant stiffness of his lips. As with breaking difficult news to his parents it was doubtless best to jump straight in rather than skirt around the point and Alex readied himself to finish what he'd started, distantly aware of just how much hung on Maria's response.

'To keep up appearances I urgently require someone to step into Augusta's place for the evening and that is where I was hoping I might prevail upon your good nature.'

Even as he reached the end of his sentence he knew the enormity of what he was asking, putting himself completely at her mercy, but it was the only way he could think of to avoid the unpleasantness he knew his mother had every reason to fear. Once the *ton*'s gossips set to work the rumours would fly, casting aspersions on the family name and all connected to it, and his parents' embarrassment would be known all over the county.

If Maria agreed to help him save face, however, it would stop any whispers before they started—but as Alex waited for her reply, feeling her skirts brush softly against his leg as she took a startled step backwards, he knew his motives ran far deeper than avoiding some malicious mutterings.

If she agrees to a fake engagement...could there be a possibility she'd entertain a real one?

Immediately he reined himself back, although the question echoed inside his head like the chime of a bell. It had occurred to him the very same second he'd realised he was free of his obligation to Augusta and now he could think of nothing else, his head feeling oddly light as he took in Maria's widened eyes.

'You want *me* to pose as your fiancée?'

'If you would consider it. I realise it's asking a great deal, but it wouldn't be for long and I'd be greatly in your debt.'

She blinked up at him, the gears turning in her mind almost audible. Clearly there was a lot of thinking going on behind her stunned face, but she didn't give anything away, the blankness of her countenance not allowing him any clues until she finally spoke—a little unsteadily, as if still processing her surprise, but with the same determination he'd come so quickly to expect.

'What would I have to do?'

He wasn't sure what the sensation that passed over him was called, only that it made his head swim more than ever. 'Not very much. Stand beside me while my father makes the announcement and then suffer my company for the rest of the night, preferably as if you enjoy it. My mother will take care of the details.'

Maria listened quietly, her eyes fixed on the embroidered hem of her gown. When she looked up it wasn't directly at him, some spot over his shoulder apparently more interesting than his face. 'That doesn't sound too taxing. I just… This isn't at all what I was expecting for this evening.'

She glanced at him and then away again at once, a faint flush crossing her cheekbones, and Alex felt something sharp beneath his ribs. Perhaps he'd asked too much of her, his own feelings making him act far more rashly than he ought. Just because his own heart had been touched by their unlikely friendship didn't mean hers beat faster likewise, his desire to keep her close perhaps blinding him to the truth.

Maria had plans for the future that didn't include him, he realised bleakly, her resolve to join her father and brother in the running of their estate the very reason they'd met in the first place. There was nothing to say she'd want to stay at Milbrooke for longer than she had to, their mutual attraction perhaps nothing more to her than a pleasant distraction while she waited to make her escape. Even if she granted him this favour and stepped into Augusta's shoes for one night that didn't guarantee she'd accept him for real, her mission to win the acceptance of her father surely still sitting at the very forefront of her mind.

His throat convulsed in a painful swallow as he tried again to find a smile that didn't want to come. 'How stupid of me. You must be thinking about home and what your own parents would say to such a wild scheme.'

Her beautiful, disobedient curls gleamed as she shook her head. 'Not at all. If our engagement is only to span one night, it will be over long before I reach Norfolk. My mother might even be pleased I managed to snare a man after despairing of me for so long—and a viscount, too. She won't know whether to be horrified I let you slip away or proud I caught you at all.'

Alex's brows rose swiftly. 'So...you might consider it? I know it's pushing you further than I have any right to and I'd understand if you'd rather not—'

A young couple passed by their alcove, the woman holding her sweetheart's arm as if without it she might die, and Alex watched Maria's head turn to follow them. They must have been newlyweds judging by their utter indifference to everyone else in the room, so wrapped in each other that they seemed more one person than two. There was something touchingly pure in their devotion and perhaps that was what helped Maria to decide to grant him clemency.

'I'll do more than consider.'

She looked down at her gloves, her hands clasped in front of her so daintily it took all the self-control Alex had left not to capture them in his own far bigger grasp. 'Given your kindness to me during my stay here, I'll even go so far as to agree.'

Maria feared her weak smile would melt away completely as she followed Alexander to the centre of the ballroom, the other couples participating in the waltz apparently far more interested in her than the dance about to begin. Eyes were trained on her from every direction and she might have been tempted to run if Alexander's hand hadn't sought hers at that very moment, drawing her towards him so invitingly all thought of escape was forgotten.

'Everybody's looking at me.'

'You've just been announced as my new Viscountess. By this time tomorrow the whole town will be talking of your beauty and then shortly afterwards feeling very sorry for me when we quietly call off the engagement.'

Alexander's voice was soft and she couldn't completely stop herself from wilting at the delicious sensation of warm breath against her skin. Confusion still coursed through her, the shock of his outlandish request lingering to make it difficult to think, although as soon as he'd asked for her help she'd known she would give it to him without hesitation.

How could she refuse? In truth there was nothing he could ask that she wouldn't be prepared to grant him. He'd been so generous it seemed the least she could do in return… although if she was honest, daring to truly examine what lay deep down inside, she had to admit one other reason for agreeing to stand at his side and accept the congratulations she didn't really deserve.

An excuse to make believe.

When Alexander had asked her, with such sweet hesitance that only made his request even easier to grant, she had wondered if she was still awake. It was like something from a dream and even knowing his proposal wasn't real couldn't take away the dizzying wonder of hearing him say the words, so heartfelt and earnest her legs had felt weak. She was only playing a part, yet it was *almost* enough, so close to what she really wanted that to refuse would have felt like missing a once-in-a-lifetime chance.

Now, as they took their places, she risked a secret glance

up at his face. She'd assumed he would seem more at ease now the crisis had been averted and yet something still lingered in the set of his jaw, a slight tension in the chiselled line she had to think quickly to draw herself away from.

'I confess I still don't completely see how this pretence is better than simply keeping silent.'

Alexander exhaled shortly. 'A dignified end to a respectable match doesn't draw much comment. Holding a ball specifically to announce one and then saying nothing *does*.'

The band's violinist made a few tentative scrapes and then a merry waltz floated through the air, the rest of Alexander's explanation almost drowned out as the couples around them began to move. 'There would be too many questions and the last thing my parents want is any suggestion of scandal. Your acting as my fiancée tonight will be of great help all round.'

Maria was about to reply when a sudden blaze of heat choked back the words. Alexander's hand was at her back, his palm pressing against the silk to light up every last nerve, and when his fingers laced with hers she wondered if she'd be able to remember how to move.

The music was loud, but the rushing of her blood was louder. Alexander was so *close*, just as he'd been that fateful afternoon in the billiard room, the memory of it coming now to make her stumble. One false step and she'd be in his arms completely, no chaste little gap left between his body and hers and nothing to prevent her from feeling the firmness of his chest held against her once more. All that had happened that evening left her dazed, guilt and elation mixing to make a heady brew, and Maria's thoughts spun through her mind just as Alexander spun her across the dance floor, the strength of his grip the only thing anchoring her to events that seemed too strange to be true.

Perhaps he misread her dazed silence. As he looked

down at her, she saw him hesitate, her own eyes battling the urge to stray down to his mouth.

'My mother especially will feel greatly indebted to you. If there's something she values more than propriety, it's tact—and in helping her avoid any disagreeable rumours you've made a formidable friend.'

'I'm glad of it.'

She tried to lift her lips into a smile, although they felt suddenly too cold to move. For all the Countess's importance it was her son's good opinion Maria really valued, her most secret fear spilling out before she could force it back. 'And you? Are you still my friend, despite the unpleasant tale I brought before you tonight? If I hadn't been in the study you would still be marrying Miss DeVere. I know some of the fault lies at my door.'

Alexander's face clouded at once. 'Surely you can't think that?'

His dark brows drew together, the look he cast her raising goose pimples on her bare arms. 'In truth, you did me a bigger favour than I ever dreamed possible. Augusta never wanted to marry me nor I her, both of us only going along with it because we thought there wasn't a choice— but we were wrong. There's always a choice if you're brave enough to make it.'

Maria swallowed against a lump that rose in her throat. There was something in Alexander's tone she couldn't quite name, a low note that stirred the hairs on the nape of her neck so delightfully she almost shivered, but all attempts to figure it out were lost at the sudden intensity of his unbroken stare.

Still a willing captive in his arms, she felt herself stagger as his thumb traced a soft trail down her spine, the gentlest of touches but leaving flames in its wake, and she burned as he bent his head lower to murmur against the shell of her ear.

'And as for your question…there can be no doubt. I still hold you in the highest regard and you can be certain nothing will ever change that.'

He drew back, his eyes seeking hers, and the expression in them robbing her of the ability to reply. A shadow had fallen across the blue, seeming to darken them with unspoken desire that echoed the longing beginning to circle low in Maria's stomach. The music was still playing and the people around them moving with elegant steps, but nothing could break through the indefinable connection that held the two of them apart from everything else, the rest of the world carrying on while Maria and Alexander were frozen in a moment neither wanted to end.

She watched him take a ragged breath, the rasp of it more rousing than anything she'd ever heard. Both were thinking the same thing, she could have sworn it: how easy it would be to bridge the final gulf between them and come together for another kiss just as passionate as the first, their hunger for each other a maddening itch only a statue could have resisted.

Alexander's voice was hoarse and Maria found a shaky smile to hear him confirm everything she suspected.

'I said I wouldn't impose on you again.'

'Who's to say I'd think it an imposition?'

She felt him lose his footing, her boldness making him stumble over the practised steps, although a curious emptiness began to spread through her as she gazed up into his tense face and realised she had nothing left to lose.

This isn't real, after all.

He wouldn't *really* marry her. It was as he said and as she knew all too well. Their engagement was a ploy to avoid shame for the Earl and Countess and would be abandoned once its purpose had been served, a farmer's daughter having no place at a viscount's side.

She would leave Milbrooke Hall tomorrow when Carew

came to claim her and Alexander, too, their time together almost at an end and the thought of parting from him a dagger thrust she had no choice but to endure. To think anything else would be to believe in a fairy-tale, more fit for children than a grown woman with her own plans for the future, and the most painfully bittersweet weight settled over Maria's breastbone as she made up her mind.

Why shouldn't I give in to fantasy one last time? One final taste of heaven before I have to return to earth?

It was a split-second decision, but the timing couldn't have been more perfect. Twirling across the floor, they passed a wide window framed by floor-length velvet curtains—and it was the easiest thing in the world for Maria to draw Alexander behind one of them, so quickly nobody else in the room noticed them disappear.

There was no need to explain what she wanted.

Alexander reached for her and she was in his arms at once, but far closer than she'd been as they danced. Half of society was watching as the handsome Viscount and his shy bride-to-be took to the floor for a respectable waltz and there was nothing respectable in the shudder that coursed through Maria as Alexander's mouth came down to steal every last trace of restraint.

His fingers wound through her hair and pulled her to him, one hand on the back of her head and the other so tight around her waist it was difficult to breathe, but she wanted to press closer still and her heart sang to hear a muffled groan in Alexander's throat as she deepened their already soul-wakening kiss. It was what both had been waiting for and there seemed little point in fighting something so *necessary*, a yearning neither had any hope of overcoming without giving in to its pull.

Alexander's breathing was fast and harsh although his tongue danced with hers as deftly as a swallow tumbling through the sky, Maria feeling as if she, too, was falling with nothing to stop her. Her hands clutched at his lapels, the fine silk of her dress pressing against his shirt, but neither pausing to think of the tell-tale creases their passion would leave behind, only sensation and instinctive need driving them on as one flimsy curtain stood between them and utter disgrace.

If Mrs Bartlett could see her daughter now it would mean a one-way trip to a nunnery, Maria realised in the one faraway corner not entirely taken up by delight, but then Alexander's lips trailed a scalding line from her mouth to the dip between her collarbones and everything else vanished completely from her pleasure-drenched mind.

Her whole body was trembling when Alexander abruptly pulled back, his fingers no steadier as he raked them through his disordered hair.

'I can't—I can't go on any more. One more moment and I might forget myself completely and I have far too much respect for you to do that.'

Maria steadied herself against the wall, the meaning behind Alexander's careful phrasing almost as exciting as his kiss. Clearly the same fire flooded his veins as she felt in hers, so heated and so wildly *unacceptable* she might almost have been ashamed.

But it doesn't really matter. In less than twelve hours I'll be gone—and then I shall never see him again.

Unhappiness surged in to douse the longing holding her in its grasp, but she tried desperately not to let it show, her chest rising and falling quickly as she watched Alexander try once again to flatten his dark hair. If this was to be their last night together, she wanted him to remember her with the desire he clearly felt now, not as a miserable young woman whose eyes had begun to sting, and, gathering all the self-control she had left, Maria forced herself to nod.

'I understand. Perhaps it would be better if we returned to your guests now before anyone has time to miss us.'

Before Alexander could reply she turned to the curtain, tweaking it aside to look beyond. Nothing seemed to have changed in the two snatched minutes that had made her legs feel weak and with a strained smile over her shoulder Maria slipped away, moving blindly through the crowds with her head down so nobody would see the tears threatening to fall.

Chapter Seven

Maria's legs felt like lead as she silently opened the kitchen door and stepped out into the freezing yard, carrying her small leather bag. In the pale early morning light the snow gleamed far less brightly than it had only a day before, much of it churned into dirty slush by boots and horses' hooves, and there could be no doubting that it had melted enough for her to leave.

Carew's letter had instructed her to wait for him, but she couldn't risk meeting Alexander. One look would be her undoing, a single smile enough to steal all her resolve, and she had to escape before he saw the agony the prospect of parting from him had etched into her face. If she rounded up the turkeys now, she could be on the road before the sun had fully risen and intercept Carew on his way to Milbrooke, at least sparing her the shame of Alexander witnessing the scolding she knew the reunion would bring.

Or would have once, anyway.

Alexander's appreciation for her just the way she was cycled through her mind once again and as she made her way across the slippery cobbles Maria felt painful gratitude well up. Perhaps she wasn't such a troublesome disappointment after all. She was strong and capable, Alexander's admiration managing to outshine every feeling of inadequacy, and she almost managed a grim smile to think *this* time she wouldn't take her brother's reprimands lying down.

Her time with the Viscount had made her more determined than ever to pursue her dreams and even though she'd be leaving her heart behind she could take comfort from knowing the memory of him would stay with her for ever, the ghost of his kiss still lingering on her lips as she unbolted the stable door.

It was dark inside and she was just wishing she'd thought to bring a lantern when the crunch of boots from behind made her turn.

'This is the second time I've found you in here. If I didn't know better, I'd think you meant it to be the last.'

Her heart sank as she returned Alexander's direct gaze, although she made herself step back out into the yard. Standing in the greying snow was far colder than the stable, but Maria barely felt the icy breeze, the feeble dawn sun lighting Alexander's rugged profile far too strikingly for her to notice anything else.

He glanced down at the bag in her hand, his dark brows already pinched in a frown. 'Were you going to leave without saying goodbye?'

'I thought that would be easiest.'

She could hardly speak, her voice almost lost amid the whistle of the wind and stirring of the birds in the stable behind her. The most curious of them approached the open doorway and she made a half-hearted attempt to usher it back with one foot, Alexander never taking his eyes from hers.

'Since when have you taken the easiest route? The woman I was so enjoying getting to know never seemed to back down from a challenge.'

Maria's chest tightened at the unhappiness in his voice that he tried to hide behind his usual good humour. She'd hoped to spare them both this moment, although now Alexander was before her she couldn't help but drink in every last detail of his handsome face, committing it to memory so she would never forget so much as a single hair. The temptation to reach for him was fierce, but she forced it back, an ache growing inside her to know she couldn't give in.

He cared for her, of that she was certain, but that didn't change the facts. Alexander was still a viscount and she was still a farmer's daughter, and just because Miss De-Vere no longer stood between them didn't mean every other obstacle had been shattered. Their kiss the previous night had been the most perfect of heart-breaking farewells and she braced herself against a flood of misery as she tried to find something to say.

'I have to go. You were kinder than you needed to be in letting me stay for so long, but now my brother is coming to fetch me home. I have to go with him.'

The shake of Alexander's head came immediately. 'Not if you don't want to. You could stay here.'

Maria's eyes widened, but he went on before she could open her mouth. 'Goddard has left my employ. He resigned his post last night. That leaves the position of estate manager open and I'm offering it to you.'

His words spilled out in a rush and Maria saw a hint of colour rise in his face, for once quite unlike the confident man who always seemed so at ease. What her own expression was at that moment she didn't know, too amazed to think while everything she'd dreamed of since she was a little girl was held out for her if she was brave enough to take it.

'You can't mean that.'

'Why can't I? You said yourself you have a good understanding of running an estate. I can't think of anyone else I'd rather have to take care of mine.'

Alexander didn't look away—not even when she took a step backwards, her immediate flare of breathless temptation chased out by bitter regret.

'I—I couldn't. It wouldn't be proper.'

'What's improper about it?'

His face was so earnest that Maria had to turn away, disappointment and longing rising like bile in her throat.

A vast emptiness opened up inside her, a gaping void swallowing all her baseless hopes. Surely he had to know such a thing could never be acceptable in spite of how much they both might wish it. She could hardly live in Mr Goddard's old quarters, a part of Alexander's household but neither servant nor guest. The whispers would start at once and scandal was sure to follow, an unmarried woman having no place working so closely with an unmarried man.

She only realised she was gripping the handle of her bag far too tightly when the leather began to bite into her palm. 'It just…isn't *done*. A single woman…'

The rest of her sentence was lost on the breeze and Maria didn't chase it. Instead she stood like a marble statue, cold and stiff and yearning to move towards Alexander, although she knew that in truth she could never touch him again.

For an indistinct time neither of them spoke. A chill wended its way through Maria's core that had nothing to do with the frost still glittering on the dirty ground, a pulse of pure, crystal despair throbbing with every beat of her heart until finally Alexander broke the silence.

'I've considered that.'

Gazing down at the slush around her boots, Maria heard him give a dry cough. His voice was oddly strained, but she didn't look up, too blinded by misery to see what was coming.

'What if you weren't a single woman any longer? What if you came to live here at Milbrooke Hall permanently— as my wife?'

Alex felt as though his heart was going to burst through his ribs as he watched Maria's face set into a mask of surprise. Her eyes were stretched wide and her lips parted on a soundless gasp, and he could scarcely stop himself from pulling her into his arms at the innocent wonder in her frozen countenance.

All night he'd wondered how to ask her, endless scenarios passing through his sleepless mind until he couldn't take it a moment longer. The unanswered knock at her bedroom door at dawn had warned him to move fast and relief at having found her before she could slip though his fingers almost brought him to his knees, reinforcing what he'd realised for certain as they'd danced. That he couldn't live without her and that he would do everything in his power to persuade her to stay.

She stared at him now as if he'd just asked her to jump over the moon or something equally impossible, stumbling over her words when at last she found her tongue. 'But… It was *pretend*. I understood that. A man like you can't really marry a woman like me.'

'Can't? That's not a word I thought you believed in.'

He pushed a hand through his hair, frustration running through him. It wasn't her fault she thought herself unworthy. That dubious honour belonged to everyone who had ever told her she aimed too high with her aspirations for the future, to a society that imposed nonsensical rules on who a man could and couldn't love according to the accident of his birth, rules Alex had almost been a victim of until Maria had come into his life to show him another way.

'Let me tell you something. *Any* man would be fortunate to marry you. A farmer, a viscount, even a prince… There's nobody in the world set above you and if you haven't guessed how I feel about you by now then I'm not sure you ever will.'

He broke off, breathing quickly, and his heart turned over to see Maria's now-familiar blush. It was one of the prettiest things he'd ever seen and he could have watched it all day, although the swift glance she sent him—half sweetly shy, half magnificently bold—pulled him up at once.

'I know how you feel. In truth, I suspect it's the way I feel about you, too.'

Her voice was soft, the low, wonderful words inviting him to bend down to catch them, although when he took a pace forward she held up a slightly unsteady hand. 'But what about your parents? You were to marry Miss DeVere. I have none of her position and very little to match her wealth. I'm hardly much of a substitute. Wouldn't they be angry?'

Alex resisted the urge to take her by the shoulders, to make her look up into his face and see the honesty with which he laid himself bare.

'My parents' opinion is nothing. As much as I respect them, I've learned at last that the only person who ought to choose who I marry is me. I've made my decision and let me tell you—you are *nobody's* substitute.'

Every nerve felt as though it was on fire as he waited for Maria to speak, her downturned face hidden from him by her swathe of flaming hair. He longed to tangle his fingers in it, even in the dim light the curls glowing like real copper, but he dredged up the last remnants of his flagging self-control to give her space to think.

How many minutes passed Alex would never know for sure. It felt like several hours and eventually he couldn't contain himself any longer.

'So…do you have an answer?'

His throat was dry and his innards in knots, hardly able to keep upright as he watched her nod.

'Yes.'

Heaven help me.

'And that answer is…?'

She finally, *blessedly*, raised her eyes from the ground and muttered a single syllable that lit fireworks in Alex's churning stomach.

'Yes.'

The icy wind and dull snow vanished as that one word

hung in the air between them, the power of it eclipsing everything else in the frozen yard, and for one painful heartbeat Alex couldn't move. Rooted to the spot, he could only stare as Maria's mouth lifted into the most beautiful smile, her petal-pink lips capturing every thread of his attention and the urge to kiss her crashing over him as unstoppably as a tidal wave.

If he could only make himself move surely she would be in his arms before he'd taken three steps—a theory that proved to be true when she met him halfway, the distance between them closing with a finality nobody could ever hope to undo, and he held her against him as if his life depended on keeping her close.

Blindly he cupped her cold cheek, rejoicing to feel the softness of her skin against his palm once again, but his plan to guide her mouth to his was thwarted by a finger held to his lips.

'I have one condition.'

Maria's voice was just as shaky as her hand and yet the determination in her green eyes was every bit as staunch as he had come to expect—and admire. 'I began my journey with the intention of selling these birds to the highest bidder. Only by bringing the money home did I think I could persuade my father to take me seriously.'

She gazed up at him steadily, although her breath hitched as he lightly kissed the finger against his mouth.

'I remember.'

'That is my condition. The purchase of these twenty turkeys—' she nodded at the birds now scratching around the yard '—is the price of my hand. I'd like to follow through with what I started, even if it seems unnecessary.'

The temptation to laugh was strong, but Alex caught himself just in time, almost carried away by the dizzying elation that sang in his veins. A few birds were nothing to him, but for Maria they represented so much more. Independence and success, the knowledge that she had achieved what she'd meant to, and he would rather have cut out his tongue than laugh at something so important to the woman he'd grown so quickly to love.

'Those are your terms? That's what I need to do to claim you as my wife?'

He brought his other hand up to rest over her waist, feeling her shiver against him as he gently brushed his thumb over her lowest ribs. His blood was growing warmer with every second that passed and Maria seemed to feel it, too, her slender throat moving in a dry swallow.

'Yes.'

Bending his head, Alex murmured into her ear, delighting in the floral fragrance of her hair that he wished he could bottle, 'Then you have a deal.'

Maria turned in his arms and then pure, molten relief swept through him as finally she allowed his mouth to come down on hers. It was a softer kiss than the night before, when the spectre of separation had made them cling together as if they knew they were doomed—now there was only light and hope for the future, dazzling joy that flooded both with molten gold, and Alex could hardly bring himself to speak as Maria drew back to smile up into his rapt face.

She was so lovely in her happiness that he had to kiss her again, revelling in her sigh until he straightened up and made himself look stern. 'I have a condition of my own. I will buy the rest of your flock, but they will never end up on any Christmas table.'

Maria's brow creased. 'Then what—?'

'I couldn't live with myself. I owe these birds a great debt. Without them I never would have met you and it would be ungrateful indeed if I rewarded their service with basting.'

He looked down at them, their glossy black feathers stark against the snow. A couple pecked around his boots while another inspected the bag that had dropped from

Maria's hand, so self-important Alex's attempt at seriousness slipped at once.

'You can have the money to send to your father, but the turkeys will live out the rest of their natural lives here with us. I think, given the circumstances, it's the least we can do.'

The future Viscountess Stanford laughed, her arms still around him and the top of her warm head pressed delightfully beneath his chin. 'You're far too sentimental. I'm afraid you'll never make a good farmer.'

'I know. Fortunate, then, that I have an excellent new estate manager to help me. How soon can you start?'

* * * * *

*If you enjoyed these stories,
you won't want to miss these other
Historical collections*

Get 4 FREE REWARDS!

We'll send you 2 FREE Books plus 2 FREE Mystery Gifts.

FREE Value Over **$20**

Both the **Harlequin® Historical** and **Harlequin® Romance** series feature compelling novels filled with emotion and simmering romance.

YES! Please send me 2 FREE novels from the Harlequin Historical or Harlequin Romance series and my 2 FREE gifts (gifts are worth about $10 retail). After receiving them, if I don't wish to receive any more books, I can return the shipping statement marked "cancel." If I don't cancel, I will receive 6 brand-new Harlequin Historical books every month and be billed just $6.19 each in the U.S. or $6.74 each in Canada, a savings of at least 11% off the cover price, or 4 brand-new Harlequin Romance Larger-Print books every month and be billed just $6.09 each in the U.S. or $6.24 each in Canada, a savings of at least 13% off the cover price. It's quite a bargain! Shipping and handling is just 50¢ per book in the U.S. and $1.25 per book in Canada.* I understand that accepting the 2 free books and gifts places me under no obligation to buy anything. I can always return a shipment and cancel at any time by calling the number below. The free books and gifts are mine to keep no matter what I decide.

Choose one: ☐ **Harlequin Historical**
(246/349 HDN GRH7)

☐ **Harlequin Romance Larger-Print**
(119/319 HDN GRH7)

Name (please print)

Address   Apt. #

City   State/Province   Zip/Postal Code

Email: Please check this box ☐ if you would like to receive newsletters and promotional emails from Harlequin Enterprises ULC and its affiliates. You can unsubscribe anytime.

Mail to the Harlequin Reader Service:
IN U.S.A.: P.O. Box 1341, Buffalo, NY 14240-8531
IN CANADA: P.O. Box 603, Fort Erie, Ontario L2A 5X3

Want to try 2 free books from another series! Call 1-800-873-8635 or visit www.ReaderService.com.

*Terms and prices subject to change without notice. Prices do not include sales taxes, which will be charged (if applicable) based on your state or country of residence. Canadian residents will be charged applicable taxes. Offer not valid in Quebec. This offer is limited to one order per household. Books received may not be as shown. Not valid for current subscribers to the Harlequin Historical or Harlequin Romance series. All orders subject to approval. Credit or debit balances in a customer's account(s) may be offset by any other outstanding balance owed by or to the customer. Please allow 4 to 6 weeks for delivery. Offer available while quantities last.

Your Privacy—Your information is being collected by Harlequin Enterprises ULC, operating as Harlequin Reader Service. For a complete summary of the information we collect, how we use this information and to whom it is disclosed, please visit our privacy notice located at corporate.harlequin.com/privacy-notice. From time to time we may also exchange your personal information with reputable third parties. If you wish to opt out of this sharing of your personal information, please visit readerservice.com/consumerschoice or call 1-800-873-8635. **Notice to California Residents**—Under California law, you have specific rights to control and access your data. For more information on these rights and how to exercise them, visit corporate.harlequin.com/california-privacy.

HHHRLP22R3